PRAISE FOR

Rose of No Man's Land

"Compellingly honest and told with a voice so pure that it would be ignominious to overlook it . . . A sincere achievement."
—*San Francisco Chronicle*

"*Rose* [*of No Man's Land*] is balls-out from the start. . . . Not for the faint of heart, Tea's writing is raw, funny, and tragic, but never forced. **A-.**"
—*Entertainment Weekly* (Editor's Choice)

"Trisha Driscoll has more adventures in one day than most of us do all year. When the fourteen-year-old vows to make a friend, she never imagines it'll be Rose, a chain-smoking mall rat who introduces her to the scary world of hitchhiking and first love."
—*Teen People*

"[Tea] follows the snarky and disillusioned fourteen-year-old Trisha as she learns about life, love, and getting out of the house."
—*Ms. Magazine*

"Tea uses vivid language games to show the rawness of being a teenager in a world of disposable mall jobs, television addicts, perverts, and late night tattoo parlors."
—*The Other Magazine*

"*Rose of No Man's Land* is a manic valentine to the flashiness and grittiness of malls, tattoos, and instant girlfriendship. . . . Michelle Tea's exhilarating punk rock prose had me flying through this book. As always, she finds the beautiful in places no one thought to look."

—Pam Harcourt, *Books To Watch Out For*

"Michelle Tea's brain, an intricately designed punk rock word machine, endlessly calculates human motivations and cultural meanings of the inanimate. She dangles this soul research overhead like an endless spit string from the lower lip of a torturous older sibling. She weaves from it the young girl tales of outside of American society that give voice to riot hags everywhere. No man's land is the hilarious, scarily gorgeous, deliciously creepy, cold, squishy, heartbreakingly fucked up teenage bliss of finding the one true hardass love that gets it."

—Lynn Breedlove, author of *Godspeed*

"Gritty, animated, original, and disturbing, this allegorical tale of friendship and belonging is hard to put down."

—*Library Journal* (starred review)

"Flashes of brilliant writing and some scenes worthy of David Lynch remind readers of Tea's very considerable talent to shock and amuse."

—*Booklist*

"Tea is brilliant in making the stakes for Trisha abundantly clear as she discovers sex (and, concurrently, her sexuality), drugs, and the emotional gains and losses attendant to each . . . a postmillennial, class-adjusted *My So-Called Life*."

—*Publishers Weekly* (starred review)

"The novel shines with a kind of beatnik deference to drugs and lust and dangerous youth." —*Kirkus Reviews*

"Like a laser vision searing through the minutiae of splintered bus stop benches, wasted mall trash, and television family psychosis, Michelle Tea lets us inside the heart of female energy and intelligence and we fall hopelessly in love." —Thurston Moore, Sonic Youth

"When fourteen-year-olds recite Michelle Tea's glorious suburban ballad to each other, they'll go AWOL. They'll tear off their *Baby* T-Shirts, spit in the lens of reality TV, and torch their favorite malls. May the rest of us—the furious, the underemployed, the unwritten amazons, the still-lost grown—follow the girls' brigade into the scorched glory and ripped-open language of *Rose of No Man's Land*, a place, with any luck, that has a no-returns policy."

—Katia Noyes, author of *Crashing America*

"Such gorgeous prose and dead-on dialogue. Her characters are so believable, you hold your breath for them at times. I ate up every word. How does she do it?"

—Beth Lisick, author of *Everybody Into the Pool*

"Tea's prose is unflinching, sort of a stream-of-consciousness, capturing the life of this complex young girl so well that you'd swear it was another of Tea's memoirs."

—*Time Out New York*

"A riotous coming-of-age novel . . . do[es] for working-class teenage lesbians what S. E. Hinton's *Rumble Fish* and *The Outsiders* did for greasers and street-brawling tough guys."

—*The New York Times Book Review*

"People unfamiliar with her work call her prolific, the greater national literati call her transgressive, and her fellow San Franciscans call her iconic. Whatever you label her, Michelle Tea . . . fires out her poetry and prose with a manic energy that blurs the line between fiction and memoir, author and reader."

—*SF Weekly* (Best Local Writer selection 2006)

"Tea's novel transcends the category of young adult fiction and escapes being some alternate-universe version of teenage chick lit. Pay attention until the very last page, sister; it's worth it." —*Seattle Weekly*

"Tea has filtered first kisses and blue-collar camaraderie through her engaging charisma, transforming them into rapturous punk odysseys." —*The Village Voice*

"[Tea] is, as always, realistic in capturing what it means to be young and searching for both empowerment and enlightenment by whatever means you can."—*Curve Magazine*

"Saltier than shrimp ramen, seedier than a Jerry Springer marathon . . . laced with caustic humor and lyricism."

—*The Advocate*

"Told in the giddy, stream-of-conscious voice of Trisha Driscoll, *Rose of No Man's Land* is a tonic taste of what many girls at fourteen are looking for . . . hers is an unforgettable twenty-four hours." — *Santa Cruz Sentinel*

"Tea quickly draws her readers into the world of fourteen-year-old Trish, who narrates her own tale with a blend of innocence, sarcasm and self-deprecation—and now and then a flash of perfect insight. . . . Tea is skilled at making us all feel as vulnerable as Trish."

—*The Daily Hampshire Gazette*

"In her fiction, as in her life, Michelle Tea knows a girl can never find salvation on her first try. . . . There are lessons in her first night of bright lights and brighter hopes, but she won't learn them fast enough to keep her safe. That's okay, because safety is not the point of being this kind of girl."

—BookSlut.com

"What distinguishes *Rose* are the undercurrents of sexual tension and confusion, the honest portrayal of blue-collar life and the truly original scenes Tea has crafted."

—*Time Out Chicago*

"Tea expands her horizons with this engrossing work of fiction, a hardscrabble story about lost innocence and the bittersweet glories of a first love . . . [a] tale of beautiful angst . . . Rich, witty, outrageous fun: this is another remarkable and outstanding accomplishment for Tea."

—*The Bay Area Reporter*

"[Rose] is convincing as one of those intense, powerfully magnetic people who can readily suck the more passive Trish into her powerful and potentially damaging orbit."

—BookReporter.com

"Michelle Tea has this ability to perfectly capture the most painful, awkward and excruciating moments of adolescence, wring out the essential essence of that time, and create sentences that unerringly strike to the core yet can also leave you laughing. . . . *Rose of No Man's Land* is a nasty, sweet, queer love story for the Really Real World."

—*The Skinny*

"With its manic and witty prose, readers experience a new-found evolution of girlhood amongst the wreckage of pop culture's burnouts in broke-down America. . . . *Rose of No Man's Land* should be praised for its subtle maturity and brutal honesty . . . a gorgeous portrayal of the corruption and reconfiguration of a young, lost soul trapped in Americana."

—*Falls Church News-Press* (Virginia)

"[A] confident foray into fiction . . . Tea's writing, as always, is 'raw, funny and tragic.' What's more, 'it's never forced.'"

—*The Week*

"Highly addictive, fast paced, and a guilty pleasure of sorts."

—*Mountain Xpress* (Asheville, NC)

"Raw charisma, a poetic voice, and an adventurous spirit fuel her stories."

—*Utne Reader*

"Hyperkinetic and hilarious . . . [told] in a voice that feels dark, funny, and totally true."

—*Girlfriends*

"Tea recounts her hero's wild ride with gritty wit and not a single disapproving sentence . . . There's more to growing up in grim suburbs than depicted in those Baby-Sitters Club novels. This is the realistic, if hyperkinetic, flip-side."

—Richard Labonte, Q Syndicate

Rose
of No Man's Land

Rose
of No Man's Land

A NOVEL BY MICHELLE TEA

A Harvest Book
Harcourt, Inc.
Orlando Austin New York San Diego Toronto London

www.HarcourtBooks.com

First published by MacAdam/Cage in 2005.

Library of Congress Cataloging-in-Publication Data
Tea, Michelle.
Rose of no man's land/Michelle Tea.—1st Harvest ed.
p. cm.—(A Harvest book)
1. Teenage girls—Fiction. 2. Lesbian youth—Fiction
3. Poor youth—Fiction 4. Dropouts—Fiction I. Title.
PS3570.E15R67 2007
813'.6—dc22 2006017183
ISBN-13: 978-0-15-603093-9 ISBN-10: 0-15-603093-4

Text set in Minion
Designed by Dorothy Carico Smith

Printed in the United States of America

First Harvest edition 2007
DOC 10 9 8 7 6 5 4 3 2

For Ali Liebegott

One

People always say to me that they wish they had my family. Like my family structure, or my lack of family structure or whatever. What they mean is, they wish they never had to go to school or clean their houses, or they wish they never got into trouble with their parents. Serious trouble, like when you get grounded or your favorite thing gets taken away and locked in a drawer somewhere. I guess they wish their parents didn't give so much of a shit and since mine clearly do not give any sort of shit at all, they're jealous. Really these people are massively wrong. It's like when guys say, "Oh if I had tits I'd stay home and play with them all day, I'd never get out of bed." Believe it or not I have actually heard my Ma's boyfriend, Donnie, say this. I heard him say it with a mouth full of ham salad from Shaw's, the pink mayonnaisey mush that he eats by the spoonful like a modern caveman. He doesn't even bother to make a sandwich out of it and it's not because he's on one of the no-bread diets like my sister, Kristy. Donnie just has a natural aversion to civilization. I'm surprised he doesn't dig a stubby finger into the hammy glop and eat it like that, that's how gross he is. Instead he shovels it into his mouth with a big silver tablespoon. I always know when Donnie's been eating 'cause the sink is full of spoons. So Donnie said, just days ago, with his eyes on my mom's boobs, "If I had tits I'd stay home and play with them all day, I'd never get out of bed," and all the vowels were compromised by the ham salad tucked into his cheeks. The sort of funny thing is that all Ma does is lie around and fiddle with her boobs, but it's because she's a hypochondriac and she's terrified she has breast cancer all the time. Whenever Donnie's not around she's flat on her back on the couch, her nightgown hiked up and the spectacle of her breasts splat on her chest, her hands meditatively rubbing the skin inch by inch, pressing, somber and focused like when she'd look through my and Kristy's hair for bugs when we were little. So it was sort of ironic to hear Donnie say that to Ma of all people. Her summery nightgown does sort of showcase her boobs so it's not like she doesn't have some responsibility here. I thought the mere reminder that she had them would have made her hands fly nervously to case them for tumors, but instead she just smiled a weird, lazy smile at Donnie and gave him a slow-motion swat. I guess she liked it as most females enjoy it when their boyfriends make appreciative comments about their breasts. I have found that thinking about Ma like she's just another girl in the world, like any of the girls going on about their boyfriends in the bathroom at school makes me less horrified that she is in fact my mother. When I start thinking of that word, *mother*, it's when I can start to feel empty and panicky and filled with big scary nothing feelings. So mostly she is Ma, the girl on the couch, so afraid to be sick that she's brought it onto herself, kept company in her make-believe illness by her food-eater boyfriend Donnie.

Ma says about Donnie: "At least he doesn't bother you girls." By "bother" she means "try to have sex with," and she says it like we, me and Kristy, should drop to our knees and kiss the peeling linoleum and prostrate ourselves to the patron saint of creepy dudes for sending us such a winner. I think the biggest problem between me and my family (by which I mostly mean Ma, my mother, the girl on the couch) is we have really different standards. For example, I would like to think it's a given that your mother's boyfriend doesn't try to have sex with you. I know that this isn't always the case — look at the Clearys across the street. Their stepdad had actually been doing it with one of the older sisters until one of the younger sisters called the police I think and it was like the whole family got hauled away somewhere, I don't know what happened to them. I don't think they would put an entire family in jail for something like that, but the Clearys are gone, their house and the rumors left waiting for them. I would like to think that we do better than the Clearys, me and my family. I guess you could call me inspired. I'd like to think that you don't just let creepy guys into the house, not ever, but to hear Ma talk about it, it's a real crapshoot and the fact that Donnie hasn't tried to get it on with me or my sister actually makes him a great man as opposed to simply not a criminal in that particular arena. Ma says I'm ungrateful and also unrealistic. That's the part that gets me. I am ungrateful, it's true. I'm not proud of it, but I don't think that gratitude is something you can fake. I mean, people do. I see people being pretend grateful all the time, like at school, and I don't know how they don't just puke all over themselves from the toxic phoniness of it all. I think I'd rather be honestly ungrateful — realistic. I think I'm realistic. I hate when Ma tells me I'm not. We both think we're being realistic, me and Ma, and only one of us can be living in what's generally acknowledged as reality, and most of the time I'm pretty confident it's me. But sometimes, like if I'm feeling particularly bad, she can trip me up with her insistence that I'm living in a dreamworld, and I start to consider that maybe Ma's world is the real one. And that is a deeply spooky thought. That's creepier than a hundred million Donnies all put together in one room eating a lifetime supply of ham salad from Shaws.

My original point is that sometimes people at school — who I rarely talk to yet they seem to know the whole story about my family — make it sound so great that I can do whatever I want. In reality, it's not so hot. Maybe the grass is greener, but I think it would be great to have a Ma who did get at you to do your homework and saw to it that you woke up by a certain time of the day, who didn't let you drink cans of beer in the house. Maybe if I did have that sort of Ma I'd really hate it, it's true that people really seem to hate their Mas for just these reasons, but there is something very anxious about the way things are so blown open in my home. It's like I really could just do anything I want. Or maybe it's more that I could just *not* do anything, and it would be no big whoop. It's not about going out and robbing the Cumberland Farms on the corner or getting pregnant with some loser's kid. It's more that I could sit in this bedroom of mine, plopped on my skinny bed, for a solid month before anyone noticed I haven't left the house in so long I'm green. I could be one of those people who never gets off their mattress. I could be a high school dropout, and believe me, don't think I'm not considering it. My high school is a complete joke but at least it's something to do. It seems like on the outside of high school there's nothing but time. Big, dark, eerie time, endless amounts of it. I guess that's life, and I'll wind up there soon enough, I might as well not quit high school. After high school comes life. Don't ask me what I'm supposed to do with it.

My *original* original point is that I missed the last day of ninth grade. I'm not terribly sentimental, but I'll never have another last day of ninth grade again. I missed it. Lately little things like that have been making me incredibly sad, the sort of sad you feel when you see a real old man at the Walgreens buying a single carton of milk, or a tiny box of ice cream. Something individual-sized. First of all I think it's incredibly sad to be buying food from a Walgreens. It's just not a place to find nourishment. It sort of makes me mad that Walgreens sells food at all. It seems greedy, like it's not enough to take your toothpaste money or your birthday card money or medicine money, they're going to get in on the food racket too, selling really lonely food items to sad people too old to hike over to a real supermarket. I was behind an old man at Walgreens last week, one who was buying a little red pint of milk and a tiny box of vanilla ice cream that looked like it got packaged up in about 1950. Just a weird blanched picture of a dish of ice cream on the cover. It didn't look too appetizing. The man's hands were sort of shaky when he paid for it and then he walked out real slow. The sliding automatic doors were open forever, it was like a performance, the old man leaving. I wasn't the only one watching him. There was a big lady in front of me buying antifungal foot cream, and she shook her head and muttered something tense and regretful. I was behind her with a box of Walgreens brand tampons, which are not great but are definitely the cheapest, and when it was my turn at the register I could barely find my dollars in my pockets, I was so wrecked by that old guy. I know in my head it doesn't make any sense, that just because someone is old it doesn't make them automatically great or holy. Just 'cause you have the elderly shakes doesn't mean you're God. Not to bring everything back to Donnie again, but he'll be an old man someday and it pisses me off to imagine a totally regular girl trying to buy a box of feminine hygiene products moved to tears at the sight of him buying ice cream at Walgreens. Which will totally be his story: eighty years old, alone, buying individually packed, ill-nourishing food at a big drugstore. And nobody should feel sorry for him because he creeped his way into his own destiny for sure. My point is the old guy is probably an asshole, but the sad I felt off him was wicked powerful. I tried to talk to Kristy about it and predictably she said it was just my period and I should get that pill they make for women who get too emotional during their period. I told her that pill is just a bunch of Prozac stuffed into one pill, but she didn't listen because she's four years older than me and thinks that makes a big difference between our brains.

Even though Kristy sort of made a joke out of it, I do think it was my period that helped me feel that sadness off the old man. I think that when I have my period my body gets sort of weakened, from losing all the blood and also from the energy my insides are spending cranking it all out, and it's like some invisible shield I'd propped up around me sort of melts away and all the sadness of the world rushes in. I think I psychically protect myself most of the time so I don't go crazy from the constant awful that surrounds us, but when I have my period I'm all ripped open and raw enough to feel the deep, deep sadness of everyone, assholes included. It's truly terrible. Maybe if everyone walked around being in touch with each other's hidden pain it could work out and even be beautiful, but it doesn't feel safe to be the only compassionate person on the planet. And when I have my period, that's exactly what I feel like — some weird psychic girl, an anti-superhero who can feel the tragic vibes of everyone she bumps up against in the world. I try to stay in my room when I have my period, but even that's no good 'cause I eventually have to walk to the bathroom to piss or to the kitchen to scavenge a scrap of food from our dusty cabinets, and chances are I'll see Ma, all spaced out on the couch, watching television with her sparkly eyes wide open, unfocused, like the glowing box had finally hypnotized her, sucked her brain out her eyeballs, and she's not even watching anymore, just staring, lobotomized.

Most of the time I don't have my period and am not trapped in a chemical sadness over Ma and her various ailments. Kristy hates when I refer to Ma's ailments as such, because she is a hypochondriac, but then Kristy does not fully grasp the nature of hypochondria, which truly is much more than our mother lolling about on the couch in a progression of polyester nightgowns. Ma has made herself sick with her hypochondria, like actually sick on the inside of her body. And even if that's not true, being a hypochondriac is at the very least an illness in itself, a mental illness. Which is worse than having a kidney infection or a gallstone 'cause it can go on forever, and in the process you lose all your friends for being crazy.

When I woke up this morning my bed was bright, full of sun, and the alarm clock on my nightstand was blinking on and off, on and off. I could feel in my body that it was really late, not morning anymore. I could hear someone, Ma or Donnie, in the kitchen making food. Lying in bed, woken up naturally, without the loud static jabber of the alarm scaring me awake, my senses were super sharp. In that moment, just before my brain snapped together, it's like my body was an animal body, and I could tell just by breathing through my nose, catching the hot wet smells coming from the kitchen, that it was pasta or ramen, something you boil that fills the place with balloons of damp cooking steam. Lunchtime food. As my brain cranked to life, everything — my observations, the sunlight, the repetitive flash of the clock, and the starchy, humid air — coalesced, and I screamed. I hollered for my mother. I felt all this instant anger. The day was mostly gone and I couldn't get it back and it made me feel cracked like I wanted to smash something.

I heard Donnie singsong from the kitchen, *Deborah, ya daughter's hollering for you . . .* and I heard Ma yelp, *What?* over the television hum. It sounded like a talk show, the rise and fall of boos and cheers. I knew Ma was not going to get off the couch. I would have to go to her. I checked to make sure the T-shirt I'd slept in covered my ass, which it mostly did, and I stomped out into the house. I can't help but think of my bedroom as not quite part of the home we all in live in. It's like my own wing, separate, velcroed to the rest of the place, detachable. Like I could hit a button and my bedroom would shoot away into outer space.

In the kitchen Donnie stirred not one but two spice packets into a single-package serving of ramen noodles. He always did this, which meant a few things. It meant there were opened packages of ramen noodles stacked in the pantry, all missing their flavor packets. Donnie wasn't going to eat them later, so I guess they were being thoughtfully saved for me and my sister. And ramen is a carb, which is a real no-no on Kristy's diet, so I guess they were piling up for me. A packet of plain ramen actually isn't so bad with some salt and a little margarine, if you're really starving, but still, it's the point. It's a rude practice. Nobody in our house made ramen like you were supposed to, with the broth, like a soup. Even Kristy, when desperate, sort of dusted the bowl of cooked noodles with the flavor packet and then scarfed it down, but Donnie's noodles were positively encrusted with the stuff. They were crunchy. I don't know how he could eat it. It was like pure MSG with an afterthought of noodle. He loved it. He made happy and excited noises in his throat as he ate it, moaning and gurgling at once, like the noodles were strangling him from the inside and he couldn't have died happier.

So I stomped into the living room. Ma moved her eyes from the screen to greet me. It was Sally Jesse Raphael. A bunch of girls were crying because their moms dressed like teenage skanks. Ma, Today Was My Last Day Of School, I told her. I tried not to be totally accusational because it really gets us off on the wrong foot.

How was it? Ma asked.

I Didn't Go! I shrieked. I know I sounded really blameful but I couldn't help it, I blew it, and once my voice goes to a place like that there's no coming back. I Overslept Because Someone Blew A Fuse And The Alarm Didn't Go Off!

Oh, your sister did that, Ma said. *She plugs too many things in, it's an old house. She had that camera going, and the blowdryer, and everything went out. Donnie had to go down into the basement and hit the fuse box.*

Don't thank me, Donnie held his hand up like he was a big hero but also humble. The MSG paste from his lunchtime ramen had collected in the crook of his mouth like a cold sore.

Well, Why Didn't Someone Wake Me Up Or Check My

Alarm Or Something? Didn't You Know My Alarm Wouldn't Go Off?

Donnie started nodding vigorously, tapped his greasy head with the tip of the fork he was eating from. He swallowed a clot of ramen. *I did think of that, I did. And then I forgot. It slipped my mind.* His tongue shot out like an undersea monster, eyeless and newborn. It scraped the bit of flavor packet from the corner of his lips and retreated. *Sorry, kiddo.*

On the television a newly made-over skank mom walked onto the stage in a khaki pants suit and subdued golden jewelry. Everyone cheered. *That doesn't look so hot, either,* Ma observed. She was done with me. *But I don't think much would look good on her. What do you think, Don?*

Donnie investigated the controlled chaos of the Sally Jesse Raphael show. The skank mom's daughter was crying great tears of salty joy at her mom's new look. I could sort of identify with her, which made me mad.

Hello! I made my voice extra slicey, to cut through the television haze they'd been marinating in all morning. Hello, I'm A Real Person Here In Your Living Room Who Missed The Last Day Of School For The Entire Year. That's A Little Anticlimactic, Don't You Think? And It Would Be Really Cool If You Could Admit That It Was Your Fault.

Oh, here it comes, the blame game, Ma sighed. Ma loves self-help books. She doesn't have the attention span to actually finish one, but she gets in deep enough to fish out some groovy new lingo.

It's Not A Game, Ma. It's Real. I Really Missed School. It's Really Your Fault.

Ma arranged herself into more of a sitting position, less of a lying position, her fighting stance. Her shimmery nightgown was a deep cranberry, and her long brown hair fell across the lace at the throat and on her shoulders. When I was wicked little, me and Kristy loved to fish all Ma's slippery shiny nightgowns from her top, most mysterious drawer. The drawer with all the nothing-colored fabrics wound together in the wood, the technical-seeming items like bras with their hooks and straps. All of it stunk up from the tiny pillow of dead flowers buried in the center, a stale, sweet smell. The nightgowns Ma lives in now are the same ones I used to play dress-up with. I have a memory of Kristy swimming in that particular cranberry number, her lips smacked with some sort of matching lipstick, making me walk behind her with the hem of the gown clutched in my hands, lifting it from the grubby floor.

Well Trish, how about being in the solution instead of the problem, Ma sighed. *Can you go to school now? All this time playing the blame game with me, you could be putting on some pants —*

Which, maybe you could do anyway, huh? Donnie cut in, scrunching up his nose like *I'm* the creep of the house.

Ma smirked. Now that Donnie butted in on her behalf she was going to act like she won the fight. She's such a bully. She's got great eyes. They're a real spooky green color. People leave you alone when you got eyes sharp like that. It's a color they give to witches in horror movies, to illustrate their evil powers. Of course I did not get the spooky-eye gene. I got brown. Just Forget It, I spat.

Your sister was in your room with her camera this

morning, Ma told me. *I thought she was waking you up. You kids aren't babies. I didn't know I needed to check on you all morning. I was still sleeping. I don't know what's wrong with me, it's like I got mono or something.* She sunk back into the collapsed pillow that held her head.

If You Had Mono, I said, We'd All Have Mono.

Her eyes rounded. *Don't say that!* she said. *God forbid. You feel tired, Don?*

Nah, Donnie shook his head. Donnie wears a pair of wire-rimmed glasses. They slide down his greasy nose all day long and I have a suspicion he wears them only to look smart. But Donnie doesn't look smart. You can spot his smartlessness twelve miles away, like a throbbing neon sign.

Maybe you need a battery clock, Ma suggested. *Since the fuses blow.*

They sure do blow, Donnie chuckled and nudged Ma with his bowl. Ma chuckled back. They really are perfect for each other.

Why don't you put it on the wish list, Ma suggested. *Battery alarm clock.* The wish list is a worn and crumpled piece of yellow paper that lives on our fridge. It's pinned to the metal with a plastic banana magnet. On it is scribbled everything we need. The scribbles take different shapes — the perfectly sculpted handwriting of Kristy; Ma's faint, looping script; Donnie's quick jots. They're marked in pencil and ballpoints and fuzzy markers that bleed through the back of the page. It reads: *canisters, DVD player, stepstool, cordless phone, new sheets, towel rack, towels, blender, diffuser, George Foreman grill, humidifier, dehumidifier, security system.* Some of the earlier items from years ago have faded away, though Kristy periodically rewrites the whole list in her neat penmanship on a clean piece of paper. The banana magnet is weak, so the wish list frequently falls off the fridge and gets stomped on, kicked under the table, then picked up with food-stained fingers and dropped atop the table, where it gets eggier, more coffee-stained and dusted with ramen flavorings before being hung back on the fridge. The weight of the page slowly drags the banana magnet down the length of the pukey green refrigerator. The fridge is avocado-colored, Ma has told me. A shade that was big in the '70s, when everyone loved to eat avocados I guess. I have never seen an avocado, but if the fridge is any indication, they can't be too appetizing.

I turned and stomped away. I took tiny, hard steps and felt satisfied by the way the rickety house rocked beneath my annoyance. The way this house moves, it's like a living thing we all live inside. I think about it a lot in that way, especially at night if a wind hits it and it shifts and squeaks. Like it's restless and trying to communicate. I think that the house is aware of us and likes me best, is on my side, feels sort of sorry for me. I rattled myself into the kitchen and plucked the wish list from where it sagged, knee-level, on the fridge. There were no pens anywhere. I rifled through the junk drawer and came up with a mostly dry purple marker that still smelled faintly of grapes, a souvenir from grade school. I pushed the scratchy tip to the page. *Battery powered alarm clock.* I stuck it back on the fridge. What a joke. Sometimes an item will miraculously fall off the back of a truck. Sometimes Ma will hit on a Scratcher and we'll cross something off the list. Last year we got a hot-curler set that Ma and Kristy had seen on TV. It hadn't even been on the list, it was a spontaneous purchase. There were about fifteen desired objects ahead of my alarm clock. I wasn't holding my breath.

In my room I sunk onto my bed but not too hard. Kristy once made a big show of flinging herself onto her bed and wound up busting the frame and the box spring, and now had to sleep on a mattress on the floor. It doesn't pay to show strong emotions in this house. I eased myself onto my bed even though I'd have preferred a full-body slam, some sort of rough and complete contact. Maybe I should take up a sport, something aggressive like rugby, which I heard is wicked violent, but I don't think they have that in America. At least not in Mogsfield. I don't know if Mogsfield has anything aside from cheerleading, actually.

It's going to be a long summer.

Two

I found out from Kristy that Kim Porciatti tried to kill herself. Kim Porciatti didn't go to my school, Mogsfield High, and she didn't go to the vocational school like Kristy, the one called "the Voke." The vocational school frowns on that nickname because it sounds too trashy. They're trying to get people to call it "Metro Tech" instead, short for the Eastern Metropolitan Technical Vocational School. That's the school's real name but not even people who go there can keep it straight. It sounds like some sort of government institution you could learn to fly planes and fix air conditioners at. As opposed to a run-down high school for pot-smoking hicks learning plumbing and girls with bad hair and no future studying data processing. People get real excited about the Voke at first, because it's so different from regular schools. Girls who go there say things like, "Oh it's just like real life," with this sort of superiority as they exhale a plume of Marlboro Light. But once the novelty wears off you realize you're actually working a really shitty job you're not getting paid for. Companies hire the students to process their data for wicked cheap. They pay the school, and the students — all girls, in data processing — do the work and never see a dollar. How is that even legal? I guess the really great bit is you're getting taught how to process data, which is supposed to be a valuable job skill. Except you learn how to do that in like fifteen minutes and then for the next three years that's all you do. Then you graduate and find a job doing more data processing and you do that until you die, either from natural causes like cancer or some deliberate suicide, whatever comes first. It's fucking depressing. Plus, learning that someone you know tried to kill herself will put you in a dark space, even if you didn't particularly like the person.

Kristy's shop at the Voke was not data processing, it was cosmetology, which if you ask me is the only reason to go to the Voke, and the reason most every girl does. That shop doesn't start 'til junior year, though, so you essentially piss away two whole years of your life learning something you have absolutely no interest in, like drafting and design, killing time until junior year. And not every girl gets accepted to the cosmo shop, either, so there are a lot of ruined female lives at the Voke, a lot of bitter data processors. You go in dreaming of being a hairdresser and you leave a dental assistant or a glorified babysitter — "child care technician." Those girls spend their entire high school life watching the teachers' kids. For free. For their education.

Kristy made it into the cosmetology shop because that's how life goes for her. She tends to get whatever she wants, which is why she's now going after *The Real World*, that TV show. She's positive she can be the teenaged-hairdresser-from-an-impoverished-New-England-town character, and she's been obsessively putting together her audition tape. Kristy's got this natural bossy sunniness that makes people think she is more capable then she really is. She's a know-it-all who actually doesn't know that much, and one thing I've learned from her is that if you say something in the right tone of voice hardly anyone will challenge you. Another thing I've learned is that in the event of a challenge you just stand your ground until the other person becomes exasperated, filled with doubt, or plain bored, and poof, you win. Kristy's great at that. Like that period pill argument. I am certain that the period pill — the one they have those commercials for, with the woman flipping out over something stupid like her shopping cart getting tangled in the other shopping carts — is just a huge dose of Prozac. I've given up trying to convince Kristy that it is not some genius new medicine, that it is just another way to sneak more people onto antidepressants. It is irritating to see Kristy gloating like she won the debate, but it's simpler than fighting about it forever. What the fuck do I care anyway. It's not like I'm going to take the stupid pill.

Kristy learned that Kim Porciatti tried to kill herself because she does Bernice O'Leary's hair and Bernice manages the Ohmigod! store at the mall. It is sort of sad to think that you can be the actual manager of the most popular store at the mall and still you don't make enough money to get a proper haircut. You have to drive out to the Voke — way out in East Bumfuck, the middle of nowhere, by a swear-to-god *lake* — and pay a stoned high school student three dollars to cut your hair. It seems unjust. There are two different hair salons at the mall: Jungle Unisex, which is sort of old, with a jungle motif; and Hair Universe, which has an outer space theme and a lot of neon. You'd think that the actual owners of Ohmigod! would pay for their managers to get a fancy haircut since it's such a big frigging deal to work there. Ohmigod! sells miniskirts and fake-flower hairpins and anorexic-looking sandals. It's very bright and plays old music from the '80s and it's supposed to be really fun, like some sort of disco circus. Everything that isn't striped is polka-dotted, so it truly seems like a clown place, but it's very popular anyway. More people are caught shoplifting from Ohmigod! than from any other store at the mall. Which might only mean that the girls who like those clothes are, on the whole, dumber than average and more likely to get caught. Kim Porciatti works at Ohmigod!, which is how I knew who she was in the first place. It's how I knew she went to Saint Joan, the all-girls high school, and how I knew that everyone thought she was just the greatest. Even if you don't shop at Ohmigod! — and I don't, I think those clothes are nauseating plus they're wicked expensive — you wind up knowing all about everyone who works there and what their business is. It's the sort of useless information you're always picking up in life, against your will. Kim Porciatti. I have seen her a handful of times. Her hair is always blond, maybe too bright to be real, and don't Italians have dark hair, naturally? I'll have to ask Kristy, who now knows everything there is about hair. Kristy is now officially a hair expert, in addition to an expert on period medications and the mechanics of getting onto a reality television show. Kim is blond and she always has a tan even when the world is nothing but dog-pissy snow and clouds and coldness and scrawny bare trees. It must be that spray-on tan but it looks pretty good on her. I'm trying to be fair about the whole Kim thing. On the one hand it pisses me off the way someone can get this whole little cult around them just because they look good in a fake tan and have a lawyer dad buying them cute shoes and stuffing them into a good all-girl's high school where their life isn't destroyed by guys. I mean, what did Kim do to earn all this adoration? You couldn't even say she worked particularly hard to get hired at Ohmigod! because she was popular already when she applied and that's exactly why Bernice hired her. And she didn't need the job in the first place, 'cause her parents have money and she just worked there 'cause it's cool, like being paid money to hang out in a nightclub with a bonus discount on fancy clothes. It's just not fair. Like why not decide that MaryAnn Baxter be popular? Why not select her to fall down and hyperventilate over? MaryAnn Baxter has a really fucked-up face. She got between her mom and her dad when they were having a fight and her dad flung something awful into her face. I want to say it was hydrochloric acid because that's the terrible thing people are always getting splashed in the face with on television, but who knows if hydrochloric acid is even a real thing? MaryAnn Baxter looks like she got hit in the face with pure fire. Her skin is a lot of different colors, like a car that's been stripped and primed for painting. It's sort of patchy and in certain places looks melty, like a wax candle. Thick and droopy. If you have half a brain you can probably guess that MaryAnn's not the most popular person in her high school, which happens also to be my high school. People say mean things to her in the hallway, call her "freak," write things on her locker. I swear, it's like an after-school special. Only on an after-school special everyone would learn something, and MaryAnn's humanity would be exposed and whoever was being an asshole would suddenly get a clue and life would be better. I guarantee that is not going to happen. But if life were fair, MaryAnn would be the popular one. Everyone would want to be around her because she really survived something. Like someone in a movie, she stood up for justice and got horribly wounded but carried on. She would be our hero and we would all want to help her out. Plus there is the curious dizziness that comes with looking at her face for a bit. I had one class with MaryAnn Baxter this last semester and can testify that if you stare at her for too long this certain tingly lightheadedness can overtake you, a sort of drunken feeling. I don't know why, but it's true, and why not add that to the list of reasons to be good to her: she is like a strange drug. Maybe if everyone in the world got their periods at the exact same time MaryAnn would be universally accepted for about a minute. But not even, 'cause then there's still all the guys.

Bernice O'Leary came to Kristy on her last day of shop,

for her regular fluffy hairdo, and she was all bent out of shape because her prize employee Kim Porciatti was unavailable for work and now that schools were letting out it was truly summer inside the mall and there were boxes of overpriced plastic-wrap bikinis waiting to be stocked. And then, said Kristy, Bernice started to tear up. Kristy thought it was the fumes from the perm solution that a student who'd just been smoking pot in the bathroom was liberally squirting onto the head of an old lady. This student was just dousing the lady and laughing and her eyes were all bloodshot and Kristy was thinking, Jesus, she is wicked high, and then she noticed that Bernice's eyes were all red too and maybe the perm sauce was getting to her and when she began to ask, Bernice toppled from sniffling into straight-up crying and confessed to Kristy that she didn't really care about the bikinis, she was just so concerned about poor Kim Porciatti who had actually tried to kill herself.

She was really upset, Kristy told me.

Really? It sounds lousy to be skeptical of such a thing, I know, but everyone loves when something like this happens. Anytime someone tries to kill themselves or crashes their car up drunk driving, they're suddenly everyone's best friend. And I felt a bit of dread, because everyone was already trying to be Kim Porciatti's best friend and now that she'd gone and tried to kill herself I knew it would be unbearable. How'd She Do It? I asked.

I think she cut her arms.

Which Way? I asked. The Phony Way Or The Real Way? Kristy rolled her eyes. *Everyone knows about that,* she said. *I'm sure it was the real way. No one cuts their wrists except cutters.*

Maybe She Was Just A Cutter, I suggested. Maybe Her Parents Caught Her Cutting Herself And Got The Wrong Idea. I sort of liked that theory. I know the whole cutting thing is very trendy right now but still, it gave Kim Porciatti a dark side I hadn't thought she had. I shared my theory with Kristy.

Oh, suicide isn't dark enough for you? she asked. She had an unfriendly look on her face.

It's So Showy, I said. A Cry For Help. I had to resist the pressure to feel upset about it. No doubt every high school in the area was about to declare a regional day of grief at the very idea that someone as cute as Kim Porciatti could feel emotional pain. Then I remembered that high school was out now, and such mourning would play out at the mall if anywhere, and I thought it was poor planning on Kim's part to make such a dramatic statement when no one was really around to take notice.

You're cold, Kristy said. *Hard.*

Don't Blame Me, I said. Blame The World.

Three

The Square One Mall is our mall. If you think about it, it's a crummy name for a mall. Like, "back to square one." It's where you go when your really big, visionary plans don't work out. What I really like is that at the side entrance there's a great, lit-up neon sign propped above the doors that glows, "MALL." It's generic, yet glamorous. Square One's got the regular things that most malls have. There's an Ohmigod! and then stores that sort of aspire to be Ohmigod!, places like Eternally Eighteen and Tight Knit. These stores should be embraced for generously offering cheaper versions of the crap on sale at Ohmigod!, but everyone is so frigging self-loathing it's some sort of social crime to buy the cheaper outfits.

There's a Lotions & Potions for natural skin stuff and

a Dark Subject that sells clothes for kids who want to make you think they're really dark, scary people with tortured inner lives. There's a bunch of other weird places I'm not really interested in, like a hobby store, stuffed with miniature vehicles, that I've never seen anyone go into. Sometimes a Mr. Rogers-looking guy with a button-up sweater stands at the edge of this shop and peers out into the greater mall. A little track of scalp is displayed by the side part of his neat, nerdy hairdo. He looks like he time-traveled into Square One from some gentler year. He stands before his hobby shop and looks over at the giant video game store where all the boys are having a big testosterone fest trying out various games in which they street fight, run over hookers, and in general make some mayhem. His little ships and gluey planes are no match. It's too sad, really. There's a craft store where mom-looking women shuffle around putting bouquets of plastic flowers and pipe cleaners into their shopping baskets. A dull bookstore. They have a giant shelf when you first walk in, all the covers are every different shade of pink, from the faintest fingernail-pink to a more brassy, unnatural fuchsia. Those are books for females. They have pictures of high-heeled shoes on them, or caricatures of little dogs, or ladies holding teacups or martini glasses, and the pink is whimsically accented with bits of lime green or jolting orange.

There's a food court in the middle of the mall with a lot of top-rate crap-ass options. There are carts throughout the place that sell really useful things like cell phone covers that have pictures of girls who look like Kim Porciatti in Budweiser bathing suits, or miniature wigs you somehow stick into your hairdo for maximum hair effect, or imitation designer pocketbooks that don't fool anybody and still cost a bunch of money.

I went to the mall on the evening of what should have been my last day of school, to assist Kristy in the scoring of a job at Jungle Unisex. I'd stayed in my bedroom all afternoon, going quietly crazy in my head. I was filled with rage at my jackass family and also starving, but would not go out into the kitchen and face the torn-open packages of ramen, not to mention the slack, crusty face of Donnie and his concubine, my mother. It's true — I laid around and felt very sorry for myself. An activity I could expect to dominate my summer. When Kristy came home from her last day at the Voke we had a gigantic fight. Kristy had been working on the videotape audition that she hoped would get her onto the cast of *The Real World.* She ingeniously stole a video camera from some media room at the Voke no one even knew was there. She found it while looking for the storage room that held the bulk 40 volume peroxide. So as if life isn't hard enough, she's been sticking that camera into everyone's face, filming our home, getting every single sick and dysfunctional element onto video so that some stupid MTV person fascinated with white trash people will see that Kristy is the real thing, stick her on the show, and wait for her to say ignorant things to the black person and the gay person. She'd been in my bedroom that morning, taping me oversleeping as a symbol of family laziness. It's so deeply unfair. I may not have such a clear life plan as Kristy, with her *Real World* aspiration and cosmetology career, but I am not our Ma and I do not enjoy spending the day in bed. I would have loved for Kristy to wake me up so I could not miss my last day of school, but I guess that didn't really support the angle of her video: the one ambitious person in a welfare family, please save her.

We had a big fight, and Kristy promised to be more fair and let me speak for myself in her dumb video if I came with her to the mall, because Donnie doesn't let us drive his car alone. That's how I wound up in the food court, my ass plopped on a molded plastic bench, getting sort of carried away with my thoughts. I thought, how would I like to be represented in Kristy's video? Perhaps as a quirky sisterly sidekick. Maybe as a brooding and mysterious person with an artistic disposition. I've never done anything artistic, but it seems that being an artistic type can excuse you for being abnormal. I thought that maybe *The Real World* would enjoy having an actual, blood-related pair of sisters on the show. What a great way to ensure a dysfunctional family-style household. But there's no way Kristy would go for it. She was trying to escape, after all, not bring a fragment of her own screwed-up family along with her to Los Angeles or Miami, wherever they set up those fancy houses with the pool tables and swimming pools and beanbag chairs for the stars to slump their skinny, hungover bodies in.

Donnie's car is a Maverick, deep green, the color of the bushy part of a stick of frozen broccoli. I think trashy old cars like that are back in style the same sick way that mullet hairdos are. Like it's wicked cool and funny to be a stupid moron with bad taste and no money. I've gathered this from my limited watching of television and my observations of people at the mall, and I tried for a minute to get into it, having lived my entire life among stupid morons with bad taste and no money: like, maybe my whole life is actually completely cool and I myself am too authentically cool to have realized it. Donnie practically has a mullet hairdo and here he is tooling around in this muscly car. It all fell pretty flat, though. I don't care how much the world loves the *That '70s Show*, that era is over and the only people still living it are too broke or retarded to move on and get with the more contemporary era. People like Donnie, who in real life are not so cool.

In my lawless house, where teenaged children are free to imbibe liquor and slag about without any purpose whatsoever, Kristy is not allowed to take Donnie's car to the mall alone. I am required to chaperone, plopped in the passenger seat. This is the only real time me and Kristy hang out anymore. We used to hang out a lot but then she became upwardly mobile, what with her plans to look good and make friends with certain people and get into the cosmo shop at the Voke so she could eventually be a hairdresser to the stars — after she becomes a star herself by getting on *The Real World*, of course. The supposed reason for Donnie's car law is that it's somehow safer, as if my presence ups Kristy's driving skills to a NASCAR level, but it's just a way for Donnie to get us out of the house at the same time so him and Ma can get romantic in front of the television. In real life it is actually so much more dangerous to have me in the car with my sister, feeling bullied into running her errand, resentment building and cresting into a slap-fight that sends the car careening off the road. Which only happened once and we didn't actually crash, but still it was scary to feel the general mutual annoyance and frustration sharpen into something that felt so angry and crazy that we'd start slapping each other in a moving vehicle. It was seriously a pretty deep experience. I had told Kristy she looks like our father. I could hardly remember what he looked like, he left so long ago and Ma tore his face out of all the old photos in our thin photo album, but I had some memories and in most of them his hair is too long and needs a shampoo, and his face is sleepy, his skin gummy and slumped on his cheekbones, from the drugs he was on, I guess. Telling Kristy she looked like him was the big-gun insult I always held inside my mouth until she really, really pissed me off. It bothered her more than anything, because she's so vain and because our father was such a jerk and also not too attractive and really most of all because it's true: Kristy does look like him, but in that strange way that really good-looking people can sort of resemble somebody very homely. Our father is a ghost that haunts her face. She doesn't always look like him but his genes flash to her skin's surface often enough that she knows it is true when I say it and it enrages her. So she swung at me with her thin hand wide open and then I got to tell her she looks like dad but she's crazy like Ma and then she swung again, wildly, one hand on the wheel, the other flailing out for my face, but I'm part of this family too, I'm part of the whole sick churn and clench of it, so of course I grabbed her hand, and, having two to work with, slapped her back. And I made it, I got her right in her cheek and the car veered off the road.

The whole thing was very disturbing and we sat there

in the car for a while, hazards on, Kristy trying hard not to cry, her whole body tense and vibrating with the effort and only because I was there beside her and she didn't want to crack like that in front of me. I wanted to apologize and ask her if she was okay, maybe cry also, but I didn't want to soften toward her. What if she stayed hard and took another swipe at me? So I just stayed quiet and swallowed a bunch and waited for her breathing to regulate. Eventually the tears in her eyes dried up and she was able to blink without them rolling down her face. She was able to push her hair back and pull some air into her lungs and get the car back onto the road. While I waited for Kristy to get it together I ruminated on some pretty unpleasant thoughts, thoughts about DNA and about being Ma's daughters. Daughters. There's a word. Daughters. It sounds like a deep-fried pastry. Something not too good for you, nuts stuck to it with sugar thick as paste. Something stuffed with soggy fruit.

Ma's never hit either of us — she's way too tired for that — it's the DNA of her mental illness I worry about. If it's been passed down to me and Kristy, some little viral strand of it. Not her exact brand of crazy, hypochondria, but something else, some tendency toward negativity and brooding and wanting to whap my sister while she's behind the wheel of a moving vehicle.

At the mall, in the food court, I watched Kristy as she walked out from the long, fluorescent-lit hallway that leads to the public bathrooms. The bad lighting flattened her out like a greenish paper doll and it was so weird to see Kristy

— who, it is generally agreed, is wicked pretty — looking crappy that my stomach startled me by clenching in worry for her future. I guess I am invested in Kristy and her *Real World* plans, even though the complete self-obsession surrounding it can get on my nerves. I don't actually get any happiness out of seeing my sister fail, seeing her stuck here instead of on the television where she longs to live. Watching Kristy swish skinnily down the fluorescent tube, I thought, Fuck, I hope Kristy's not turning to bulimia or some other tired-ass grasp at beauty-at-any-cost, 'cause her coloring looked a lot like my own does after I pound too many beers in too short a time period. I mean, she looked ill, like she just vomited. But as she exited the weird, tunnelish hallway, the red and purple and electric orange glow from the food court neon lights warmed her back up and she looked pretty again. Her hair was long and smooth and the highlights her cosmo partner gave her didn't look totally phony, her hair wasn't flying up with electrocution static even though I'm sure she was just in front of the dull metal mirror in the girls' room going at it with a hundred brushes. The way she runs her eyeliner pencil over the inside of her lids made her eyes look bright and shiny. She got Ma's special eyes, the green ones, they look like jewelry her face wears. I just can't do that with eyeliner, because no matter how much I concentrate and steady my hand and tell myself calming words, my eye thinks it's going to be stabbed and it blinks itself shut like a clam. A couple tries of this and my eyes become teary and totally useless. I tried to draw the black pencil along the outside instead but it just made my face look clownish and dirty so I gave up. I don't like makeup very much anyway so it's no big whoop, though it really bothers Kristy, who is practically a spokesperson for makeup, being a cosmetology graduate and all. She acts like my choice not to wear lip gloss is some sort of sociopathic break from civilization, as if I've decided to never again wear a tampon and just bleed all over everything instead.

Fresh from the bathroom, Kristy stood before me, smiling with her glossed-out lips. It's aimed at me but it's really for her, a wide, together smile that was a summons for her inner troops to gather and prepare to charge. That smile was a bugle call, da-da-da-da-da-DA! *Ready, sister?* she chirped. Honestly, I didn't think that having your makeup-less, super-nonglamorous, actually rather awkward sister trail you into a job interview with a video camera was a great idea, but that's Kristy's way. I almost admire it. It's her strategy to stand out so much that she can't be ignored. Kristy will be the only potential employee who brings a camera crew to the interview, and this, combined with the natural spectacularness of her personality, will get her the job. Plus, we were getting really crucial, really real footage for her *Real World* application. Kristy already had way more video of her unamazing life than *The Real World* would ever need. She'd already made a veritable documentary of herself. I feared that the camera was adding an obsessive focus to her normal narcissism and now she'd never stop talking about herself. It would go on and on and the tapes would pile up, the audition deadline long past. We would forget that there was a time when Kristy was *not* accompanied by the whirring machine. The video project would slowly be revealed as a mental illness, the magnitude of which our family has never seen.

Get it ready, she instructed me as we moved away from the food court and toward the leafy entrance of Jungle Unisex. Kristy's shoes made a sharp clack-clack-clack on the mall floor. My flip-flops made a flatter, slappy noise. I pulled the video camera up to my eye and this great thing happened. It was like I wasn't really there, not anymore. Voom, I'd become the camera. I hadn't wanted to make a big deal out of it, but I was sort of dreading going into Jungle Unisex. It's just not the sort of place I feel comfortable. I appreciate all the big green plants and the stuffed carnival tigers mounted on the walls and the flashy zebra wrapping paper they tacked up like wallpaper — I'm not totally uptight. It is definitely a wild place to walk into, but then you have to deal with all the girls who work there. They've got their hair all done up and when they move their hands it's all flash, a blur of silver scissors and shiny nail polish nails shooting light. They look like comic book superheros casting some sort of power from their palms. They've got full command of the space. I've walked into the place from the relative calm of the mall, suddenly in some bizarre tropical clubhouse that is really not my scene. The girls looked me up and down. I could just feel them giving me a makeover. Immediately I could feel the exact place that a greasy lock of my very unstyled hair brushed against my cheek, the faint friction summoning a zit from the skin there. My skin suddenly felt like it had a weird film over it, like the skin of a dirty pond. My clothes felt soft against my body in that way that only really dirty clothes feel, like the dirtiness is wearing the fabric thin. This is how I like my clothes to feel, but on the inside of Jungle Unisex it stopped feeling comfortable and started feeling hampery. Needless to say, I do not have a pedicure. I may instead have athlete's foot, and I'm always in my flops, my peely toes all hanging out. Ta-daa. But, with Kristy's stolen video camera pressed to my face, it all felt unreal. It was like something I was watching on TV, which was perhaps a good omen for Kristy. An older lady with brown hair, the bangs sprayed up in a thin fan said, *Can I help you?* She cocked her head and her hair fixture sort of wobbled with the movement, but didn't fall. She had makeup welling in the creases of her face, maybe a couple shades too dark, triple-pierced ears hung with gold hoops, and a few rows of gold around her neck. She must be loaded, I thought. I made out a charm in the shape of a blow-dryer hanging off one thin chain.

Hello, I'm Kristy Driscoll, Kristy chirped. Her hand shot out toward the woman, who backed away from it before realizing that Kristy was trying to shake her hand and not steal her jewelry. Kristy pumped the woman's hand while gesturing to me with her free one. I moved in close, making sure I got both of them in the frame. Without that camera I'd have been staring at my flops, but now I was able to really inspect the woman's face, I could look straight at her. It made me a little giddy and I even hit the slidey zoom lens close-up button till the top of her peacock hairdo got chopped out of the picture. Now she should be on a television show. Who even looks like that? Actually, tons of people around here look like that, but nobody on television does. Which is even more of a reason this fan-haired woman should have her own show. *This is my little sister, Patricia,* Kristy jabbered on. *She's videotaping me because I'm auditioning for* The Real World, *do you know that show?* The woman paused and turned toward me. The frame became filled with her suspicious expression. She took a breath and held her hand up toward the camera the way that actual celebrities do when the paparazzi charge at them as they're leaving the yoga studio. Kristy jumped in, *It's a great show, and if I get picked I get to go and live on MTV in another town, and it would be really wonderful for Mogsfield and for the whole region to have a local person on a national TV show, talking about local issues.* Kristy nodded, as if the movement of her head could somehow hypnotize the woman into nodding her own head. *The producers just want to know what my life is like here in Mogsfield, so my sister is following me around with a camera, would that be all right?* Her head was still bobbing but now her face was scrunched too, in that way girls scrunch when they need something. I don't use those tactics. Or maybe I have never needed anything that bad.

The woman got her hand back from Kristy's polite grip of death and was fiddling nervously with herself, first touching one of the thin gold necklaces resting on her tan sternum, tweaking a charm, then patting the stiff crest of hair on her crown. *I wasn't ready to be on television,* she admitted a bit shyly.

Oh, this won't be on television, Kristy assured her. *This is just for the producers to see. But who knows, if I get picked maybe I could get MTV to come here for haircuts!*

The woman smiled. *That'd be something,* she said. *All*

right. It's pretty weird, you know, but I'm a flexible person. I'm Mercedes, by the way. She turned and looked deeply into the camera. *Mercedes Patron,* she said intensely. Her delivery gave me a little shiver. Who knew I would actually enjoy helping Kristy, ever?

We followed Mercedes Patron and her excellent name through the salon and into a tiny back room. Along the way I trailed the camera across the incredible jungleness of the place, and got a swipe or two at some ladies getting their hair chopped. For the first time ever in my limited history of visits to Jungle Unisex, the hairdressers smiled at me. Of course they were smiling at the camera, but it was my eye that caught them.

The back room smelled like shampoo and was hot and rumbly and loud from the washer-dryer stacks banging around a load of towels. It was hard to figure out where to cram myself to catch the best shot. I tried crouching down beneath where Kristy and Mercedes sat on aluminum folding chairs, but Mercedes waggled a bony finger sporting a curling gold *M* into my lens.

Aaah aaah ah, she snapped. *Too many chins down there. Shoot from above.* I fumbled to my feet, wondering if perhaps Mercedes had been a soap opera star or something. She was so cozy with the camera. I wedged myself into a corner and zoned out for most of the interview. It was pretty boring, just Kristy talking about herself and her love of hair, and Mercedes nodding and making the occasional cooing noise as she fell under the spell of Kristy's charm.

Well listen, Kristy, she said at the end of a short monologue in which Kristy detailed her glee for shampooing the heads of strangers — how it must be aromatherapy from the shampoo or something because it just really relaxes her and people have even suggested she go to massage school because she scrubs their heads so wonderfully — *What if I train you, here at Jungle, and you win this television contest and then you leave? I need a commitment.*

I saw this indignant flush rise up in Kristy's face and I had a feeling she was having the same thought I was having, roughly: you expect me to pass up a reality television career to work at fucking Jungle Unisex at the fucking Square One Mall in fucking Mogsfield? For, like, six dollars an hour? Something like that. My thought included a mention of dandruff and other scalpy bits being lodged beneath fingernails and also the general poisonous odor of the place, the perm solutions and the peroxide, but Kristy is immune to these things. I watched my sister through the eye of the camera as she took a breath and assured Mercedes that she probably wouldn't get picked because millions upon millions of young people from all over America try out and there's only a tiny handful of slots and really she's applying mostly because she believes it's good to aim high in life, even when the odds are stacked against you. Watching Kristy spin it into a platform to display her unconquerable spirit was pretty impressive. Especially because Kristy is wicked superstitious and into affirmations and positive thinking, and it must've just killed her to say out loud that she didn't have much of a chance of getting on *The Real World.* Kristy believes that saying things out loud makes them true, and it's an interesting idea, especially when you consider Ma and her hypochondria and her illnesses.

Lady Mercedes was quiet. *Well,* she finally spoke. *I like your energy. You come back after the weekend and we'll get you started. You know, shampoo and sweeping, and when you pass your boards we'll see what happens.* Then she winked, but it was mostly for the camera. I pulled back to get a nice shot of Mercedes Patron brandishing her scissors and generally making love to the camera. If nothing else, my footage could possibly be worked into a nice little commercial for Jungle Unisex. Mercedes slipped her shears into the brief apron bowed around her waist, and abruptly turned away. *This person will not come with this camera every day, capiche?*

Four

Back in Donnie's Maverick, Kristy hit the steering wheel with the palms of her hands, smack smack smack. *Fuck!* she screeched. A long clump of hair was snagged in her glossy lower lip like a mouse in a glue trap. When she tugged it away it left a strawberry snail trail across her powdered cheek. From my view behind the camera, the gloss smear caught the setting sunlight coming in the windshield and made my sister's face look glittered. I just couldn't stop it with the camera. I understood part of Kristy's obsession with it; I didn't want to put it down either.

This Is Great! I enthused. I Can't Believe You Have This Now! I wasn't taking her steering-wheel-smacking fuck-outburst too seriously. Watching someone through a camera sort of makes them look like they're acting, and I don't take Kristy's outbursts too seriously anyway.

Fuck, she repeated, this time a mutter, and jammed the key into the ignition. It was like me and the camera weren't even there. I thought, Kristy is so good at ignoring the camera, she'll really be perfect on *The Real World.* I hope that quality of obliviousness comes through for the producers. *I can't believe I said that out loud,* she said darkly, steering us out of the parking lot. The neon bulbs of the MALL sign dazzled the rearview and then were gone. *That was so negative. I can correct it, though. Right now I can.* She took a deep breath. A fruity smell wafted through the car on her exhale. Kristy's like a living, breathing air freshener. *I am going to get on* The Real World, she spoke in a controlled voice. *I am going to get on television. I am going to be chosen for* The Real World. Truly, this seemed to relax her. That's the benefit of living in a dream world, I guess. You can just keep telling yourself all sorts of happy lies and cheer yourself up by believing them. I thought that Kristy and Ma had two halves of the same mental problem: Ma told herself bad things and believed them, and Kristy told herself really fabulous things until she was totally stoned with delusions of grandeur. But Ma's anti-affirmations did seem to come true. Maybe Kristy was right.

Five

Later that night I stared at myself on the pixilated screen of Kristy's ripped-off video camera. There I was, on my bed with sheets twisted around my legs, the same blue flowered sheets I've had since I was a kid, so faded now that they looked gray on-screen, you couldn't really make out the little blue petals unless you knew what they were. I'm wearing one of Ma's old T-shirts, a Weight Watchers T-shirt she still had from after she was pregnant with Kristy and before she got knocked up with me, when our dad was around. The accidental arrival of Kristy inspired a self-improvement spurt. Our dad tried to stop shooting drugs and Ma went to Weight Watchers, which I always imagined as a long, pink room filled with those machines ladies used to strap around their asses to jiggle the fat away. The T-shirt has a faded cartoon of a woman with a very big, blond head and a very small body and it says, "I'm A Loser!" It's sort of hilarious to imagine Ma working out. I think the most exerting thing she does is occasionally have a fight with Donnie, but the two of them get along pretty great considering what problematic personalities they both have. Life is peaceful in the parlor, the two of them lazing on the couch, all the action on the television.

On the little screen that pulls out from the side of the video camera I observed myself, innocently sleeping, completely unaware that Kristy was recording me. I felt bad for the girl on the miniscreen, me. There's something terrible about the idea that you can be lying in your own bed, your mom's old T-shirt tugging up around your ribs so that a boob's almost popping out, mouth ajar, so vulnerable really, just trusting in that basic way that it's okay to be sprawled out like an animal in sleep, and meanwhile someone's training the sights of an evil camera on you. On the screen I twitched and smacked my mouth together. It sounded gummy, like an old person without their dentures in, and my mortification deepened. It is definitely the better deal to be on the other end of this machine. Just when I became very afraid that the me on the screen was about to make a really gross noise or scratch my crotch, the angle shifted and zoomed in on a small pile of mess beside my bed. There was the pair of jeans I'd kicked off before bed, and the history book that I didn't turn in splayed open and slashed up with the Easter egg ink of highlighter pens. A leather bracelet with a rusty snap, and the real centerpiece — a cluster of green glass beer bottles, all clanked into each other, propping each other up like a gang of drunken friends. The longer the camera rested on them, the less like beer bottles they appeared. They became like a sort of sculpture, green and round and deliberately arranged. As I noticed this effect and felt on the verge of some brand-new thought about it, the camera moved again, sort of violently this time, a dizzying swoosh around my blurred room as Kristy twirled and aimed the machine at her face. Her voice when she spoke was hushed. *My sister, Trish,* she whispered, *is a teenage alcoholic.* Another kaleidoscope spin and there I am again, only this time my sleeping posture and gaping mouth look very different, look like the posture and mouth situation of a teenage alcoholic. Now I looked passed out rather than simply asleep. I couldn't believe I slept through this. The camera zoomed in on the digital alarm clock on my nightstand, the time uselessly flashing midnight. Then there was Kristy's face again. *She's in denial about her problem,* she husked into the camera. *It looks like she's not even going to make it to her last day of school.* And Kristy capped off the drama with a final shot of me, sprawled and unattractive. I bounced in the frame as she backed out of my room and into the hall. Then static.

God Kristy, I Can't Even Fucking Believe You! I charged her bedroom. I didn't care about the camera anymore and so I threw it onto her mattress. Why Didn't You Just Plant The Bottles In The Bed With Me? That Would've Really Helped You. I swear you could see the idea of it flash across her face. The camera, my betrayer, was still streaming out its footage, the flipped-around screen showing our entrance into the dimly lit interior of Jungle Unisex,

Christmas tree twinkles and soft tubes of light snaking up the animal-print walls. Kristy reached over and pressed the red Power button, twirled the blank screen back into the camera's body, like a bird wing tucked away after flight.

Well, you must admit you have a drinking problem, she said calmly. *It might be exploitative of me to film you like that, but what am I supposed to do? They want to see my life and this is my life.* She shrugged a dramatic shrug like some new twitching dance move, a jolt that tensed her whole body and shoved her shoulders up to her ears. *This is my life, Trisha! How do you think it makes me feel?* I took a deep breath, swallowing the Fucking Bitch sitting in my mouth like a wad of gum with all the flavor chewed out. Do you see what I am up against here? The delusions, the martyrness of it all?

You Cannot Film Me Again Without My Permission, I said sternly. You Let Me Miss School, Which Makes You An Asshole. If You Want Me To Keep Helping You With Your Stupid Project, Which You Know Is A Waste Of Time Anyway — Kristy's face shimmered at this, the same sort of shimmer I saw before she tried to smack me in the car, and I steeled my voice like my words were slaps too — You Know It Is, Kristy! But If You Want Me To Help You've Got To Stop Being Such An Asshole! God! Now I was screaming. I know it's the worst because it gives everyone an excuse not to listen to me because now I'm officially hysterical and crazy, but oh well. It's like my voice just wanted to get louder. I don't have a lot of control over this stuff.

Hey! There's Donnie's voice, shrill and whining out of

the other room. *Stop calling each other assholes!* His mouth sounded characteristically filled with unswallowed mush.

Really, Trish. Kristy looked at me. *You drink too much.*

You Barely Drink At All, I accused, as if this was a sort of teenage sin, and, really, it might be. How Are You Qualified To Judge Too Much?

You don't know how to leave it for weekends, or parties, she sputtered, exasperated. *Drinking during the week, on school nights, means you have a problem!* I didn't know how Kristy thought she'd fare in a *Real World* house filled with the youthful alcoholism and sloppy sex and constant fighting the show is famous for. I guess she could maybe worm her way in with the Controlling Older Sister angle, always freaking out on everyone, but really, didn't she understand that she'd sort of be the joke of the show? Kristy exhaled a long, sad sigh.

We already had this fight, remember? Earlier? She held the camera in her hands; lovingly she lifted a corner of sheet from her bed on the floor and rubbed the glass lens.

Yeah, Well, I Hadn't Actually Seen The Footage. I Hadn't Actually Seen How Gross It Is And I Hadn't Actually Known You Were Framing Me As An Alcoholic. Fuck!

I stomped out from Kristy's room — which is papered with pictures of models from magazines in little bikinis and shit. You would totally think she was a lesbian if you saw Kristy's room, but she hangs them up to inspire herself to keep not eating bread and to do sit-ups. It's a little overwhelming to walk into. It could almost be an art project about how fucked-up the whole world is about women's bodies and sex, but it's serious. Some sort of church of the female stomach. I crashed back into my own room, paint chips spraying from the door jamb as I slammed it shut behind me. My room is fairly bare, the way I like it. I think it's embarrassing to hang stuff all over your walls. They're like little flags, posters. You can take a peek into Kristy's room and after the initial creepy horror you feel at the assault of glossy, skinny females staring sulkily at you, you understand what nation Kristy belongs to. Or what nation she wants to belong to, or wants you to think she belongs to. I don't want anyone to think they know who I am just because they saw my bedroom walls, so I keep them empty. Once I was going to paint them purple. I scratched *purple paint* onto the useless wish list sledding with its magnet down the fridge. My walls were just the regular dirty white brand of walls. A little patchy in places, a little drippy. White paint clogged the wire squares in my window screen. My bedroom floor was scuffed linoleum, the pattern just as faded as the one on my bedsheets. Only a vague image remained, some shapes and lines repeating endlessly. It was old, our house. All the ages of the past shone through in the worn-out corners: today's wallpaper peeling to reveal long-ago wallpaper. It seemed a good candidate for a haunted house, all the evidence of olden days still visible. Some old lady ghost could creak right inside and be comforted by the same old tub with the eagle-claw feet still in the bathroom, the green paint she'd slapped onto it while she was alive molting, flaking the linoleum like dandruff.

So many other people had lived where I live, and it never even freaked me out that probably some of them died in there, maybe even in my own bedroom. I always thought that something kept us lucky, and maybe it was that we were being watched over by a gang of ye olde ghost grandmas, all swirling around in otherworldly housecoats. All the months we didn't pay the rent on time and we were still here. Ma fake-sick all the time and she never got cut off, never got real-life bad sick either. Me only giving half a crap at school and still I got by. Being underage but never having a problem getting the beer I wanted, always that excellent swept-away feeling there in the bottle and I was good with it, I hardly ever puked and never, ever got blackouts. It was a real low-key sort of luck we had going on, my family. No megabucks sweepstakes won, no long-lost relative who croaked and left us suddenly loaded. It was a sort of loser luck, I guess, the luck of the cigarette-smoking ghost-grannies who shuffled the scuffed linoleum, but I'd take it over no luck at all.

Ma made the sound of the television swell against the hateful hollers of me and my sister. Passive-aggressive for sure, but I'd rather Ma communicate her irritation by cranking up Jerry Springer instead of sending Donnie in to do some pretend-Dad song and dance. Still, the blast of talk show hysteria made all my jumbled anti-Kristy feelings surge higher and larger until my insides were chaos. My immediate instinct was to gather my beer bottles and run screaming into Kristy's room and hurl them at the paper bodies on her walls, terrifying but not actually hurting my sister with the rain of green glass. But I am so contrary I rebel against even my own impulses, so instead I slowed down. I nudged my door deeper into the sticky frame. The rising heat and humidity would swell the door and goo the paint, effectively sealing me into my bedroom. Slowly I moved and breathed toward the beer bottles. The fluttering plastic handle of a grocery bag poked out from under my bed. I tugged it out and laid the bottles inside, dumping the drippy remains down my throat first, so that they didn't spill out and dribble through the holes in the bag, making everything sticky and stinky. I tied the handles in a knot and continued to clean my room. I folded my limp jeans and placed my leather bracelet on my bureau. With my bare hands I gathered the gray dust bunny puffs that formed against my walls. I tossed them out my open window and watched them blow along the nighttime pavement like tumbleweeds. Everything was fine. Who cared about missing the last day of school, anyway? It's not like I was particularly in love with any of my teachers. I was also not very connected to my classmates. I'm what they call on television a "loner." On television most people are suspicious and even scornful of the loner, but one or two key people tend to be intrigued, and if the loner manages to avoid becoming a victim of circumstance, he or she often prevails. It's not so bad. I only needed to locate the one or two key people who would find my lonerness interesting and befriend them. And then learn to identify the precarious circumstances that could victimize me. I thought: this is my summer plan. I decided it right then, sitting on my bed, which I had more or less made — tugging the sheet up over my pillow and then sculpting the fabric around the pillow so I could see its distinct shape, like in magazine pictures of beds. The air that came in my window smelled like summer trees, like their limey-green leaves. It smelled like the tar in the street that had turned gooey under the sun, the whole world softened in the heat.

My burst of self-willed calm and optimism was so inspiring I was moved to paint my toenails. Just for the fuck of it. Who's the teenage alcoholic now? The girl sitting in a cleanish room, enjoying some fresh air and giving her toenails a little color? I don't think so. Soon enough there was the sound of pressure against my door, a heaving, creaking sound, and it appeared the rickety door with its globbed-on paint dried in drips and blobs would split down the middle. The thing popped open and Kristy fell into my room. She did not have the video camera. How's that for turning over a new leaf? For trying to be a humane person in the world? Though what a redeeming shot it would've been: me in my cleaned-up room, the beer bottles bagged up and tucked away, waiting for disposal. Me actually painting my toenails, a well-adjusted female activity. The red pooled on the tiny nails and made them look like candy. I imagined feeding my candy toes to some sort of salivating boy who liked girl-feet. *Your toes look like Red Hots,* he would murmur excitedly. I gave a bitchy glance at Kristy and returned to my feet, shaping the puddles of polish with the brush, stopping the excessive paint from rolling down onto the skin of my toes.

Wow, Kristy said humbly, and I relaxed. *You're painting your toenails.* I shrugged like I did it all the time. *If you want, I'll do your fingernails for you. A manicure.*

Did They Teach You That At The Voke? I asked, and she shook her head.

I already knew it. Kristy moved to the end of my bed

and sat down on it. Many times Kristy has tried to buy my bed frame off me. She's had jobs forever and has more money than anyone in the house, and she deeply regrets the temper tantrum that caused her own bed frame to crack down the middle, the wooden slats gutting the shabby box spring. She offers me insultingly low prices to part with my bed. I'll never do it. My primary activity is lying around in bed, so you could call my bed and all its parts my number-one possession. Cash would be nice, but I got by without it. There was always some dried-up ramen bricks in the pantry, waiting to be plunged into a pot of boiling water. I'd never starve. Ma liked to brag about this fact. She'd say, *You kids don't starve.* She'd say it like she wanted a prize, like she wanted the mother-of-the-year award for not starving her children. But she was right, we didn't starve, not so long as the big ramen factory kept slapping up those bunched-up nests of noodle. I bummed beers off Donnie when possible, I didn't need much. Kristy could buy herself her own damn bed frame anyway, if she didn't spend her money on endless beauty products and douche-bag clothing from Ohmigod!, but she's got her priorities, I guess.

Trisha, what are you going to do? she asked me, arranged on the edge of my bed like a little canary. Her voice had a made-for-television-movie heaviness to it, like I'd been diagnosed with breast cancer and she wanted to know what treatments I'd be pursuing. I capped the polish and set the bottle on my nightstand, began wiggling my toes to accelerate the drying process. The last time I painted my toes I didn't wait long enough for them to dry properly. I put on a pair of socks and then my sneakers, and at the end of the day the polish had dried with the socks stuck into it so they were attached to my feet by these smears. It looked like something horrible and bloody had happened to my feet and I dramatically limped into the parlor screeching, My Toes, My Toes! and scared the shit out of Donnie and Ma. Ma in particular was affected by the joke and seemed to have a hard time viewing my feet as healthy ever sense. She insists I have athlete's foot and a toe fungus but really they seem fine, just a little peely. I worried that Ma's hypochondria might be branching out into Munchausen Syndrome by Proxy, like Eminem's mom. And look how fucked-up he turned out.

Are you going to give me the silent treatment? Kristy asked. Her voice was tender like a Hallmark card. She loves to play Big Sister.

No, I Just Don't Know What You Mean, I said, staring at my crimson toes.

I mean, what's your plan for the summer? Like, my plan is to work at Jungle Unisex and pass my boards and complete my application for The Real World. *What's your plan?* She gave me a sisterly smile. I shrugged.

I Don't Know, I said. The plan I'd just made, to find people intrigued by my essential loner nature, seemed both complicated and embarrassing. Like, my plan is to find a friend. God. Kristy shook her head impatiently, making the layers in her streaky brown-blond hair shift and tremble. Kristy cut her own hair, using an impressive configuration of mirrors. She wouldn't let any of the girls in her cosmo shop do it because she said they smoked too much pot, but I bet she was paranoid.

No, Trisha, she said intensely. *You need a plan. You can't sit here like this in your room, with those two out there all day. You'll go crazy.* She slapped the bottom of my feet. *You need a job.*

Oh, Kristy, I groaned.

You need to pay attention, she said, and if possible her voice got even more intense. *You need to look for all the bits of your personality that are like Ma's and you have to work against them or else you could end up just like her. And it worries me that you don't have a job, Trish. You're old enough. I've had one for years. You can't lay around all summer like she does.*

Our mother doesn't work. She hasn't really ever, and her mom didn't work either. It's like a family tradition, not working. A few years back she'd actually freaked us all out by going down to Joe's Club and managing to get hired, and for a minute that was really exciting. Joe's Club sells basically everything you could ever need, and workers get a discount on the already cheap stuff. The possibility of such material riches almost made me anxious. We could get a DVD player. Cassette tapes in bulk, for hardly any money. Giant-sized bags of potato chips. Oh, the luxury of a giant new bag of chips. One you pull open with a pop, releasing the greasy-salty puff of potato chip air from inside. You can snack 'til you're stuffed and not worry about leaving enough for the other hogs, there's just so much. A pirate's treasure, an endless magical bag of chips. The Joe's Club thing opened up these wondrous possibilities, possibilities that were then slaughtered because of Ma's back problems, how the job aggravated them. And the thing about back problems is doctors can't even say if they're real or not. I mean, if Ma's lying they can't prove it, but they also can't give her the big Bad Back Award. It's a weird gray area, the back. Ma brought hers back to the couch and that was the end of my Joe's Club dreams. I did console myself with one of Ma's new painkillers, which was sort of nice. Ma had to hike down to the welfare office, all doped up on them, and explain her failed attempt at rejoining society to her caseworker, getting back on track with the flow of paperwork and aid that came regularly through our door slot. I just lay in my bed, feeling heavy and wobbly like a pan full of Jell-O.

All in all Ma doesn't have it so bad. I mean, if I'm right, most people work all week to scavenge two brief days of the kind of living Ma has all the time. It's like she's on a permanent vacation. I have to admit, this lifestyle has a queasy pull for me, sort of like the last beer or two of the night — I know it's not so good for me, but I want it anyway. Even the kind of wanting is similar, a sort of familiar and comfortable and even physical want, like I've already had it and I want it back, intimate like that. Like that lying-around life or bottle of beer was mine some time ago, was ripped away, and I'm just working to get it back. I know that Kristy's right to ride her own ass so hard, and that she's right about me too, but the conversation still shakes me up and makes me sort of frustrated. Because it's just not that easy for me. I can't just crash out into the world with a smile and a flip of hair and make shit happen. I don't know how to be like Kristy, who seems to understand the crucial way to be if you want to get things in this world.

Kristy, I Don't Know How To get A Job. Nobody's Going To Hire Me.

Kristy's eyeliner-wide eyes grew larger in alarm at my words. *Well, to start, stop talking like that,* she hissed her voice like it could put out the fire my negative sentence had sparked. *You shouldn't even think like that, Trish. But you really, really shouldn't talk like that.* She took a breath. *Okay, say this: people are waiting to hire me.*

Kristy, I groaned.

Say it!

People Are Waiting To Hire Me.

That's good, that's good, she encouraged. It was nice of her to ignore my tone and the toss I gave my eyeballs. And really I think it's great that Kristy has this tie to the cosmos, this ability to indulge her hocus-pocus emotions without feeling like a total goon, but I don't have that power. Even though it was just Kristy, who has seen me naked and smelled my farts, I felt the way you do during those naked-in-class dreams that seem to be a universal human experience. Like she'd lodged a telescope into the parts of my person most hopelessly riddled with loserness. *Say it again,* Kristy beamed, *but really like you believe it!*

People Are Waiting To Hire Me, I repeated. This time I made my voice louder and didn't roll my eyes. I couldn't help the tone, though. Tone is generally beyond my range of control.

Trisha, my sister gasped. She looked like a soccer mom whose brat had just head-butted the ball to glory. Proud. *We are going to get you a job!*

Six

On the morning of the next day, at an hour I usually don't wake up at without the requirement of school, Kristy was putting the finishing touches on her new project, me. My hair, which she was unable to handle without making intense squeals of grossed-outness because of the dirt, was weaved into some ladylike hair sculpture on the back of my head. It felt heavy and fragile, like a small animal was pinned to my scalp.

I do believe that in your case, dirt might be working as a styling agent, Kristy mused.

See? I said. If We Could Find A Way To Bottle My Funk We Could Sell It To Hair Salons And Be Rich.

Kristy snorted, wiped my organic hair grease from her hands with a dishrag. *Hold your breath,* she ordered, and I sucked air into my lungs and squished my eyelids tight as suffocating clouds of Aqua Net shot from the giant can and engulfed my head. When she was done, Kristy tipped her own feathery head upside down and blasted a gust onto her own hairdo. *Okay!* she said proudly, her hair settling back around her face, somewhat stiffer. She plonked the can down on her dresser. Once I watched some girls in the bathroom at school take a lighter turned up high and spray a cloud of Aqua Net at it. It transformed into a swirling ball of fire, suspended for a moment in the air, then vanished. It was maybe the best thing I'd ever seen. I thought of it whenever I saw Kristy's can, but am generally too scared of burning the house down to try it myself. From what the girls in the bathroom were saying, if you fucked up the fire could somehow be pulled back into the can and explode in your hand and then you're dead or all burned up.

I could feel what Kristy had done to me, and I didn't want to see it. The makeup felt like a thin, cracking dryness on my face, like the time I used Ma's clay mask, the way it slowly tightened itself over my skin, a shell. My eyelids felt heavy and fragile and my lips felt smeary. Miniature chandeliers of earrings swayed against my neck. If I looked down I could see my boobs, a part of my body I generally like to pretend does not exist. There they were, curving out from the anxiously low-cut and fluttery fuchsia top Kristy had ordered me to put on. The boobs looked, from my rather aerial point of view, like someone else's boobage. I resisted the urge to run my fingers over the fleshy domes, just to feel the touch and understand that they were mine. I felt disoriented and flushed. Maybe all the hair spray had clogged the flow of oxygen to my brain. I slid off the stool I'd been perched on and picked awkwardly at my bottom half — underwear wedged into my crack and a skirt composed of ruffles that barely covered my wedgie. Air pooled and streamed around my excessively bare legs. It felt like an awful lot of exposed skin. Kristy's pink flip-flops, made of a thicker cut of foam than my regular flops, the straps dotted with shiny circles, were on my feet. I looked at my toenails. They had started all of this, hadn't they. They had seen it coming.

Woo-hoo! Donnie cackled in the doorway. He slapped his hairy thigh, making the stringy fringe of his cutoffs waggle. His grody feet were bare and I imagined he was trailing evil foot problems across our linoleum, shedding general ill-foot health along his way. *A transformation!* he continued. *Kristy, you gotta film that! You gotta do a before-and-after. You gotta put that on your resume!*

Kristy, who like me does her best to treat Donnie with consistent scorn and disdain, allowed herself a little smile, a quick bask in Donnie's compliment. *You're right,* she bobbed her head and snatched at the video camera, flicked the screen open, and hit the button to get it rolling. She scanned me with it, from the tips of my flops to the shellacked braidwork crowning my head. I stared at the camera accusingly, contemplated flipping her off, but instead said People Are Waiting To Hire Me, in a voice dead people would use if dead people spoke.

Donnie blinked. *You're getting a job?*

Yes! Kristy snapped.

Well, that's great! he enthused. *It'd be good to get some more money rolling in around here. More money for the bills and the groceries.* Kristy glared at him and my stomach sank a little bit, a hot-air balloon that got nipped by a bird and was slowly descending to earth. The idea of having money of my own had begun to grow on me. I'd found myself sliding into quickie daydreams: my own six-pack chilling in the fridge, new flip-flops, maybe a pair of terry cloth wristbands. The thought of having to subsidize Donnie's ham salad and Ma's television killed it, gave me a trapped and futile feeling. I thought about how Ma had broken it down for me a while back, how when you work, the government took a bit and then, I don't know, some other part of the government took another little bit, and then you've got your bills and whatever and soon there's nothing left. It seemed like this was happening already. Already Donnie had his sights on my wages and nobody'd even hired me yet.

Can we take the car? Kristy asked. Donnie dug into the pocket of his cutoffs for the ring of dangling keys. He tossed them to Kristy with a quick, sharp nod. God, he thinks he's so cool, it's really embarrassing. Like, you're embarrassed for him. He feels no embarrassment, you feel all of it. How's that for fair? But I guess that's just one more way losers like Donnie make the world a lousy place for the rest of us.

Seven

Back in Donnie's Maverick we cruised along in the heat. Kristy did scientific calculations regarding wind. Like, would the air blasting in the rolled-down window batter the shape and sleekness out of my carefully sculpted hairdo? Alternately, if we kept the window cranked up tight, would the simmering heat melt the hair pile into a sticky, chemical hairball? We compromised by pulling the window down just a tad, just enough to breathe, to stir the ashes in the Maverick's ashtray — a busted ashtray, permanently jammed out and piled high with butts and their charred dust. It was so humid inside the car that we fanned the air in front of us, which was better than having the wind gusting in and blowing shit around, causing us to inhale Donnie's old cigarette ashes. Terrible stuff involving cigarette ash has happened in the Maverick. One time I was riding in the back and Donnie was smoking like he always does — the car was his safe space for smoking; Ma wouldn't let him do it in the house 'cause of her self-diagnosed emphysema — and he flicked the edge of his butt out the cracked-down window and *whoompf,* a chunk of ash soared into the backseat and, seriously, right into my mouth. It was hot and it was not soft and powdery like I imagined an ash to be. It was sort of hard and crunchy. I spit as much of it from my mouth as fast as I could, but some of it had just stuck wetly to the inside of my cheek, had dissolved or something, and ugh, it was the most disgusting thing ever to happen to me. My mouth felt burnt and filthy afterward. Thankfully I was in the backseat by myself and nobody saw this humiliation.

Kristy parked the car expertly in a yellow-lined slot in the mall parking lot. We climbed out and examined each other. You Have Ash On Your Shoulder, I informed her, and dusted off the bunched, sky blue cotton of her T-shirt. She squinted her eyes at the top of my head.

Oh no, she murmured. She moved toward me, her heavily glossed lips puckering into a blowhole. She started huffing fruity-scented puffs onto my head, just up from my forehead. The hair there was pulled tight in a side part, secured with vicious bobby pins, creating a sleek plain for the updo to erupt from. Kristy blew and blew onto this one spot on my head, the blows becoming increasing hard and focused until it felt like a form of torture and her face turned a tomatoey red.

You're Going To Hyperventilate! I whined. What Is It?

It's a big ash, it's really stuck in the hair, it's stuck in the spray.

Just Leave It, I said. I was already exhausted. I wanted to go home and get out of this outfit. The air was climbing up my bare legs and spiraling around my nude arms, skimming my exposed cleavage. The sun was all over me and I could feel it flushing and stinging my sensitive Irish skin. Kristy shook her head firmly. She's like the only perfectionist in the history of our family. The whole family, the ancestors, all the way back to Ireland. She's a mutation, a genetic aberration.

No, Trisha, you don't go out to get a job with your head looking like an ashtray. Jesus. Kristy started to do that gross thing that mothers do, though our mother never did it 'cause she was too freaked out about germs. She licked her finger and instead of rubbing a bit of smudge off my cheek she got her finger really lubed up with a whole bunch of spit and brought the shining, slimy thing down on my head. Her face was all crinkled, like it hurt her to do it to me. *I'm so sorry,* she genuinely apologized. I could feel the giant wet drip of her spit plopped onto my head, doing its best to dissolve the ash trapped in my hairdo. This was amazing. This was not a great start to my career in being an employee. If we had belonged to some ancient religion that respected omens I have no doubt we would have known to turn back right then, to clamber into the ashmobile and zoom back back home, perhaps stopping at a packy along the way and persuading an adult with loose morals to buy us a four-pack of weekday wine coolers. Here's where Kristy's a hypocrite: she gets all up on my ass about beer, but she just loves wine coolers and Zimas.

Oh! Kristy bit down on her bottom lip in pure joy, like the sight of me was so intense it pushed her to self-cannibalism. Her front tooth scraped off a bit of fruity lip gloss. She licked it away and smiled. She rubbed her lips together, smearing more gloss over the little crater the tooth had left. She smacked them together with a suction-cup sound and squealed. *You look great! Great! I have big feelings, Patricia. Big, lucky feelings.* She grabbed my hand and led me in the direction of the side entrance. The many neon bulbs of the sign were no match for the relentless sun above. The sun sucked away all the shine of the lights, blasted everything out with its glare. But I knew they were glowing underneath all the summertime, and when the sun fell down later the lights would rise like a bunch of red moons in the sky above the mall.

Eight

Bernice O'Leary ruled Ohmigod! Kristy led me into the store, pointing out the manager like we were in the forest trying to spot deer. *There she is!* Kristy whispered, like we could startle her and cause her to dash off into the communal dressing room. She was partially obscured by a freestanding jewelry rack holding Ohmigod! jewelry. She had at her feet a cardboard box full of plastic-wrapped fake-pearl necklaces from China, and was tearing into bag after bag with the jagged corner of a box cutter and lifting the necklaces into the air like midwifing a child. She held the necklaces so gently, gazed at the shiny plastic beads, and her breath fluttered the fat sateen ribbons meant to bow around a girl's neck. One by one, slowly, she hung the necklaces onto the hooks in the rack. She draped them over the prongs and straightened them neatly. Also at her feet was a wire basket she tossed the old, unsold spring jewelry into, carelessly, meanly, like she was pissed at the cheap rhinestone necklaces, the hemp chokers, and faux-bronze crucifixes for being such failures. The chains dashed and twined against each other in the basket, earrings were separated from their partners, plastic disks cracked, paint chipped cheaply from metal. Teensy backings for pairs of iridescent fake-crystal studs were knocked from their posts and rolled out the gaps in the basket's weave. Bernice was all decked out in Ohmigod! clothes — the capri pants and metallic belt, the sparkly shirt, a pair of fuchsia earrings shaped like stars swinging out from her hair on silver chains. She had the clothes, but somehow, she didn't have the look. Maybe it was because Ohmigod! caters to seventeen-year-olds and Bernice had to be at least thirty. But I think it was more than that. Bernice O'Leary had put the bright clothes onto her round body the way a worker puts on a unifrom. If she was working at Dark Subject she'd be wrapped in a cobweb with bats flung from her earlobes. She might as well have been wearing a smock. I wondered what Bernice wore on her days off. If all this glitz looked fake on her, I tried to imagine what looked real. All I could come up with were sweatpants.

I watched Bernice at work. The curves of her cheeks were red, like she'd been in the cold or had recently been slapped. She was totally engrossed, practically hypnotized by the pearlescent sheen of the baubles. I could really understand why Ohmigod! has such a huge shoplifting rate. I felt like I could have grabbed an entire rack of rainbow terry cloth rompers and strolled cooly out of the store, never distracting Bernice from her love affair with the beads. But I was wrong. My hand slunk up to rub the soft terry cloth nubs and tinkle the silver zipper and wham, up shot Bernice's head, like she had some sort of sick sixth sense reserved for retail managers at busy malls. She arranged her face in an interesting combo of welcoming smile and suspiciously squinting eyeballs. *Hel-lo,* she said to me, clanking a fistful of necklaces in greeting.

Bernice O'Leary, Bernice O'Leary, Kristy singsonged, her voice like a Disney princess, dripping flower petals and plump, chirping birds. Bernice swung her focus over to my sweetly smiling sister.

Oh, Kristy! Oh, I'd been hoping to see you around here, girl! I don't know what I'm supposed to do now that your cosmo shop is all closed up for the summer! Look at this! She brought her fingers up to her bangs, which were fringing into her eyes. *I shoulda had you go shorter with these. They've been making me crazy!*

Well, you are so lucky I'm here then! Kristy beamed. *And, I'll be working at Jungle Unisex starting next week!*

Oh. Bernice's smile fell a bit, but then she propped it up with some reinforcements. *Well, good for you. I guess that's what ya went to school for, huh?* She layered the beads, now extra shiny with a scrim of Bernice O'Leary palm sweat, onto an empty hook.

Well, I can't cut in a shop 'til I take my boards, so I'll be just doing shampoos and sweeping up over there 'til I pass. But maybe I can bring my shears by the store after you close up or something?

Rattle, rattle. Bernice's happy fists shook a new handful of jewelry. *Oh, you're the best, girl! I'm so glad, oh my god, these bangs are about to put my eyes out, you know? And I could come see you at Jungle, I could, but I don't like that place so much. No offense. The girls are bitches over there. They gave my mother a perm that burnt her scalp, swear to god. I tell her to go to the Voke, but she doesn't listen. She doesn't want kids working on her.* Bernice shrugged.

It's temporary anyway. I'm trying to get on The Real World.

Yeah? How's that coming?

Good, good, real good, Kristy shuffled and flipped her hair. She took a breath and plunged into a vat of lies. *So Bernice, I was wondering, how's Kim doing? And, how are you doing too? It must be wicked hard, being so close with someone who does something like that. And now you got one less girl working here, and school's out and there must be a ton of shoplifting to worry about...*Kristy's eyes went doe-y, all green mush. They seemed as compelling to Bernice as the baubles she'd been stacking. She stared at my sister, her face went sort of slack and then her blotchy red cheeks rippled with a quiver of sadness. I thought, great, fucking Bernice O'Leary is going to cry. I just didn't feel like I was close enough with the woman to witness something so intimate. And there's Kristy, drawing it out of her like a slow poison.

Oh. Bernice's "Oh" was a gasp of air, a shaky, verbal shrug. She peered at my sister from behind the thin curtain of bangs. *Oh, it's hard, sure,* she nodded. *Kim, she's like my little sister here, you know? Such a hard worker too. You wouldn't believe it, but it's true. And she brought in a lot of business. It's just dead without her. Oh* — this "Oh" was a fishy, shamed gasp at having used the word "dead" in conjunction with Kim Porciatti. A fierce flush flooded her round cheeks and a drip of cry spilled over one of the eyes, and was quickly sopped up by her hair. Kristy was nodding a therapist's nod, melodramatically concerned. She took a deep breath, and then, as if just remembering me, spun around and pushed me toward the weeping manager.

Bernice, do you know my sister, Patricia?

Oh, no, girl, I didn't know you had a sister! Older or younger?

Younger, Kristy purred, and patted a strand of hair above my ear like I was a little doll.

Oh, that's sweet! You're lucky, Bernice nodded at me. *Kristy's a good kid. What a great big sister she must be, huh?* I nodded my head dumbly. My outfit was draining my IQ.

Patricia was close with Kim. IS close with Kim. This has been wicked hard on her too.

Oh — Bernice's neck bent out, giraffelike, toward me. *Oh, no. Have you seen her? Will you tell her to please call me — when she can! No rush, no rush. It's just that, she hasn't called at all, you know, and I don't want to replace her.* She laughed. *Who could replace Kim? Right? But I need to know when she's coming back. And how she is, just any word from her would be good. Do you know . . . why? She did it?*

Uh...I stammered. Fucking Kristy did not even tell me the extent of the untruth she had planned. What a total scam the job-getting activity would be. You think she would have briefed me on it. I mean, what if I just turned around and said, Kristy, Why Are You Such A Rotten Lying

Liar? Why Are You Lying About A Suicide Victim? Why Are You So Evil? But Kristy was my sister, knew me well, had banked, correctly, on the fact that I would be too frozen in fear to protest the ecosystem of lies springing up around me. I would be paralyzed and easily maneuvered.

Oh, that's tacky, huh? Bernice seemed embarrassed. *I'm sorry. Patricia.* She looked at me close. *Have we met before? Have you come in here with Katie and Yolanda?* She meant Katie Adrienzen and Yolanda Peters. Katie was Kim's best friend, they were like a famous friend-couple, always together, dressing in complementary outfits, sort of looking-glass doubles of each other. Katie was dark where Kim was blond, she was already filled with curves, I mean boobs, while Kim was skinny like a lanky supermodel, her chest concave in a way that looked glamorous, not undeveloped. Yolanda was a couple years younger than Kim and was being groomed by Kim to be, like, the next Kim. She was mini-Kim. It was pathetic. I nodded.

Yeah, I Think I've Been In Here With Them, I mumbled.

Kristy whapped my arm with her clutch purse. *Of course you've been in here! It's only your favorite store!* She turned her smile to Bernice. *She's nervous to be meeting you. Ohmigod! means a lot to her, and she's still freaked out over Kim and all...*

Sure, sure.

But anyway, I was thinking — why doesn't Patricia here help you out while you're waiting for Kim to come back? I mean, I'm sure if you had to replace her, temporarily, Kim would want one of her friends to take her place. And I know it would be Patricia's dream to work here, right

Sis? She's shy! But, she's a great worker. Loves fashion. And is sooo motivated!

You look like you love fashion, you do, Bernice mused, nodding her head.

It took every mental muscle in Kristy's brain for her to not blurt and take credit for the giant hoax of my outfit. I saw her struggle with it, her mouth tense.

You really want to work here? Bernice asked. She kept blowing upward gusts of breath to knock her hair from her eyes. She peered at me hopefully from behind her outgrown hairdo. I couldn't believe it. It was too easy. My sister was a genius, a dark genius.

Who Doesn't? I gushed.

It's true, Bernice said, *This is the most popular shop in the mall. That poor thing Debbie who works over at Dark Subject has been trying to get hired here since Christmas. Those freaks have been making her crazy. Did you know the lady who manages the place got her teeth filed down to look like vampire fangs?*

Oh my god, Kristy said in that deep, gossipy shit-talking voice.

Honest to god. A dentist did it. Can you imagine? He should get his license revoked. I mean, isn't that illegal? As a cosmetologist, what would you do if someone came to you and asked you to make them look like a circus freak?

I'd tell them to go see a psychiatrist! Kristy said.

Bernice O'Leary sighed then, in the grip of a moral dilemma. Her bangs shagged limply, she allowed them to curtain her vision. She looked down at the mess of jewelry at her feet. *I did promise Debbie the next opening . . .*

But it's not really an opening, Kristy reminded her.

It's not really an opening, Bernice agreed.

It's for Kim, Kristy said gently. *And you.*

It is, Bernice nodded. She looked at me. I tried to make my eyes go round like Kristy's when she's trying to be extra sincere, but they felt only bulgy and I think I alarmed Bernice. *Don't cry!* she gasped, reaching out and touching the bare skin of my arm. I shrank back. *I know this is hard,* Bernice said. *Suicide, god! Who commits suicide in this day and age, when there's so much help available? I mean, we got medicines now . . .* She took a firm breath. *Come in on Monday, all right, girl? I really do need the help.*

Nine

Family time! Ma hollered from the couch in a cartoony-sweet voice. It was the voice that gave birth to Kristy's saccharine singsong. *Family time!* There was real glee in Ma's voice, I heard it as I rounded the kitchen and entered the living room, the room with the shades perpetually drawn so there wasn't glare on the television, the room with the spotty beige wallpaper and the scuffed-up wooden floor and the couch — the fat and battered and stained and slightly funky-smelling most important piece of furniture in our house. Ma was stretched out on it like always but she was literally stretching, her whole body pulled taut like a cat, her muscles vibrating with the pull, and when she relaxed she did not fall back into her usual fetal curl before the TV. She shook herself out and propped up straight. I remember when I was smaller, when I would see Ma pop out of her ennui like that, a bright smile and a slight gust of energy. I would feel a real swell of hope in my heart. I would think: she's better. Her face would be rosy, and instead of a brow cramping with the weight of possible illness, instead of the general downward cast her face took beneath the unfathomable heaviness of all that can befall a body, she'd have a simple, innocent smile on her face. Not a big grin, nothing manic, just a sweet openness. It felt like she was waking up from a long, dark dream of illness and mental nuttiness. It seemed possible in those moments to start over again, as a family. Not get our dad back — I wasn't too interested in having some strung-out stranger joining us. What I wanted was the three of us — me, Ma, and Kristy — starting off on a new foot, a more hopeful spring in our step. But they didn't last long, these bursts of attention and openness. Eventually I came to identify them as moods, nothing more than a swing in a new direction. Mood swings. It's weird that these little moments that had led me to believe that Ma was maybe better were ultimately what brought me to the conclusion that she is hopeless. Even her bursts of cheer are symptoms of her mental illness. Nothing about Ma is well, and still I can't help it. When she snaps out of it for a second I like to be there. It stabs that little place in my heart that wants a real normal Ma so bad, I can't stop myself from sitting before her like a dumb puppy-daughter sucking up her smiles and her interest. So I did; I wandered into the room and there she was, flushed and beaming. Who knows, maybe her and Donnie got it on while we were at the mall and she's blissed out on some gross sex wave. Best to avoid the couch just in case. I sat down on the edge of the coffee table, shoving over a small pizza box containing half a congealed pizza, the cheese run onto the cardboard and dried there thick as wax. It still smelled good, though. I hadn't eaten anything yet. Kristy wouldn't let me eat at the mall because she was certain I would spill greasy food onto my borrowed finery and, honestly, I'm such a slob I couldn't really make a convincing case in favor of taking the chance.

On the ride home in the Maverick I enjoyed the way the open window tore at the hairdo. The hairdo had done its job and could now be dismantled. I enjoyed the feeling of it wobbling in the breeze, and I enjoyed the way my life suddenly felt cracked a bit more open. I guess I had something to look forward to, something new, something novel. It was pretty wild that me of all people was now going to work at Ohmigod! I was going to have to somehow continue the enormous lie that got me hired, but I had just started thinking about my life in terms of movies, you know? And this seemed like a real cinematic turn. Kristy was too proud of her bullshitting abilities to do anything human like check in with me and make sure it was okay that she had just scammed me a job atop a hill of deep falsehoods, so we buzzed home in silence, the wind creating a whirl of ash that made the car feel like the inside of a souvenir snowglobe. Once we pulled up to the curb on Lincoln Street I was out of the Maverick and rocketed into my room, the shabby house trembling under my super-sized flip-flops. Out came the evil bobby pins. I examined their nubby tips for specks of dried blood because I swear

Kristy had secured them to the actual tender skin of my scalp, it had hurt so bad. But the small, crimped pins were bloodless. My hands probed the mysterious updo, digging out pin after pin, all buried beneath the tacky twist of hair. There seemed no end of pins to be found there. They accumulated on my dresser, snagged with dry strands of damaged hair. When I finally had retrieved them all I shook my head like a dog shaking off wet, in hopes that my hair would flutter back down to normal, but no. It stuck out all over the place, bent and sticky. I looked like a madperson on a TV show, with the kind of hair they put on someone to demonstrate insanity. In the bathroom I flushed the makeup off my face with some palmfuls of tap water, and I peeled off the ruffly and revealing high-fashion clothing, pulled on some sweats, and dug Ma's old Weight Watchers T-shirt out from the ball of sheets on my bed. Better, normal. My own normal, since Kristy and her kind would insist that it's not so normal for a fourteen-year-old American female to lounge around in sweats without a friend in sight, no gang of girls dying to slumber party at my crappy house, sticking each others' bras in the freezer or whatever weird-ass things girls do when they stay up all night together, getting wigged out on sleep deprivation and making out with pillows. No gang of girls, and, if I may be honest, no boys either, as in, I could give a crap. I'm seriously not interested. And I know that is seriously abnormal, but I'm not going to lie. I'm not so good at lying. Which makes me a little anxious in regard to my new employment at Ohmigod!, since it does seem like my primary job requirement is to be an ace number-one bullshitter, so I better get good at it quick. I better learn how to properly sashay in a pair of platform flip-flops. I better learn how to be a girl.

Ma hollered her *Family time!* cry from the living room and I put the brain-twister aside and went to spend a bit of bright-time on the couch with her.

Ma, I Got A Job, I started. *Oh yeah?* she asked, part happy, part skeptical. The skeptical part is always there — it's the part trying to sniff out the potential disease or festering bacteria in any individual or location or concept. I've learned not to take the skeptical tones personally. Yeah, I'm Working At The Mall Now, At A Clothes Store. Ma squinted her glittery green eyes at me, like shards of beer bottle glass. *So you and Kristy, both working at the mall, huh?* I nodded my head. The salty-grease stink wafting up from the pizza box was starting to really get to me. I hooked my fingers into the crust of a triangle and wrenched it from the cardboard. *Women of the world, my daughters,* she said with a smile. She said, *You two don't take after me, that's for sure. You must take after your father. He didn't have any problem just going out into the world, did he? Clearly he didn't.* I bit into the tip of my pizza. Extra cheese. My teeth really sunk into the thick mass, yum, it was excellent. I love cold pizza. I love it better cold than hot. I was ignoring Ma because she was being what they call passive-aggressive with that comment. Like me getting a job is the equivalent of abandoning the family and running away to Louisiana to get high in a swamp like our dad did. That's Ma, though. One hand is petting your head while the other's giving you a pinch. *What's up with your hair?* she asked.

Kristy Did It For Me. You Should've Seen It. I Looked

Wild, Like A Fashion Model. It Was All Up And Fancy.

You look like a homeless person now, she commented.

I Know. I bit into the pizza again. I looked forward to eating it all the way up to the bubbly crust, and then splitting the crust open and dousing the fluffy insides with a ton of salt. Better than those pretzels you buy from a cart at a carnival. Where'd The Pizza Come From? I asked. It wasn't every day that you come home to find such riches left out on the coffee table.

Donnie brought it home. He got some work off his cousin. She sighed happily. Donnie had a cousin who owned a couple houses in Malden, and sometimes when a water heater exploded or a toilet got especially nasty he'd call Donnie over to help him fix it. I don't know what it is about guys. They do seem to know how to do things. Even a certified loser like Donnie has the ability to patch up a busted water heater. It's not a lot, but still, it's maybe more than Ma. Though I guess Ma had kids, so that's something, right? God. It's so Tarzan and Jane, it's really depressing. I think I'd like to opt out of the whole man-woman thing if possible. And it does seem possible, right now, when I'm mostly just a kid, but I know at some point the kid is going to melt right off my body, and then what? I'm a woman? It's too overwhelming to think about.

Ma leaned over and gave me a hard kiss on my cheek, she really dug her lips into the skin there and I let her. It felt nice to be loved by Ma. Her hands dug into my gunked-out hair and rubbed my head a bit and I closed my eyes and let myself feel small. It was a real sweet moment. When it ended I hurried out of the living room, my pizza crust clutched in my hand. In the kitchen I grabbed the big tube of salt and shook a stream of it from the metal spout into the tender center of my pizza crust.

Ugh, Kristy said, entering the room. The camera sprouted from her face like a terrible growth. *Tell the camera what you're eating.*

Pizza crust, I shrugged. The camera ran the length of my body, and I could feel it soaking in my bare feet, the sweats, the ratty T-shirt, and my crazyperson hairdo.

Kristy, I said, trying not to whine. You're Not Being Fair. You're Taking Me Out Of Context.

Kristy shook her head, the camera still firmly pressed to her eye so that it too shook in seeming disapproval. Her free hand gestured dramatically to the kitchen around us, the grease-heavy curtains and the clutter of the kitchen table. *No, Trish,* she said ominously. *This is it. This is you, and this is your context.*

Family time! Ma hollered from the living room. Kristy sighed, let down the camera, and hit the Pause button.

There's Pizza, I offered helpfully.

Kristy shuddered at the suggestion of something bready. *Ugh, no thanks.* She hesitated, waiting for Ma's next yell. *What's she doing?* she whispered.

You Know, I said. Sitting Up. Waiting For You. It's No Big Deal. I gulped the rest of the crust and grabbed a half-empty glass of water from the table to wash it down.

Nasty! Kristy said. Ma's summons from the living room had made her edgy. *That's been there forever.*

It's Just Water.

Gross, Trisha. Really. You've got to learn how to be a bit more civilized if you're going to keep that job. And I laughed, because though Kristy was right, I was going to have to learn to act like some sort of regular human girl for my time at Ohmigod!, Kristy was deluded if she thought my spot there was anything but doomed. The job was unkeepable. She's In A Good Mood, I said, and jerked my head in the direction of the living room. You're Going To Have To Say Hello To Her Sometime, It Could Be A Lot Worse. *Yeah,* Kristy said uneasily. She hit that Pause button again and the camera whirred back to life. She followed it into the living room. *Hello, MTV!* our mother cried happily from her spot on the couch.

Ten

Monday morning I tried to reason with Kristy. I told her that it was ultimately preferable to come into work smelling like cigarettes than with your face all puffy and red and its makeup muddied and streaked because you were crying about smelling like cigarettes. Through the entire philosophical discussion Donnie leaned far back in his seat, one arm draped lazily out the window and the other gently riding the steering wheel, a burning Marlboro clenched between his yellowing cigarette fingers. *I'm doing you a favor,* he pointed out, and by "pointed" I mean he used his burning cigarette as a little pointer, jabbing its ashy tip in Kristy's general direction. *I do your mother a favor, not smoking around her and her illness, and this is where I get to smoke. You ride with me, you ride with smoke.*

He chuckled as if he'd just created some identifying catch-phrase for himself, like "Ay caramba!" or "Hasta la vista, baby." You ride with me, you ride with smoke. What a genius. Kristy didn't want smoke all over her clothes and her hair and neither did I, but I don't indulge in dead-end fights. Donnie wasn't going to toss his butt out the window and onto Route 1, which whizzed by beside us, sort of sad and abandoned-looking in the daylight. At night, forget it. I've never been to Las Vegas but I can't imagine it's any better than Route 1 and the lit-up theme restaurants propped up alongside the freeway. There's a Chinese restaurant that I heard has a frigging river running through it. A place called The Ship, which is on the inside of an I-shit-you-not ship. Another buffet sort of place that has a fountain inside and colored lights flashing below all the spouts, making the water glow red and blue and purple and a person playing a big, white organ in the middle of the whole thing. Route 1 is crazy and at night everything is neon. It's pretty exciting. In the day it's just sort of blammed out.

So Donnie was stinking up our hair and skin and fashionable clothing and Kristy's about to make the whole problem aesthetically worse for herself by bursting into futile tears. Too bad she didn't bring the camera. It would have been great to get a shot of Donnie, the back curls of his mullet getting blown by car-window wind into the giant pores of his sweaty cheeks, his cigarette, and his cheap plastic sunglasses, saying, *When you ride with me, you ride with smoke.* If *The Real World* didn't just take immediate pity on her and whisk her off to TV-land then probably they'd at least have called Child Protective Services and warned them that a perfectly good teenage girl was being left in the care of a mulleted loser in Mogsfield, Massachusetts. But on the order of Mercedes Patron, Kristy had left her camera behind.

Don't Do It, Kristy, I hollered at her from the backseat. Don't Cry! No Crying! Jungle Unisex Has So Many Stinks In It, Nobody's Going To Smell You Anyway. It's true, I thought. All the perm-solution smells and the bleach and the hair colors, not to mention the gentler odors of shampoo and conditioner, hair gel and spray and spritz, and the smell of the ladies who work there, their perfumes and lipstick and powder smells. Who's going to notice a bit of second-hand-smoke stink on Kristy?

Donnie dumped us off outside the side entrance, my favorite one with the neon-bulbed mall sign. Instead of saying good-bye he exhaled a gigantic cloud of cigarette smoke — I swear, he must've been holding it spitefully in his lungs since we turned into the parking lot five minutes ago. He breathed it out the window and it hung there like a toxic glob, stuck in the humid air outside his car window. Then he flicked the butt by our feet and peeled off. Me and Kristy stood there staring off after the Maverick, a lacy, blue smoke from the tires blowing into the cigarette smoke, creating a sort of smoke soup in the air around us. The little butt lay smoldering on the cement until Kristy daintily stepped on it with her sandaled foot. She smooshed it and then scuffed the ashy mess onto the ground like dogshit off her shoe. *Could start a fire*, she murmured. Kristy, I said. I felt like I had to bring her back. The ride in the car with Donnie and the smoke had clearly unhinged her. You're

Going To be Great, Dude! I clapped her on the back, which was bare. Kristy was wearing a terry cloth haltery-thing that scrunched across her boobs and cascaded over her butt. Resting on her chest were a couple of gold chains — one hers and one she'd pilfered from Ma's dresser. She was biting Mercedes Patron's style a bit, in a friendly way. I thought it was pretty smart of her. My own style was a little weird, if you ask me. A T-shirt that had the word "Baby" across it in that airy paintbrush style, like the kind you get at the state fair in Tewksbury. Like most everything Kristy owned, it glittered a bit. I had her old jean skirt on too but she wouldn't let me borrow the one piece of her clothing I actually liked, a little belt with metal squares all over it. The squares are loose and Kristy was sure I'd knock a bunch off as I clumsily stomped through my day. I don't know how fashionable I looked, though. I thought I looked kind of trashy, like some girl spending the summer hanging out at the parking lot carnival down on Revere Beach. I actually love the parking lot carnivals — I mean, I love any carnival, who doesn't, but that one on Revere Beach is sort of the bottom of the parking lot carnival barrel. One of the times Ma tried to implement some authority in the house was after the last shooting down there. She forbid us to go but we were like, Yeah Sure Whatever Ma and then she went, "Well, okay, then win me something," and that was that.

I insisted on wearing my own flops because you wouldn't think the extra few inches on Kristy's would make a difference but my heel kept sliding off the back and then my ankle would sort of twist around my heel like a contortionist foot and I swear I would have sprained my ankle if

I'd worn them to my actual first day of work, so I had my own regular-sized black plastic flops on, my hair back off my face in a ponytail so it didn't get my skin greasy, and ta-daa, I'm ready to go.

Kristy gave me a quick, fierce hug at the spot in the mall where our paths split. I watched her enter the darkly glowing cave of Jungle Unisex, then continued my way down the faux-brick road that paved the inside of the Square One Mall. Bernice O'Leary was hanging out by the gates of Ohmigod!, her eyes squinting through her bangs at her wristwatch. I felt a tiny clutch of panic in my throat. Was I late, was I going to get canned before I even started? I had to be on time, Kristy was fanatical about getting us into the Maverick, chop chop. That's what she said, *Chop, chop,* clapping her hands together like some sort of military person. Also, *Quick like a bunny!* And she hopped behind me, herding me out the living room and onto the front porch, her sandaled feet snapping at my flip-flops, threatening to give me a flat tire and knock me down the stairs.

Bernice gave me a big-assed smile when she saw me, but that little clench stayed there in my throat, all fisted up tight. I thought: welcome to the workforce, Trisha. Like school but worse 'cause it's really pretty hard to get fired from school. You've got to set the place on fire or beat up a teacher, and even then . . . Not so hard, I imagined, to get fired from a job, especially a place like Ohmigod! Bunches of spazzy, fashioned-crazed girls are just waiting for you to get the ax so they can strut their resume over to Bernice and take your place like you were never even there. I couldn't think about it. My work at Ohmigod! was doomed, founded on a giant lie I could not hold up forever. That's how it worked on TV, anyway. Fools always got found out. The pressure was on to uphold Kristy's massive fib and be a good worker, whatever a good worker was. For real, no wonder Ma just stayed on the couch.

Patricia! Good morning! Bernice chirped. She tenderized her voice. *How's Kim? Have you talked to her? Is she feeling any better?* I took a breath. I wasn't expecting Kim questions so early in the morning. I figured right then that though I might be getting paid minimum wage to hang tropically flowered dresses and metal jewelry all day, my real job was to be Bernice's connection to Kim.

Kim Is So Sorry, I started. Bernice's eyes widened. Maybe she was in love with Kim Porciatti, I suddenly thought. Maybe she felt a lesbian love for her. Usually I hate it when kids say shit like that in school, like if someone is at all nice to a person of the same gender then bam, they're a fag for them or something, but really there was something so gasping about Bernice's interest in Kim, even considering the dramatic effect suicide attempts had on people.

You talked to her? she breathed.

Yeah, I said. Yeah, She Told Me To Tell You — I pointed at Bernice for affect — That She Is So, So Sorry She Hasn't Called.

Bernice's head was nodding furiously. *It's okay, it's okay, tell her it's all okay. She's got enough to deal with right now. She needs to deal with getting better.* Bernice tucked a swinging chunk of fluffy hair behind her ear.

Um, Yeah, I said. I nodded. I furrowed my brow. This was serious stuff, suicide. Bernice rolled up the giant gate and there stood Ohmigod!, shrouded in darkness, the shapes of the many dresses and bikini ponchos ghosty in the shadows, reflected endlessly in the dim mirrored poles scattered around the store.

Stay here while I turn off the alarm, Bernice told me, gently placing her hand on my shoulder before diving into the dark store. God, she was touchy. I was going to have to get used to it, the hands of Bernice O'Leary. The wind of her movement stirred the edges of garments as she slunk down the main aisle and disappeared as thoroughly as a dive underwater. It was undeniably spooky, Ohmigod! all shut down and creepy-quiet. Then blam blam blam the supersonic lights flashed on overhead and the room was screaming with color, fuchsia this and safety orange that and every ugly shade of green human tinkering has brought to the color wheel. The music slammed on too. The theme to that movie *Pretty in Pink.* Was that it? Was I in an eighties movie? If Molly Ringwald had been going through that drama in Mogsfield she would've ended up with her ass kicked at some horrid teen dance club on Route 1, Ducky would've been fagbashed, she would've never found that cool woman who gave her the dress, and her father would have been a more serious loser, like a molester. Molly wouldn't have made it to the dumb prom at all — she'd have gone out with some other fuckups, gotten a little too wasted, had sex with someone regrettable, and wound up pregnant.

Okay, okay, come in! Bernice shot toward me with a big grin on her face and her arms akimbo, gesturing toward the glory of Ohmigod! like ta-daa! Like the store was a big party she'd thrown just for me. I felt myself relaxing a little, even in my stupid outfit. In fact, my stupid outfit was largely responsible for this fresh sensation of relaxation. Normally I'm not so relaxed in places like this. But really, on the rare occasions I'm forced to enter a shop like Ohmigod!, or perhaps am simply curious and drawn into the musical blare and general sensory overload, I don't get treated too hot. In my sweats and in my flops, with my hair just kind of sitting on my head, no makeup, I look like some sort of intruder upon femininity, up to no good. The staff stare at me with undisguised hostility and wait for me to stuff a pair of capri pants down the front of my sweats and book it out the front gate. It's insulting. I actually have never stolen, not even when it would be so damn easy I wonder if the store is asking me to lift their merchandise; not even when the staff are being such a-holes that they really, really deserve to be stolen from. It's just my own little code of honor. When you walk around knowing that bunches of people are pegging you as a thief and a loser, the only thing I can think to do to get some revenge is to just not be that, to show them how wrong their puny brains are about people. But then I wonder how you go about letting those snobs know you're a good person. Do you walk up to the salesgirl at Tight Knit, the one who has been shooting you electric-blue-lidded glares for fifteen minutes straight, and tell her, I'm Leaving Now, And I Just Wanted To Tell You I Didn't Steal Anything? No, you don't. You just suck up the injustice. Or, I'm learning, you change your tune. You put on a skirt and a little makeup, take care that your shirt says something demeaning like "Baby", and the mall is your oyster.

Come here, Trishy, Bernice cried. She slapped her legs on the thighs of her fake-faded jeans so that it looked and felt like she was calling a dog. Some dog named Trishy. I followed her, hesitantly entering the chamber of bright clothes, of vertical stripes and improbable color pairings. She was rustling through a clump of hangers on a round rack. *I was just looking at your shirt and thinking this might be up your alley,* she said. She pulled out a couple hangers holding shirts embossed with some sparkly symbols. It was also all whooshed and fluffy-looking, like my "Baby" shirt. *They're astrology signs! Isn't that smart? These are going to be big sellers.* She tugged a couple more free. *I think maybe I'll do a nice display of them this morning, while you straighten.* She nabbed one with a cutesy-looking cow on the chest and held it against her torso. *I'm a Taurus. What sign are you?*

Pisces, I said. She flicked a shirt at me, a big kissy-faced fish, a girl-fish, a porno blow-job cartoon fish, its lips glittered and poofy.

We should have one day where we all wear one of these shirts! In our signs! Isn't that a great idea?

Totally. I handed the shirt back to her. I bet Bernice O'Leary was the kind of person who liked to dress identical to her friends when she was little. There's something wrong with those sorts of people. *Pretty in Pink* faded and for a minute there was silence in the store, just the sounds of Bernice rustling through shirts, the echoing clatter of gates being rattled up across the mall. And then "We Built This City on Rock and Roll" came on and trashed it.

Eleven

I was standing at a rack of shirts. They were long and slippery and had strange knots on the ends and also sleeves that seemed slit up the middle and a back that plunged as far as a back can plunge without tearing a shirt in two. This shirt should come with instructions on how to put it on. This shirt was nearly impossible to keep on a hanger, even with the helpful strings sewn into the inside for just such a purpose. I was wrestling with the shirts. It was more entertaining then some of the earlier racks, because I was pretending they were slippery eels or tiny alligators and it was my job to catch and pin them to their hanger. It lessened the tedium of the task and made the time go by, creating weird little games in my head. I was glad Bernice was out of my hair, up inside the display window constructing her astrology diorama. Every so often someone she knew would stroll by and Bernice would start yelling, Hi! Hi!, and it would sound like she was talking to the mannequins. Her bubbly voice sounded trapped inside the window chamber. I imagined Bernice O'Leary finally losing it and befriending the mannequins. This too helped me pass the time. My arms were sore from keeping them at the level of the racks, from the lifting and placing. I hadn't thought that working at a place like Ohmigod! would put a strain on any part of me — excepting the parts of my brain that fritz out after maximum color and flower-pattern overload — but I could feel my muscles aching after a half hour of the repetition. All the hangers had to be a finger apart from each other, so that the clothing fanned out in a perfect arrangement, like a chorus line of kick-dancers, each bent leg angled to reveal the next. It was my job to walk around the store and rack by rack make sure the hangers were this precise, anally retentive distance from each other. I had looked at Bernice blankly when she explained this task to me. I had been waiting for her to burst into chuckles like a big joker and cuff me on the shoulder. I had been waiting for her to say, I'm just fucking with you. I had been hoping to have the guts to ask, Are You Just Fucking With Me? But Bernice is no joke. Bernice is a straight shooter. There isn't space in Bernice's brain for hoaxes. And so I set about spacing the hangers. Sometimes the clothes had to be coordinated by color, sometimes by style or size. I imagined this was like filing, like working in a library, only with clothes. Systems of order. I zoned out. Tried to block out the music, the *Chaka Khan? Chaka Khan, Chaka Khan?* The robotic dude voice chanting, *rich . . . bitch.* The cupcake drone of *A material . . . a material . . . a material.* Girls came in and wound their way through the racks. They oohed and shrieked and pronounced certain items weird or slutty. Those were the critiques I heard most often on that, my first, day at Ohmigod!, and I considered taking a poll, a survey, a study. If only school was still in session, maybe there was a class I could apply such investigation toward. What would I be researching? The worst things for a girl to be, based on insults directed at items of female clothing by shoppers at Ohmigod!

A cluster of girls who looked about twelve but had their faces painted up like twisted, baby beauty queens were getting hysterical over by the astrology shirts, yanking them off the racks and thrusting them at one another. I felt a surge of hate. Not only had I just spaced those T-shirts out in a precise finger-length order, I had organized them by chronology of zodiac sign and then, within the signs, suborganized them by size. And the little twats were fucking it all up. And they weren't even going to buy them, anyway. I just could feel it. They were too wild, too loud. Not serious shoppers. I stomped over to them, my flops bitch-slapping the linoleum. Hey! I snapped at the gang of them. I had my official-looking Ohmigod! tag pinned above my left boob. It was the shape a *Bam!* comes in inside a comic book. It was purple, and the "*Ohmigod!*" was in hot pink, scrawled, maybe with a lipstick, as if it had been tagged there by a very passionate and heavily made-up female. You Messed Up My Rack, I scowled at them. Are You Going

To Buy One Of Those Shirts Or Are You Just Going To Fling Them At Each Other?

They stared dumbly for a moment, ambushed by my bad attitude. Then one piped up, *We can shop here if we want. Baby.* She said "Baby" mockingly and burst into laughter. Her laughter was caught on the giant pillow of laughter that erupted from the perfumed throats of her friends. They all giggled like it was the funniest thing they'd ever heard, choking on their giggles, occasionally pausing to take a gulp of air and burp out the word one more time, *Baby*, inspiring a fresh flood of hilarity. I stood there and realized that this confrontation was a terrible misstep on my part, a bold act born on a wave of low blood sugar, certainly, because I'd skipped breakfast and become horribly mean and cranky when I don't eat. I was famous for it in my household. Between this low blood sugar problem and the more recent legend of my powerful PMS, no gripe of mine was ever taken seriously within my shabby home. This pained me, this drove me nuts, so it was my duty to keep my blood levels stable and therefore not get written off so easily. The gang of girls smirked at me. They had the most basic advantage: they were a pack. I was just me, in a stupid shirt scribbled with the ridiculous word *BABY*. I was walking around with an insult sprayed across my chest, inviting the world to fuck with me.

You Just . . . You Were Making A Mess. And I Have To Clean It. The girls laughed in fucking unison, a snort-chorus.

Well, too bad for you, one snipped.

I guess that's your job, another reminded me. Meanly. It was true. I was scheduled to be at Ohmigod! for seven more hours and certainly I'd be reorganizing the racks endlessly, again and again, as hordes of shoppers rifled through the merchandise. It was my job to undo their damage. The leader, clutching a shirt with an electric-blue scorpion sprayed across the front, relaxed her fingers and let the hanger clatter to the floor.

I was going to buy it but now I'm not. Baby. And she led the rest of them out of the store. Their hands trailed out behind them, brushing and swatting at the racks they breezed past, knocking them out of their finger-length order. One little fist shot out, a hand with purple-tipped fingernails clutched at the skirt of a flowered dress, and gave it a hard yank. I could hear the plastic hanger crack as the dress sailed to a gentle heap on the floor. The hand disappeared into the horde of girls moving as one into the dimness of the mall, gone. Bernice O'Leary had come to the side of her glass bubble like a little goldfish, to watch the parade of ill will traipse by.

Trishy? she asked, frowning. Her voice bounced around her aquarium, sounding wide and hollow. *What was that about?* She climbed out of the window and trotted toward the snapped hanger, the soft puddle of fabric. She gathered the dress in her arm like a wounded animal. A bit of tulle from inside the skirt grazed her cheek. I Don't Know, I stammered. Why did I feel like I was going to get in trouble? Had I done something wrong? I felt sweaty. Bernice's eyebrows were crashed together, creating a crunch right in that space people Botox. I Think They Were Stealing. I Mean, I Thought They Were Going To. They Were Acting Sort Of Weird . . . Bernice nodded, her eyes wide. Bernice had given me a lengthy talk about stealing. She'd said, *A lot of people want what we have, Trishy. Look around.* She'd nodded her head, deeply serious. She'd motioned to the racks. *But you've got to work for what we've got, right? I mean, even we do. You've got to earn it.* Ohmigod! had a zero-tolerance-for-shoplifters policy. If I caught anyone stealing I was to stop them from leaving the store and holler for Bernice, who would go and grab Chuck, the rent-a-cop assigned to our quadrant of Square One. Then I guess they got hauled away to a room underneath the mall. It sounded really creepy. I had felt pretty uncomfortable at the idea of confronting someone shoplifting, but after my run-in with the twelve-year-olds I wondered if I was going to have a hard time *not* starting fights with the customers.

Bernice looked stressed, her eyes zooming around the store and landing on the astrology rack, the Scorpio shirt getting dirty on the linoleum. I Asked Them What They Were Doing, I told her, And They Freaked Out And Started Throwing Clothes Around.

Bernice gasped. *Oh, Trishy,* she said. *Oh if that happens again, you holler for me. Good job, good job!* She lifted the cracked hanger from the rack and dropped it onto the fluff of the dress. *I'll take care of the dress,* she told me. *You reorganize those astrology shirts, okay? I knew those were going to get a lot of attention. Right? Didn't I? After that you can take your fifteen minutes.* And Bernice shuffled to the rear of the store and the music track jumped to a Pat Benatar song and a new gang of girls bounded into Ohmigod!, jacked up on hysterical girlness, their lips melting on their faces like Popsicles.

Twelve

The weird CD-thing that Ohmigod! plays in an endless rotation was playing Sheena Easton. "Strut" was on and I was getting ready to take the fifteen-minute break Bernice had promised me. My head felt empty and deranged from having no food and the high-intensity fluorescent lights running in strips above my head. I think on some deep and sickening level I can perceive their endless flicker, their strobe, and it makes me feel a little nuts. Bernice was in the bathroom and when she was done I could split, grab a candy bar, and head outside for a little normal light. So "Strut" was playing and this girl, she sort of actually strutted into Ohmigod! like she was pretending to be a model. Very dramatic. And I started getting very judgmental about her in my head and looking for the rest of her irritating pack of girls. Then I realized that she was actually alone. She was holding a big army bag and wearing a bizarre outfit of bright stripes. The top was striped with orange and green and yellow and the bottom was a stained khaki and the whole thing was too big for her. Her hair was dark but it was all smashed under a hairnet like an old lady. She looked greasy. I noticed this as she strutted toward the register at the back, where I'd stopped moving and started just staring. Her makeup, mostly eyeliner, had pooled around her eyes like liquid, and her face had a sheen to it. She dipped around the jewelry rack then came straight up to me and dropped her bag on the counter. The bag had things scratched into it but I was too high from low blood sugar and confusion to check it out. She spoke real low, in a voice that sounded so deep and scuffed-up it was like she was a fifty-year-old bartender in a thirteen-year-old's body. It really threw me. It was like when the little kid in that movie *The Shining* opens his mouth and that fucked-up croak comes out. She was possessed by some haggard lady, maybe Sheena Easton, whoever that is. She said, *Where's Bernice,* like she's so in with Ohmigod! she's on a first-name basis with the manager. Even though she didn't really look the type to be shopping here. And I mean that as a compliment. I immediately wanted to tell her that I'm not the type to be working here, for real, but I just went with the weird moment and I stammered that Bernice was in the bathroom. *Cool,* she said, her voice still low and gravelly. You could almost expect a stream of smoke to sort of wisp out of her mouth. She held up her hand and in it was a wiry bracelet with some beads clattering on it. Most of the beads had fallen off of it — it was a pretty bare and unremarkable item from the sale basket. She said, *You're going to ring me up for this,* and laid it on the counter. Then she flashed the second item at me, a black flower, a sculpted rose with a giant red rhinestone in its center. It was a pin with a green stem shooting out a couple thorns and a single green leaf, a pale green rhinestone twinkling on it like a dewdrop. *This I'm taking,* she told me, and dropped it into her army bag. She had a wad of bills scrunched in her hand and pulled one crunched-up dollar free. *It's a dollar, right? Ninety-nine cents? Is there tax?* I nodded dumbly. Is it stealing if someone tells you they're taking something? That's not really stealing. That's something else. That's my problem, I guess. Bernice came out of the bathroom and slapped on her work face when she saw the thief at the counter. *Hello Rose!* she singsonged. Did Bernice O'Leary truly love everyone or was she just on automatic pilot, greeting everyone with a song and a smile of good cheer? Did Bernice O'Leary ever get in a fucking bad mood or what? I looked at her. I looked back at the girl, whose name, I guess, was Rose.

Oh, don't be confused, we'll do this together! Bernice chirped, and arranged herself behind me at the register. I had a sudden, stark fear that she was going to lift my arms for me and place them gently on the appropriate keys. What would I have done? Surely I would have just allowed her to. I was weak with hunger and now a sort of fear, because if the girl told me she was taking something and I, the guardian of the goods, did not stop her, then really I was stealing it, right? Did it matter that I didn't get to keep the rose pin? I wouldn't have wanted it. But the technicality of this exchange really baffled me. Charles Manson didn't kill all those people in the sixties but he like allowed them to or something and now he's in jail for the rest of his life, going crazy with a swastika tattooed on his face, so clearly there are instances where you can get in wicked bad trouble for a crime even when someone else, not you, committed it.

Hit Sale, said Bernice who was, thank god, not touching me. She pointed a finger at the orange Sale key. The register registered .99. She talked me through the rest of the sale. *Trishy's new here at Ohmigod!,* Bernice explained. *It's her first day. She's helping me out 'til Kim returns . . . they were good friends. Are good friends! God . . .* Bernice stuttered off. Rose raised her eyebrows, which were skinny and inky on her forehead, as if they'd been sketched on with a calligraphy pen and then smeared. Whatever was sitting so oily on her face had a smell and it reached my nose and triggered a chain of growls in my stomach. Rose smelled like food. The way you smell when you've been sitting in a diner for a while, the steam from the deep fryer sinking into the weave of your clothes, your hair, your pores. *Bummer,* Rose said to me and it took me a minute to understand she was talking about Kim Porciatti, my supposed dear friend, and then it took me another minute to realize she was shitting me. *How is Kim?* she inquired, and I responded, Uh . . . and Bernice piped up, *That's a dollar-five, hon. Oh don't you girls worry about Kim, okay? You think about happy stuff, all right? She's going to be just fine, back here in no time, right Trishy?* And to that I nodded.

Rose's hand plunged back into her sack of plunder. She fished around the bottom, coming up with a succession of pennies, all stuck with lint and bits of twigs or something, maybe tobacco. She plunked one, two, three, four, five pennies into my palm. I liked to hit the button that popped the register open. It was a triumphant sound, and I enjoyed the automatic way the drawer of money slid out toward me. I smoothed the crumpled dollar and placed it with the others, dropped the pennies in their little compartment. I pushed the drawer closed. *The receipt?* Bernice prompted me, and I tore the paper from the machine and handed it to Rose. *Thank you,* she smiled. *I work* — she started, but Bernice cut in — *Rose works over at Clown in a Box.* Rose grimaced. She swung her bag off the counter, the strap sinking into her bony shoulder. She grabbed the wire bracelet and jammed it onto her wrist. It actually looked good there. It seemed to be imprisoning the skin and bone beneath it. The leftover beads rattled when she waved at me. *Come by on your break or something,* she said. I Was Just About To Take My Fifteen, I said, glancing at Bernice. And then Rose said, *I'm on my half hour,* and that's how I wound up choking on a cigarette in the parking lot with Rose, instead of getting something to eat to level out my blood sugar. I know that from a health perspective it was not a smart decision, but in terms of my original summer plan — to meet someone, to make a friend — it seemed like the right thing to do.

Thirteen

I fucking hate the mall, Rose complained. We were behind it, just beyond the back door where employees lugged out bulging bags of trash each night at closing. Rose was sitting on the roof of one Dumpster, her knees drawn up to her chin, the arm bearing the wire bracelet clutched around her legs like she was holding herself together, the other clamped around a cigarette. She had drawn the pack from her bag and let loose a string of mouthy curses as she pulled out broken cigarette after broken cigarette, tossing them to the ground, where they lay snapped, bleeding shreds of tobacco. Eventually she found one that was torn at its top, and she ripped that bit away and fired up the cigarette with a plastic lighter. *Oh I'm so rude,* she rasped, and tipped one out of the pack for me. I held it, broken, staring at it. I thought, I should really eat some food, and Rose said, *just tear that part off,* and I did what she had done, I tore the busted top and leaned it into her lighter. Then I choked. A lot. Because I don't smoke. I'm repulsed by smoke. Smoke reminds me of all things Donnie, all things nasty and to be avoided, and yet I was unable to refuse Rose's offer. She looked at me curiously and hauled herself up the side of the Dumpster, kicking off a flutter of rust with her sneaker. I mostly just held the cigarette for the duration of my fifteen-minute break. Held it and grew neurotic about it stinking up my fingers, how my fingers would feel contaminated now, for the rest of the day. How they would turn a sickly yellow like Donnie's cigarette fingers. I looked at Rose's fingers. They seemed okay. *You must like it,* she said, looking off into the parking lot. *Working at Ohmigod!, hanging with Kim. Kimmy. That's what Bernice calls her.* I nodded, studied my cigarette. I really didn't know what to do with it. The smoke curled up and wafted over to my face, so I held it away from my body.

Bernice Ruins Everyone's Name Like That, I said. She Calls Me Trishy.

That's not your name? she asked.

No. It's Trisha. Or Trish.

Which one do you like better?

I Don't Know. I Don't Care, I Don't Think.

I'm trapped, Rose said, exhaling a big cloud of smoke. She flicked her ashes into the space where the Dumpster opened to receive its trash. *I fucking hate "Rosie," but I hate Rose too. I hate one-syllable names. It's like you're not there, really. They don't really stick or make a mark. If I were you*

I'd go with Trisha. Trisha sticks, it's got two syllables.

I Never Thought Of That, I said. I Like The Name Rose.

I'm going to change it to Alexandria when I'm eighteen, she said. *That's just three years from now.*

You're Fifteen? I asked. I was surprised. She seriously looked like twelve years old, thirteen tops. She was small, both short and scrawny, and she had that same sort of bratty swagger as the younger girls I'd fought with earlier. Hers was a grubbier version, though.

Here's what I think, Rose began. *I think smoking really does stunt your growth. Because I started smoking when I was I think eleven, and my mom smoked when she was pregnant with me. Isn't that fucked up?*

I didn't know whether to agree or not. Sometimes people ask you your opinion on things like that, but then when you agree with them they get all pissed 'cause you've insulted their mother. I just shrugged.

She was all stressed out 'cause she's a lesbian and she didn't want to be with my dad and she was going to leave him and go and live with all these other lesbians in Vermont but then boom she got pregnant with me and so I guess she thought that meant she'd never get to be a lesbian. So she smoked a ton. I think it stunted me. I was a preemie. I lived in a little tank for like a month.

Wow, I said. Did Your Mom Ever Get To Be A Lesbian? I asked her. She nodded and threw her cigarette into the Dumpster. It was still burning. A thin stream of smoke slunk up from inside.

Give me yours, she commanded, and I did. I had to resist the urge to smell my fingers because I'm sure they smelled just so unbelievably gross. *You don't even smoke, do you?*

I shook my head. My day had been filled with lies, I figured if I had the option to get out of one of them I should take it. *Well, if you ever want to try it again let me know and you can try again,* Rose offered generously. *I love to smoke.* She took a big drag off my cigarette. *My mom is a lesbian right now,* she said. *But she still smokes a ton. She never stopped being stressed out. I guess it's really stressful to be a lesbian.*

I Bet, I nodded. I hadn't really thought about it. I didn't know any lesbians besides maybe Bernice, but I wanted to let Rose know that I was cool about her mom being one. I'm Not, You Know, Racist Against Lesbians, I told her.

You mean "prejudiced," she told me. *You're not prejudiced against lesbians. Racist is against like black people or Puerto Rican people.*

Oh, I'm Not That, Either.

Rose nodded and more smoke gushed out of her mouth. She nodded and shrugged and exhaled all that smoke at the same time.

No, But A Lot Of People Are Around Here, Right? I asked. You Know? But I Don't Think I Am.

That's cool, she said. *I'm like a quarter Puerto Rican so I can't be racist.*

Oh, I nodded. Cool.

Rose took a thick drag off my cigarette and flung the smoking butt into the Dumpster with the other. *I think I'm subconsciously trying to burn this fucking place down.*

Really? I asked. I admit I was sort of taken aback and flustered by Rose's general attitude. I know that I can be very abrasive, but Rose was coming at it from a different angle. It had never occurred to me to burn the mall down but now I was wondering why not.

Thanks for the jewelry, she said, jumping down from the Dumpster and wiping sooty rust flakes from her ass. The khaki shorts she wore were so baggy they looked like they would slide right off her if the knobs of her hips weren't there for them to hang onto. *You were so sharp with that, that was cool of you. I was going to explain everything but then Bernice showed up.*

Yeah, I Know, I said, and thought about telling her I was nervous, or about making a crack along the lines of, Yeah, nice of you to assume I'm sympathetic to thieves, but Rose was plowing straight along. She had her own internal agenda. You could see it even as an outside spectator. There was a lot going on in there.

Anyway, there's a bunch of us who work here and we just give each other shit. It's cool. It's like an underground economy or something.

Really? I asked.

Yeah, it's like the only good thing about working here. It's cool, though. Come by the Clown on your half hour and I'll hook you up. Then Rose smiled, something she hadn't done yet. I hadn't noticed she hadn't smiled until it happened, and it was like watching a scrap of material become twisted into a beautiful bow. Rose's face lit straight up and I swear, maybe I'm just horribly a copycat but it made me light up right back, smiling big enough to break my face, and then Rose said, *See ya,* and pushed through the glass doors and back into Square One, and I was left by the Dumpster smiling like a dork.

Fourteen

Do you smell that? Bernice O'Leary's nose was flexed upward. Her nostrils flared and contracted, flared and contracted, as she huffed the air. And then I realized that Bernice looked like one of those dogs with the hair that you pin up with little barrettes. I swear. Something about the shape of her nose, her underbite, the way her floppy, overgrown hairdo begged to be secured back from her face. I shook my head at her, wondering at the state of my own hairdo. It had been windy out behind the mall. I touched it carefully.

I smell cigarettes, Bernice crinkled her nose and sucked another gust of air up her powerful little nostrils. *Trishy, you don't smoke, do you?* She looked horrified.

No, I Don't, I said, and I was being honest but the truth felt like a lie for like the third time today. Maybe that was the way of the working world. Always slaving away under the boss man or woman, waiting to get axed. It makes a person nervous. I was all nerves, and my continued abstinence with the foodstuffs plus my run-in with nicotine had me actually trembling a bit.

But I smell cigarettes. I can always smell a cigarette. Were you with Rose just now? I nodded my head. *Out back, by the Dumpster?* I nodded again. *Oh, Trishy,* she sighed. *Sometimes it's not enough to just say no. Sometimes you have to say no to people too. Do you know what I mean?*

Like, Not Hang Out With Rose? I asked. Bernice nodded.

Trishy, we have a certain image here at Ohmigod! She held up her hands to ward off my protest, but I was mute. *It's not even up to me, girl. It's in the training manual. It's in all the company material. It's the same at every store, all across the land. Go into an Ohmigod! in New Hampshire, same thing. Go to one in Boston. Go to California — I guess I don't really know if we have any way out there but, like, in Maine there's one, and it's the same thing. It's a place with standards. It's a fun place for fun girls who know how to have fun without indulging in the seamier, adult pleasures. I mean, so-called pleasures, right? Because is it really pleasurable to smoke a cigarette?* I shook my head. *It's not!* Bernice agreed. *Is lung cancer pleasurable?* This was one of those rhetorical questions, the kind you don't have to answer, my favorite questions. *Anyway, Trishy, girls who work at Ohmigod! don't, you know, drink alcohol, or smoke anything, and they keep good conduct outside of the mall. Conduct with boys. You know what I'm saying, girl?* Was Bernice asking me if I was a virgin? Was she telling me that virginity was a job requirement for Ohmigod!? The store that launched a thousand skanks? The store that sold shirts that were little more than shredded-up slashes of polyester strategically placed across boobs?

I didn't have a real orientation with you, Bernice explained, *because you're just temp, and I figured, you're part of Kim's gang so you already know what we're about here, but...*she stared at me and her face shifted. *I really don't think I've ever seen you in here, huh, Trish?* I took a breath. *But I think that's one of our shirts...*she trailed off, staring at my chest. She smiled. *"Baby." I loved that line. So sweet. I had the one that said "Bootylicious." All the glitter fell off, though.*

I'm Sorry, I said. I wasn't sure where this was going.

Trishy, you and me need to lay out some rules. Even though you might only be here for like another few days, we want to uphold the Ohmigod! code, right, girl?

Yeah.

Stay clear of Rose. She's sweet enough, but she's on the road to nowhere, as they say. Bernice chuckled. I actually didn't know "they" said that. I thought it was a song or something. *You seem like a real nice girl, one of those girls that are nice to everyone, sort of a bleeding heart type of person, would you say?*

I Don't Think So, I said. A bleeding heart?

That's what I'd say, as an outsider looking in. It's a real sweet way to be but it's also not very realistic. You really can't be nice to everyone, girl. Some people, you're nice to them and they'll take you right down with them. You think you're just giving someone a smile and then wham, before you know it you're part of a bad crowd. So watch out. Stick with the girls you already got, like Yolanda and all them, 'kay? I nodded my head. I'd been nodding quite frequently as there wasn't much I could do really but just sort of bob my head at the incredible things coming out of Bernice's mouth. The nodding was making something happen inside my skull. I swear I wasn't nodding violently or anything but it was like I'd shaken something loose inside my brain, and all these little black spots were sprinkling over my eyes like gothic confetti. My vision was being totally vandalized by some new nodding-induced neurological disorder. I got sort of dizzy and tried to lean up against a rack of clothes to take in the rest of Bernice's monologue, which at this point really sounded like the *whaaa whaaa whaaa whaaa whaaa whaaa whaaa* on Charlie Brown cartoons. So I attempted to lean against what I thought was a sturdy rack but I sort of missed the rack part and leaned into the dresses that were hanging off the rack and I went down. I hit the linoleum in a pile of shameful confusion and fuchsia-dyed cotton. And Bernice was on top of me and the lights were a seizure in the ceiling above me and she was saying, *Have you eaten today? Have you drank enough water?* And I was able to spit out a feeble no and then Bernice was gone and it was just me and the vivid lights and then she was back with a palmful of chocolate.

This is so weird, she said, peeling the delicate foil off the kisses sort of frantically. *Because Kim would get sick if she didn't eat too. So we kept these candies under the register for her. There's a few bags of stuff if you don't like these. Do you like Twix? I think there's a bag of Twix back there.*

These Are Great, I said, and they were. The chocolate felt like too much for my mouth, it seemed to come alive as it melted, grew thicker and sweeter and oozed into my teeth, it glued my mouth shut. I swallowed and Bernice popped another onto my tongue. I dug into it. Bernice was nodding. She patted my hair. She brushed it gently with the tip of her pinky. *Poor Trishy,* she said, and began unwrapping me a third kiss. And I'm not sure if it wasn't a more serious neurological freakout happening in my head, because when Bernice said that to me, I swear I almost started crying. My eyes just flash-flooded with a stinging sensation and I felt this gaping ache, as if my empty, empty stomach had elevated itself up to the region of my heart. Oh my god. I was splayed on the floor of Ohmigod! in a douche-bag costume being hand-fed chocolates by Bernice O'Leary and I was tearing up. I swallowed the last morsel in a giant gulp and got to my feet. I wobbled and Bernice put her hand out to steady me and I recoiled. I'm Fine, I said, Thanks. I sounded bitchy. Bernice withdrew her hand and looked wounded. Her palm was full of tiny shreds of silver. *Are you sure?* she asked. Yeah, Yeah. I was shaky, definitely, but I was up. The chocolate helped. I wanted more. I totally wanted a Twix. I Want A Twix, I said. I still sounded bitchy. I don't know what it was. It was like I didn't have the capacity to speak in much more than caveman grunts or something. My starving body had shut down all unessential programs, like the "tone" program that moderates the way you speak to people. Out the window.

They're under the register, way in the back, said Bernice. She was pouting like a real sourpuss. I turned to carefully walk the glistening linoleum path that led back to the register, flanked by the flutters of skirts and racks of jeans misted with fine glitter, jeans that were prefaded in the knees so you can have that one-million-blow-jobs look. *And once you've gotten yourself together, please wash up in the bathroom. Because you really smell like a big cigarette.*

Fifteen

Under the cash register, in the cluttered cubby that held the candy, I discovered Kim Porciatti's cell phone like Columbus discovered America. It had been there for a while and wasn't mine but I took it anyway. I had dragged out the bags of snack-sized chocolates and was just fiddling around under there, being a bit nosy, snooping. Not so much to look at — some cardboard boxes filled with rubber bands, paper clips. A banded stack of cards with Ohmigod!'s explosive pink and purple logo on them, "Bernice O'Leary, General Manager" printed in pink type beneath. Stacks of register tape and a baby blue feather duster clumped with frizzy dust bunnies and other sneezeables. And back behind it all, the shiny silver bundle of Kim's small phone. All folded into itself like a space-age rolypoly bug. Crouching low, I flipped it open. It was stuck with glittery stickers that said "Kim" in different colors and styles, plus a faded Neoprint sticker of Kim herself, all smiles. The phone's electronic face was dull, dead. I hit some random buttons but nothing happened. I'd never held a cell phone before so I didn't know how to make it work. Nothing I did made it light up. I was so excited to find this thing. Being in the mall all day had made me materialistic. I swear. It's easy to be down on everything when you've barricaded yourself in your bedroom, snacking on endless greasy bowls of ramen, living the simple life. Just a few hours spent in the belly of the shopaholic empire had changed me. I was embarrassed to be so impressionable. It's not like the clothes at Ohmigod! had begun to appeal to me, I wasn't totally brainwashed. It was more like — I wanted to participate, somehow. I wanted in on the action. I was all hopped up on strobing fluorescent lightbulbs and I wanted a cell phone. I grabbed Kristy's purse — she'd made me take it because the sheen of its pink iridescence exactly matched the glitter in the BABY design on my T-shirt. It was a small purse, built to hold not much more than a tiny phone. All I had in it were my house keys and a couple dollars. Kim's cell phone slid in snug and looked right at home. The pink plastic purse breathed a sigh of relief. It was complete, it was emotionally whole, a cell phone resting in its belly. I zipped it up and sunk my hands into the candy bags, rose from my squat with bite-sized chocolates falling from my fists and there was Bernice.

Didya wash up? she chirped. I thought for a moment that maybe this was what having a mom was like, working with Bernice. Someone to butt in to your business, inquire about the state of your hymen, boss you, tell you what girls you couldn't hang out with. I felt a swell of appreciation for my good ol' Ma, at home on the couch, never bothering herself with classic Ma worries like pregnancy and substance abuse. I could prance right in the door with Rose in tow, Rose could yank stolen goods from her sack, and detail the elaborate scams that brought them to her and Ma would nod and ask Rose to bring something back for her. She'd turn to me and ask why I wasn't an awesome thief like my new friend. Then she'd go back to worrying about her liver.

Bernice leaned in and took a sniff. I'm Still Fortifying, I told her. I tore into a Twix and crunched heartily. It's true that rising from squat to standing had made the dark spreckles swell at the edge of my vision. I knew better than to starve myself like this, but it had been an exceptional day. Twix crumbs cascaded down the front of my shirt, mingling with the glitter. I held the half-chomped bar to my supervisor. Would You Like A Bite? I offered, and Bernice smiled. She liked me again. It didn't take a lot. I remember Ma complaining about the work world. *You gotta kiss a lot of ass, and kiss it all day long,* she'd griped, and then made a squishy kissing noise with her lips. I guess I was kissing Bernice's ass. It wasn't so bad, really. I gave her a big smile and she smiled right back. I'd seen on *Oprah* once that women tend to mirror other people, like imitate whatever expression you shoot at them. It's very subconscious. I don't think I do it, but for sure Bernice O'Leary is a mirror maniac.

In the Ohmigod! bathroom I lathered my hands with some melony Softsoap from the pump on the sink. I made big, thick suds. I scrubbed the hell out of my nicotine fingers. I scrubbed and scrubbed like an obsessive-compulsive person. I made the water wicked hot and gritted my teeth through the steam, blanching the grody tobacco stink away. I hate to be such a wuss, I really do. I would like to be badass and free, you know, clambering around Dumpsters, thieving and smoking and being a deliberate fire hazard like Rose, but it's not so much my style.

Don't you smell like a piece of candy, girl! Bernice beamed at me. She was by the register with a pile of clothes she'd collected from the floor of the communal dressing room. I was so grateful she'd gathered the castoffs herself. I was pretty sure one of my duties here at Ohmigod! would be creeping into the communal dressing room with its shadowy corners and infinitely reflecting walls, retrieving the ill-fitting items shoppers leave scattered across the floor. Surely at some point I would have to complete this task, but I was psyched that I didn't have to right then, what with my poor health. I hate that communal dressing room more than anything. I mean, I hate it so much it's like a phobia for me. It makes me real neurotic. I'm scared of it the way tiny brats are scared of the dark. One of my first memories is Ma dragging me and Kristy in there with her, back when I was so small and the store was something different, it was called Joanie's or something and Ma shopped there sometimes. She was trying on bathing suits and so were all these other women, all of them in the dim lights and the crazy, fun house mirrors. A flashing eternal reflection of boobs and skin. The whole environment really freaked me out. And on top of it I'm crammed into this doorless cubicle with my own naked mother and all her naked-mother smells and strange hairs, and Kristy's no help because she's like totally transfixed by the mirror, even then, just gazing at herself and making faces and laughing like a miniature madwoman, and I swear I had a panic attack. It was all too much for me. I started bawling and screaming and Ma got pissed, pulled off the bathing suit, which I recall was an orange one-piece that cut high up her thigh, pulled her jeans back on, and dragged us from the shadowy room. I shrieked and then Kristy shrieked, upset that she had been yanked away from the glory of her own reflection. And communal dressing rooms only get worse as you get older. Then the weird childhood creeps merge with more teenaged concerns about your body and your clothing and what you can or can't afford and the lousy condition your underwear might be in. Not to mention the bodies, financial status, and lingerie of the other girls. Honestly, if I'd considered the communal dressing room at the time, I probably would have nixed this whole job scam right off the bat, and I planned on going in there as little as possible. I wondered even if Ma's doctor at the free clinic would write me a note verifying I have a mental illness about the space and getting me off the hook with it forevermore.

Bernice motioned to the pile of clothes, all inside out

and tangled up in themselves. She handed me a basket of hangers. It would be my job to smooth and zipper the rejected clothing and arrange them on the racks to look unworn. So that the next lady in search of a canteloupe-colored scoop-neck T-shirt could try one on confident that hers are the only sweaty armpits the fabric had ever clung to. Her boobs the only boobs to ever warp the fibers. Bernice grabbed the feather duster from under the register and walked over to the jewelry rack to stir some dust. She hummed along to the music coming in from the speakers. *Circle in the sand, goes round and round . . . never-ending love is what we found . . .*

I let myself get lost in the work. The clothes stopped being symbols for all I hated about life, they became just shapes and colors and fabrics. I began to feel affection for some of them. A skirt that felt particularly soft. A specific and peculiar shade of blue. The way the pink stitches on a sundress surprised me. It's not that I wanted to wear them, it's just that I stopped holding their prettiness against them. So they're pretty, so what? What's it got to do with me? I was just slapping them on hangers, trying my best to tune out the music because if you let that noise in it'll colonize your brain and you'll be singing Belinda Carlisle songs in spite of yourself for days. I just focused on the clothes because it made the time go by faster, and the faster the time went by, the sooner I'd be able to take my half hour and that meant food.

It was because I was such a diligent worker, such a focused caretaker of consumer goods, that I did not notice my nemeses, the feared and inevitable Katie and Yolanda, strolling into the store 'til they were practically on top of me. Katie with her long and deliberately windblown hair. Kristy has gone so far as to suggest that she positions herself in front of a fan and hoses the mane down with hair spray, but Kristy's just starting rumors. You know Katie's family doesn't have fans whirring in their house, you just know they've got air conditioning. Anyway, there's Katie and her tremendous hairdo, and also her tremendous lips, great big lips that are even more 3-D thanks to a generous slathering of deep red lipstick. Katie Adrienzen is all hair and lips. Her sidekick Yolanda is quieter, both visually and also in real life. Katie's a real talker, she's pushy and loud and used to start fistfights all the time in junior high, was a scary sort of female, but since high school she has taken up a new reserve. All that anger is still in there, though, just boiling her brains and giving her that enraged hairdo. Yolanda is tall, towers over Katie, and perhaps has compensated for the space she takes up by cultivating a meeker personality. Yolanda's dark hair was pulled back in a tight ponytail that bobbed and swayed with each loping step, and she was wearing some experimental eyeshadow job, gray misty clouds around each eye, sort of racoonish but lighter. Her eye shadow literally looked like eye shadows. I supposed she was trying to look high fashion or something. In Mogsfield. These girls were hilarious. I would have greeted them with a wall of attitude, except the longevity of my new retail career weighed on their stylish shoulders. It was Katie who looked at me first, and Katie's eyes that narrowed into mean little slits. It was Katie's pinching fingernails that clamped a thick lock of her unruly hair and tugged it back sharply behind her ear, giving her an unobstructed view of me at my humble rack, placing garments onto hangers and giving them delicate little pats, shooing away any dust or grime they might have picked up languishing on the floor in the creepy communal dressing room. It was Katie who charged toward me, and Yolanda who followed. Sometimes I thought of girl cliques as Russian nesting dolls. It was like Kim Porciatti was the main doll and inside her lived Katie Adrienzen and then inside Katie nested Yolanda.

Hello and who are you? Katie demanded. I considered saying I was Bernice O'Leary's cousin from New Hampshire, down for a summer in Mogsfield. I was opening my mouth to formulate this whopper when Yolanda piped up softly and said, *You're Kristy Driscoll's sister.* My story went right out the window. I was even going to throw in something grand like, my parents died on a white-water rafting trip and Bernice was taking care of me. They have white-water rafting in New Hampshire, right? I think that if you're going to lie you might as well lie outrageously. Plus, people don't know what to do in the face of tragedy. All the different emotions make them uncomfortable so they scoot away fast. That story would have gotten rid of them ASAP, but Yolanda called me out. I had to just be me. I nodded my head. Yeah, I said, I'm Trish. I remembered what Rose had said, about names that stick. Trisha, I said.

Not for nothing, but how did you get a job here? She looked me up and down. *A lot of girls want jobs here. And our friend actually works here already and I hope you didn't steal her job, 'cause she didn't quit. She had an emergency.*

Listen, I Know About Kim, I said. Katie's head moved back in an offended wave, like my breath was rancid.

Who are you? Trisha? You don't know Kim. I'm Kim's best friend, I know who Kim knows, and she don't know you.

I snuck a look at Yolanda, to see if she was hurt that Katie just professed best-friendness with Kim and not her. I know how competitive these girl friendships can be. I've seen talk shows about them. Yolanda looked like regular, mysterious Yolanda Peters.

I Mean I Know Who Kim Is. I said this with a strain on my voice, like I was trying hard to be patient with her being such a simpleton.

Everyone knows who Kim is, Yolanda said.

Yeah, really, Katie rolled her eyes.

I Mean I Know About All Of It, Okay? I was getting real exasperated but had to keep this whole thing low lest Bernice be lured over by the commotion and make the scene even uglier. I Know This Is Her Job, I Don't Want It. I motioned to the rack of clothes I had just been feeling so consoled by. They'd reverted back to being stupid, showy clothing for stupid, showy people. One of the dresses I'd been fawning over was almost identical to the flowery thing Katie had on. You Think I Give A Shit About This? I hissed. I Am Doing Bernice A Favor. The two girls were straining to hear me. Their heads craned toward me on their long giraffe necks. I Told Her I'd Help Her Out 'Til Kim Could Come Back. She's Got A Store To Run Here, I said. The Frigging Mall Doesn't Shut Down Because One Person Tries To Kill Herself.

She didn't try to kill herself! Katie gasped phonily.

Seriously, Don't Bother, I said.

Um, Yolanda said. She looked worried. *Her sister is Kristy. Kristy the hairdresser.*

I smirked tightly and nodded. Hairdressers Know Everything About Everyone, I bragged.

Katie sighed. I could have gotten a lot of pleasure out of that moment, but truthfully I was still scared. With them in the store and Bernice lurking about, my lie was jeopardized.

I'm Going To Leave The Second Kim Is Better, I pledged to Katie. I'm Just Doing This To Help Bernice, Then I'm Gone. Okay?

I'll make sure of it, Katie threatened. I let her have that one.

Please Don't Talk About It To Bernice, Any Of It, I said. I said it not like a question but like a statement. She Is Torn Up, You Know. About Kim. Just Don't Talk About Me Being Here 'Cause It Reminds Her That Kim Isn't.

She'll be back in, like, a week, Katie spat. I shrugged.

Whenever, I said.

Where is Bernice? Katie said, snapping her attention away from me. *Bernice?* She spun her head around, her hair fanning out from her head in glossy sheets.

Yes? I heard Bernice clatter away from the stand of jewels, and I booked it out of there. I grabbed a cluster of hangers and dashed deep into the store, getting low behind a fat rack of capri jeans. I crouched anxiously and worried about fainting again. I was proud of myself for not flipping out on Katie and Yolanda. It's hard to restrain myself when I'm in such a state and I thought I'd kept it together quite well.

Did you say hello to Trishy? I heard Bernice chirp.

Katie's voice was lower, a muffle. *Oh, well, just until Kim returns, of course!* God, Bernice couldn't help being loud. It's like she was deaf or something. There was another stream of murmur, and then Bernice chanted, *Of course, of course!* But her voice had a little catch in it, a little note of concern. *Well, I thought hiring one of you girls would be the best thing to do, just to get me through the coming weeks . . .* Bernice trailed off. I peeked around the corner of the capri jeans. Katie and Yolanda were looking at each other. If my life were a comic book, they would have big question marks hanging over their heads. If my life were a Saturday-morning cartoon, you would have heard a loud kerplunk as my stomach dropped. My poor starving stomach. It was under such stress already, and now this.

Well, yeah, Katie started, her head nodding, shaking all that streaky hair. She was gesticulating with her hands, motioning. Her voice had gotten low again.

Bernice cocked her head like an easily confused dog. *Well, she's so close with you and with Kim, I thought it was a good choice. I didn't mean to hurt your feelings —*

She's not! Katie exclaimed. Her head swung back and I ducked back behind the capri jeans but fuck, I knew she saw me. Saw me ducking and staring, saw me spying and creepy and scared. Fuck. I wondered if I should just drop the clothes I was still clutching to myself in a giant hug. I'd ruined their arrangements on the hangers. Maybe I should dump them and split, head home, start the long walk back in my skank attire, hit a packy along the way and ask some grown-up headed inside to grab me whatever alcohol the three bucks in my plastic pink purse would buy. Spend the rest of the summer lying low in my bedroom and with any luck I'd never see Katie or Yolanda ever again. Maybe I'd even conjure up an illness and join Ma in the living room for the rest of my life. The end.

I'm not getting involved in your tiffs now, Bernice said scoldingly. *This is a very intense time right now, we're all going through a lot with Kim —*

She doesn't care about Kim! Katie's voice was a hard laugh.

Katie, we can't have this talk here. I'm sorry you're upset, but this is a business. Is there anything I can help you with? Do you have anything on layaway, Yolanda?

I placed the bulky load of hangers onto the floor 'cause now I was shaking. I just didn't have the strength and I was nervous. I didn't want to lose my job already, not like this, chased out by these awful girls.

We were here to get Kim's cell phone. She said she left it here. Katie's voice was raised. Now that she had entered the yelling zone it was going to take her a little while to drift back down to her normal range.

Well, all right, Bernice said in her accommodating way and then she was flinging shit all over the counter, the bags of candy, the boxes of cards and coin rolls and inky pens and gnawed-up pencils. *I don't see it,* she said, and came back up with handfuls of register tape. I left the clothes on the floor and stood to my normal height. Bernice's hand came up with my pink purse, her terrifying fingers toying with the zipper. *Is this Kim's —*

That's Mine! I screamed toward the register, jarring the frantic gang of them, turning them toward me. My

Purse! I yelled, and smiled. I ducked back behind the capri jeans, as if I was working.

I don't know, I heard Bernice say regretfully. *Nothing else down here.* Katie murmured and Yolanda's murmurs flowed into them and then Bernice said, *Well, I really hope you girls all work it out. And you tell Kim I'm waiting for her, kay, girl?*

I heard the shuffle of Katie and Yolanda heading down my aisle, and I got low real quick and crab-scuttled to the side, a weird back-bend crawl in a crooked direction. I just wanted to stay out of their path. It was like being in a forest, low on the linoleum of Ohmigod!, the clothes stretching up all around me, hemming me in and hiding me. I located one of those circular racks and dove inside it. The chiffon dresses cloaked me, they fluttered with my breaths. When me and Kristy were little we would play hide-and-seek in stores just like this, and being encircled by a rack of clothes was my favorite place to hide. Cut off from the chaos of shopping around you but solidly in its center. I hugged my bare knees to my chest, balled up and waiting for the two to leave. I could hear them making their way to the exit. They seemed to be right by my hideout.

That fucking little liar, Katie was fuming. Her voice was sputtering like a car with a banged-up muffler, angry spurts. *She fucking lied, did you get that? Did you get all that?*

It's really pathetic, Yolanda agreed. Yolanda had more class than Katie, more dignity. You could tell that Katie would grow up into one of those road-ragers who gets court-ordered to take anger management classes. They stomped and shuffled by me, so close their wind stirred the smocks. I held my breath and counted to twenty, mentally chanting "Mississippi" between each number, giving them ample time to clear out. And then I clambered out of my hiding place. It was like being reborn, the dresses sliding over my face and revealing the stark riot of Ohmigod! I stood up straight, shook myself out, tossed my ponytail, yanked my miniskirt down and turned to face Bernice O'Leary.

Trisha, what are you doing? Are you hiding? Are you hiding from those girls? Her face was an angry smear, she was huffing. *Talk to me, girl, what is wrong with you?*

I...I'm Not Friends With Them, Bernice. They Don't Like Me. There didn't seem to be any other way out, really.

Yeah, clearly. What about Kim? Does Kimmy like you? Are you even friends with her?

Yeah, Totally, It's Just . . . Her Friends Hate Me. Because Kim Likes Me So Much.

Bernice sighed. She chewed the inside of her cheek. She blew her bangs from her eyes and stared me down. This could be true, right? Girls got in weird jealous fights over shit like this all the time. Who's best friends with who and all that. I saw it happen at school. One day there's this cluster of girls and they're all swooning over each other and then, wham, one of them has a burst of humanity and says hello to the wrong person in the hall and next thing you know you can't go into the bathroom to take a piss because the whole gang of them is having a huge fight, filling the place with wild drama, and that girl will never sit with them at lunch ever again and there will be new graffiti penned into the stall walls, about her having genital warts and being a blow-job queen or something. It's like *Wild Kingdom*, the world of girls.

I don't know, Trisha. I think this was a mistake, you working here. You're a new friend of Kim's?

I nodded.

You're new friends with Kim and you hang out with that girl Rose and now Kim tried to kill herself and all her nice friends hate you. Her eyebrows had come down low across her eyes, like storm clouds. I could see her trying to jam all the pieces together into an ugly puzzle that revealed me having some sort of suicidal influence over Kim Porciatti. *And what the hell is that?* She nodded at the pile of clothes I'd left dumped on the dusty linoleum.

I'm Sorry, I said, and dashed over to the the heap, struggled to pull the clothing up into my arms but the pieces were sliding from the hangers and the hangers were jabbing at me.

No, no! Bernice stomped her foot like a horse. *Just forget it, Trisha. This isn't a good mix. A good fit.* She took a breath. *I don't think you're Ohmigod! material. I'm sorry.*

No, Bernice! I can't believe I was whining. Maybe pleading — pleading doesn't sound quite as desperate, maybe it was just a plea but I fear it was a whine. We Just Got Off To A Bad Start. Really, I Can Work Really Well Here —

You've gotten into an argument with customers, you're throwing our merchandise all over the store, Kim's friends claim you don't even know her, the girl you hang out with is a little — well let's just say she doesn't have a good reputation in the mall and her mother, I happen to know, is not normal, and you stink like a smoker and you passed out! For all I know you're on dope and you're pregnant or something. No, this is a bad match. I really love your sister but you have to go.

Whoa. I stood there and stared at Bernice. What a fucking bitch. Did Bernice O'Leary just tell me I smelled bad? Did Bernice O'Leary just accuse me, in so many words, of being a giant douche bag? I flashed on Rose. This would never happen to a girl like Rose. Partly because girls like Rose don't get hired to work at places like Ohmigod!, but still. I couldn't imagine anyone ever trying to make Rose feel small. You know why? 'Cause there's a crucial part of girls like Rose who simply don't show up for it. They're just not available for humiliation. Maybe because they've been raised by lesbian mothers who are totally persecuted all the time so they know how to watch their back. Maybe because they haven't spent their teenage years locked in their room drinking beers and avoiding everyone. Girls like Rose don't avoid anything and so they know how to handle everything. They know how you're supposed to react when some loser like Bernice O'Leary insults you to your face. I didn't know what I was supposed to do. It seemed like not crying would be a good start. I could feel my eyeballs swell and bulge with the onslaught of tears and I was like, fuck that. No fucking way was bitch Bernice O'Leary going to make me start crying like a baby. No way was I going to burst into tears in fucking douche bag Ohmigod!, where a tiny school of girls had gathered, hesitant, on the edges of our confrontation, pretending to be interested in some ugly bikinis but totally spying on our drama. I dropped the clothes hanging in my arms to the floor and gave them a kick.

Fuck You, Bernice, I said. Kristy always tells me that swearing like that just makes you look trashy and dumb, like you don't have any better, more intelligent comebacks to fit the situation, and the truth is I didn't. "Fuck You" seemed perfect and Bernice had already decided I was some sort of skank so fuck it. I gave the clothing pile a more savage kick.

Really, I said. Fuck The Fuck Off. Go Fuck Your Fucking Self.

The school of girls burst into laughter. I shot a glare at them to see if they were laughing at me, or at Bernice, and I couldn't tell so I told them to fuck off too, just in case.

Get out of here! Bernice was shrieking now, she had her hands up, pointing and waving like a crazy person with a gun threatening to shoot up a crowd. Her bangs blew up and down on her forehead, borne on the intense breeze of her words. *I am calling security! You are banned from here! You get out of here!*

I ran toward the counter, sliding a little in my flops, praying oh fuck don't let me wipe out. It's hard to run in flip-flops, they slide around under your feet and that toe-thong is a sneaky tangle, but I made it to the counter. I ducked and grabbed my purse with Kim's phone inside, snagged a bag of candy too, just for the fuck of it, just 'cause I was crazed with starvation. It would have been nice to be able to walk out of the store with dignity but I'd already been screaming "Fuck" at the top of my lungs, so really, what the fuck. I stomped down the aisle, smacking at clothing, knocking shit off the racks onto the floor. There's something great about being at the very bottom of your own well of personal loserness. When you've already made a jackass of yourself and sabotaged whatever skimpy thing you had going for yourself, all that's left is the extreme style you see in action movies or street-fighting video games. The most atomic, apocalyptic fuck you that you can manage. I was shaking with it. Rage and starvation, the lights, the injustice of the very existence of whole groups of girls. The injustice of Bernice O'Leary. Behind it all a tinkling fear, pure scary sadness, growing wider.

Trisha! Bernice hollered. She was behind me now, herding me out of her queendom. *Trisha! You are not going to get a good recommendation! Do you hear me! I better not ever see you again!* She stopped short at the pile of kicked-around clothes, her feet skidding into the cheap material. I swung out and into the mall, almost plowing into a trio of Eminen-wannabe boys slouching toward the food court.

Whoa, bitch! One of them yelped and you'd think I'd have told them to fuck off too since I was on such a roll, but I couldn't help it anymore, I burst into tears.

Sixteen

I went into the bathroom at the back of the mall, but it was so skanky and smogged up with old exhaled cigarettes I couldn't have the nervous breakdown I'd imagined having. I set myself up in the roomy handicapped bathroom at the end of the row of stalls, but just knowing I was breathing in the out-breaths of strangers with bad habits made me stop crying and settle back into being generally pissed off. I began to see the value in smoking. You always have something to do. It seems like smokers like to smoke when they're bored or stressed, and I happen to swing back and forth between those two states all day long. Probably I'd be a great smoker, but I can't get past the stank yellow nastiness of it. Sitting in the bathroom in the secondhand fog I felt lonely and wished I had someone to share my humiliation with. I could see the charm of a cigarette in a moment like that, a little burning friend to be with you in your time of need. Really I just wished I had a beer or some other more powerful kind of alcohol. Something dark and mysterious in an imposing bottle. I could hole myself up back here in the handicapped stall, just me and my dignified bottle of exotic alcohol. People would knock on the door and I'd bark, Go Away. The smokers would come and light up. Who knows, maybe a druggie would join us in another stall. All of us in our web of chemical misery like some weird sort of anticlinic. I could have hung around the toilet for hours, not crying, not knowing where to go, philosophizing about the grossness of cigarettes and how badly I wanted to get drunk, but the longer I stayed in there the louder Bernice O'Leary's insults ricocheted in my head. And I started feeling like everything she said, like I smelled bad and was a loser, just hanging around in a handicapped stall. I wasn't exactly looking forward to going home and announcing to my family that I got fired on my first day. I knew Kristy especially would be so pissed when she heard I flipped out on Bernice. Somehow it was going to be hardest for her, trust me. Even though it's really her fault this happened at all. Even though if the world were at all a fair place Kristy would be apologizing to me with tears in her eyes and then explaining everything to Bernice O'Leary— that I wasn't a smelly, pregnant drug addict, that I'm a good kid at heart and was simply a victim of circumstance, of Kristy's lies. I stood up from the toilet and felt all the blood run cold down my body and those goddamned black spots swarmed my eyes again and I decided that all my needs — my need for food and my need to not feel like a loser, to not feel alone and trapped in a smoke-suffocating public bathroom — they could all be met if I went to visit Rose at the Clown in a Box. I pushed open the stall door. You could see the old smoke like a thin gauze the bathroom was wrapped in. Whoever exhaled that smoke could be dead by now, but their breath lived on, looking for new lungs to poison and kill. I rushed back out into the mall.

Seventeen

The food court at the mall has all the regular stuff inside it. The famous and greasy hamburger. Fried Chinese foods soaking in syrupy sauces in deep steel trays. Quick Mexican junk food, a rubbery tortilla with a fast smear of beany paste and a few honks of sour cream from the big metal sour cream gun. Pizza sitting out all day long under hot lights. One place is nothing but cheesesteaks, another place is chewy pretzels with cheap little dipping packets, and another sells cinnamon muffins and that place smells fantastic. You see those muffins all lined up behind the counter, thick sugar loops oozing over the melty cinnamon surface and oh god. I just want to lie down in them like a big sticky bed. I want to live in one. I think they've got some sort of aromatherapy contraption hidden in the back and they're pumping this addictive stink into the mall for us to follow like zombies, leaving drool trails for other brain-dead sugar fiends to follow. I figured I really deserved a sugar muffin. After all I'd been through today. I stumbled up to the counter and an older lady, like my mom's age, a little older, heavy and tired with a lot of wrinkles on her face and blue eyeshadow that matched the blue of the muffin-shaped hat that was her uniform, she helped me. Her name tag said Wanda. Her ears were double-pierced with gold hoops and the hair that stuck out from the muffin-shaped hat was blond and dry as straw from all the chemicals it took to keep it that way. I'm glad I don't give a crap about being blond. It seems like a lot of work that really damages you in the end. Look at this woman, she should be home stretched out on the couch like my own mom but here she was pushing sugar biscuits to make money for the hair dye that was destroying her hair. I know she bought other stuff with it too, like fish sticks and medicine for her dying children or something, but you can see people's lives wasting away before your eyes at the mall and it freaked me out.

I'll Have A SugarMuffin, I said. I said it sort of hushed, like it was an illegal transaction we had going on.

You want a MommaMuffin or a BabyMuffin? Or the BigDaddyMuffin special?

Which Is What? I asked.

It's a MommaMuffin and two BabyMuffins and a coffee.

Shouldn't That Be, Like, The Stressed-Out Single MommaMuffin? I asked. She didn't really laugh, but the wrinkles by her mouth got deeper for a second. I ordered just a BabyMuffin. I only had three dollars and I was hoping to get some alcohol, somehow, at some point. The lady passed me a little bag heavy with muffin.

You work over at Ohmigod! She nodded at my name tag, which I had forgotten to take off my glittering BABY shirt. BABY shirt, BabyMuffin.

I Got Fired, I confessed. Who cared? I Got Fired About Five Minutes Ago. It Was My First Job.

Oh, she said. *I was gonna give you the mall discount.* She looked at me blankly, shrugged.

Well I Sort Of Could Use The Discount More Now, I said. Now That I Don't Have A Job Anymore. The lady looked at me. Think About It, I encouraged. She stood there, thinking. She took my dollar from my hand.

I don't know, she mused. *I could get in trouble.*

Come On, I pushed her. Really. What If I Had Just Lied And Said I Worked At Ohmigod!? You Wouldn't Have Known. But I Was Being Honest. I Was Honest With You And Now I'm Being Punished For It.

It doesn't work like that, she said, and finally smiled. It wasn't a real smile, it was sort of a bitter smile, a grimace, and I thought, I bet that's the only kind of smile her face can do anymore. I thought, it's sad when the bureaucratic limitations of a huge fast-food chain is what brings a smile to your face.

Okay Whatever, I said. Thanks For Nothing. I took my BabyMuffin and turned my back on Wanda. Clown in the Box was at the edge of the food court, by the exit. I walked toward it, the stink of deep-fried everything getting stronger, the air growing oilier, as I approached. The place seemed to shiver in the distance the way a real hot highway trembles in August. It wasn't Rose but another girl at the register. She looked about twelve years old, with braces and baby fat that pushed against her uniform. The Clown in the Box name tag was a jolly plastic clown head with the employee's name stuck inside the giant mouth. This girl's name was Gina and she looked bored. She stared off in the general direction of Bamboo or Bust, the Chinese place across the court. She held a superlong plastic straw, the kind that goes with the half-gallon soda cups, and was jamming it down the back of her shirt, itching her back with it.

Welcome to Clown in the Box, what sort of summertime fun can I get for you today? The glare of Gina's braces took me off guard. They glinted with all the neon of the food court. It looked like a pinball machine inside her mouth.

Uh, Is Rose Around? I asked. I looked into the dim background of the Clown. I thought I saw a short person behind a rack of fryers but it was hard to see in the grease.

Yeah, Rose is here. Are you Rose's friend? Gina asked. She was staring at me with big eyes. She had some sort of silvery eyeshadow clumped in the corners like sleep. It went with her braces.

Yeah, I'm Rose's Friend, I said, even though it felt weird to say. Like, what defines a friend? Isn't a real friend someone who sleeps over at your house and calls you on the phone saying things like "I'm having a really hard time and I need someone to talk to." How much time would me and Rose have to spend together before we were officially friends? What sort of trials would we have to go through.

I'm Actually More Of An Acquaintance, I clarified to this girl Gina.

Oh, she nodded.

I Just Met Her Earlier. So We're Not Really Friends Yet.

But you're not, like, enemies, right? You're not here to kick her ass or anything?

No Way, I said. I wondered if Rose had lots of enemies, lots of people looking to kick her ass.

Hey. It was Rose. Her striped uniform had gotten considerably fouler since we'd last spoken. Large dark patches of oil stained the fabric, creating a kind of blobby pattern overlay with the stripes below.

Are you two friends? Gina asked.

Rose shrugged. *What's up, you on your break? Want me to hook you up?* She turned to Gina. *Trisha works at Ohmigod!* she informed her.

I saw the pin, Gina said in an oooh-goody tone, her braces flashing.

She will hook you up, Rose promised.

I Just Got Fired, I said flatly.

No! Rose gasped. Gina looked crestfallen.

Yes, I said. Fired. Canned. Kicked To The Curb.

Demoted, Gina offered.

Oh, no. Rose shook her head. She turned to Gina. *You should see the pin she let me steal today. So cool, it was like sixteen dollars or something. Wasn't it?*

I Don't Know, I said. I Wasn't There Long Enough To Find Out.

Why'd you get fired?

I sighed a long sigh. I pulled my BabyMuffin from its

sack and sunk my teeth into its gooey surface. I could feel the sugar go to work on my teeth immediately. A drizzle of caramel sweetness drooled out from the pastry and trailed down the front of my shirt. I held out the bun to Rose and Gina. Want A Bite?

No way, Rose shook her head. *I OD'd on those my first week working here. I ate so many I puked and now I can't eat them anymore.* She withdrew from the damp and spongy bun like it had very bad vibes. *I can't even smell that shit.*

I'm Like That With Peppermint Schnapps, I said.

I know what you mean, Gina said, nodding her head. She had no idea what I was talking about.

I'm Really Starving, I told them. Could I Get Something?

Totally, Rose said. *You totally hooked me up. I owe you.*

I waited in the back by the john while Rose went around plunging cages into giant metal sinks of oil. I sat on a dusty bucket of processed food glop and watched her move in her outfit. Clown in the Box sells the food you buy from trailers at traveling carnivals. They sell fried dough in both their slab and squiggle formations, served with cinnamon sugar or sugared strawberries or a pool of melted butter floating in its center. They deep fry candy bars, they deep fry hot dogs dipped in batter and impaled on tiny sticks. They deep fry cheese and there's even a sort of healthy option, the "California Platter," which is a lot of unrecognizable vegetable nuggets fried up good and crunchy. They have chicken-fried hamburgers, which I think are breaded hamburgers stuck in the fryer. It's intense. Backstage at the Clown was full of thick, sizzling sounds. Bubbles boiling up out of the oil, noises that sounded pushed from the ocean floor, hot and swampy sounds. It was a weird laboratory. People loved it. It sucked to have to wait until summer for a corn dog. Sometimes the urge for a corn dog strikes at inopportune months, around Christmas or during a March blizzard. I'm looking out at the snow, dreaming of summertime, of jerking around in a bumper car at a beachfront carnival, that electrified smell in the air, and then I get a little hungry and I think, um, corn dog. And what do I do? I go to the mall and hit the Clown in the Box and I get to eat a little bit of summertime in the freezing dead icehole of winter. I've got to admire the genius of it, even if I don't particularly love fried food.

Rose dashed around waiting on people, a huge, polka-dotted clown hat pointing in a wobbly cone atop her head. It sunk down low on her forehead. The hat's thin elastic chin band dangled inches beneath Rose's jaw. A nub of hairnet bunched out of it in the back, a twirl of Rose's hair, dark, snagged inside it like an exotic sea thing. Stripes ran down her shirt, yellow-green-orange, yellow-green-orange. As I shifted uncomfortably on the dusty plastic bucket, trying to sit in a way that did not reveal my underwear, it occurred to me that I didn't know what Rose really looked like, and she didn't know what I looked like either. We were both wearing costumes. At the counter she handed some deep-fried cheese sticks to a couple of dudes with military haircuts, and Gina rang them up. You couldn't see it from the front, but the back of Gina's clown hat had a big dent in it. Rose dashed back to a fryer and yanked it dripping from the oil. Tiny muscles percolated in her scrawny arms. She was born malnourished and grew up stunted but Rose looked like she swung from trees, both stringy and strong, like a monkey. I felt lumpy in comparison. I was lumpy in comparison. My body was soft, like it was stuffed with a thin layer of down. Ma's body was like that, and so was Kristy's. It's what drove Ma to Weight Watchers before I was born, and what inspired Kristy to swear off carbohydrates. But it didn't really bother me.

You wanted the California Platter? she asked.

I shrugged. If It's Too Much Trouble I Can Just Have A Cheese Stick Or Something, I said. Don't Put Yourself Out.

No way, Rose said. She had a paper boat full of steaming brown globs. Oil still twitched in crevices of crust. *Whatever you want, seriously.*

You Won't Get In Trouble, Having Me Back Here?

Nah, Rose dragged the back of her hand across her forehead, leaving a smear of grease. *Zack's gone for the afternoon, nobody's here except me and Gina and she doesn't give a fuck.*

Yeah, I don't give a fuck, shrugged Gina from the register.

I picked at the vegetable nuggets. I lifted a blobular crusty one from the paper boat and blew and blew until the oil shining on the stiff batter didn't look scalding. I popped it into my mouth and sucked in air to cool it off.

Hot, huh? Rose nodded. She grabbed an empty basket and knocked crumbs of fried batter onto a countertop. She swept them up with her little hand and dumped them into her mouth. *Mmmmm!* she rolled her eyes back like it was the best-tasting thing in the world. I crunched down on the grease ball cooling on my tongue. *I like to try to guess what vegetable it is,* she said, watching me chew. *The choices are broccoli, zucchini, I think cauliflower . . .*

Yams! Gina shouted back from the register.

Carrots, Rose corrected.

Yams!

They're carrots, Rose said to me. *Who even eats yams? Nobody eats yams.*

I Think I'm Eating A Carrot, I told them.

Open your mouth, Rose said. She peered inside. *Yeah, it looks orange. Marty, he usually cooks while I do the register, he said it's all just the batter but they put different food coloring inside to trick you into thinking they're vegetables.*

No, I shook my head. I probed the mass inside my mouth with my tongue thoughtfully, and swallowed. I Really Tasted Carrot.

It could be artificial flavoring, Gina suggested.

I popped another into my mouth. Rose watched expectantly. It Has No Flavor, I told her. None At All.

She nodded. *Weird, right? What are they?*

I shrugged, ate another. I Don't Know. They're Good, Though. I'm Starving.

You fit better here at the Clown more than you did at Ohmigod! Rose said. *No offense or anything. Everyone who works there is so stuck up. Even that girl Kim, I don't care if she tried to kill herself or whatever. She was a bitch. She kicked Gina out of the store once.*

What Did You Do? I asked.

Gina looked horrified. *I didn't do anything!* she said. *I never do anything!*

It's true, Rose verified. *Gina never does anything. Do*

you? You do things, right? Rose's eyes upon me seemed too much. It was like supersonic rays came at you when she looked your way. It made me feel shaky. I turned my face down toward my fry boat and scraped some batter off a nugget. The vegetable-thing beneath was a pale green color.

Sure, I lied. I Do Things. Things like sit in my room and stare at the ceiling. The ceiling, if it is stared at long enough and especially while drunk, can come to look like a weird terrain, another world, with rupturing volcano and mountain ranges and wide lakes where the paint had flaked off in chunks, revealing the pale blue beneath. There's a lot more to staring at the ceiling than you might think.

Cool, Rose said. She turned to Gina. *I'm Gone.*

Technically not for another five minutes, Gina said, looking at the clock on her register. *Can't you please wait? I hate being here by myself. What if I get held up?*

Rose snorted. *You're not going to get held up. Look, everyone's here.* She gestured around at the food court. Wanda at SugarMuffin mistook her wiggling arms for a wave and waved back. *See, Wanda's right there.*

I Hate Wanda, I offered.

What if I have to go to the bathroom? Gina continued scrolling down her list of concerns.

Go now, Rose told her. *Go, I'll watch the register.*

Gina moved down the corridor of fryers and hit the switch on the bathroom wall, sending the ceiling fan alive with a whooshy whine. The seam on the ass of her striped shorts was distressed enough to give you an idea of what color drawers she had on. Something in the blue-green family. Aqua. She clicked the door shut.

Why Don't You And Gina Trade Uniforms? I suggested.

Rose shook her head. *No way. I like mine baggy. Then I can do more of this.* She struck a key on her register and the cash slid out on its oiled tray. Rose slid her hand into the money and then down the front of her shorts. For a brief second it looked like she was playing with herself, then she swung her hip at the cash drawer and bounced it closed. Rose kept the coolest look on her face the whole time, like she was totally bored and not involved in something exciting such as stealing actual cash. She gave a quick glance about the mostly dead food court and squatted below the register. *Look at this,* she hissed, and gave her pants a quick yank down. There was a significant cash bulge in her underwear. Which was pink and shiny. The crotch jutted out and looked sort of uncomfortable.

Does It Itch Or Anything? I asked. Surely it couldn't be good to keep money all up on your hoo-ha. My mother has spoken much to me and to Kristy about the unfathomable filthiness of dollars and coins, starting when we were little kids and she caught us sucking on pennies. *Money is filthy!* she had shrieked. *People pee on money, money falls on the ground, in the dirt! People touch it with their dirty hands, sick people touch it!* She went on and on but really I couldn't get past the part about the pee. Why would anyone pee on money? I've never been able to figure it out. Maybe it's a sex thing. Rose stood up straight once more, her underwear and its stolen prizes tucked back inside her baggy Clown shorts.

No, it's not itchy, Rose laughed. *Are you allergic to money?* Her bony fingers scrambled down the front of her shorts and pressed into the balloony fabric. *I love it!* she squealed. *That's like, a hundred dollars or something.*

No Shit? I asked.

At least, she whispered. *At least. Hey. How come you got fired?*

It's A Long Story, I said. I Lied A Lot. My Sister Lied, I Lied — I remembered the cell phone stuffed into that crappy little purse. And I Stole, Too. But I Didn't Get Caught.

Rose moved closer and held her hand out for me to slap it. Behind me the door opened and the whine of the ceiling fan hummed louder as Gina exited, vainly tugging at the ass of her shorts. *Let's hang out tonight,* Rose hissed as our palms clapped together. *Can you hang out? You got plans already?*

I shook my head. No, I Can Hang Out, I said.

You can stay out late? You got a curfew?

I kept shaking my head. No, No Curfew, I Can Do Whatever I Want, I told her. I Can Stay Out All Night, Who Cares, Whatever.

Lucky duck! Gina pouted. *You guys are such lucky ducks. I don't get to do anything.*

I Stole A Cell Phone, I mumbled low, very low, almost not even moving my mouth, like Rose was a puppet I was trying to fling my voice through. Her eyes lit up at the word "stole" but her forehead crunched at the rest of my jumbled mumble. Gina lingered, leaning.

Gina, the register, Rose said. She cocked her head toward the front counter, where an old man stood squinting up at the menu boards. She leaned back in to me, close. The smell of the place had nested in her so deeply she seemed to be its source, exuding the stink of hot oil more than the bubbling vats themselves. She was fry personified. I pushed the bottom of her clown hat up off her ear and spoke into the tiny whorl.

I Stole A Cell Phone, I Need To Charge It, I hushed.

Rose stood back and appraised me, the situation. She looked toward Gina, who looked back at us with strain in her face. *Rose, one fish fry? Please? Before you go?*

Rose grabbed a frosted, bread-colored plank from a freezer and tossed it into a fry with an explosion of steam. Slick clouds billowed up and refilled the place with steamy haze. *Where is it?* she asked me. One of her penciled eyebrows was, at this point, totally gone, the hair there sparse. The other eyebrow wiggled crazily on her brow. I picked up the plastic pink pouch from where I'd tossed it into a dustball on the floor beside me. I picked the gray fluff from the strap and handed it to her. It's Inside There, I said. I Don't Know What To Do With It.

I can charge it, she whispered. *This is great, this is really great.* She paused, thinking. *We can call all over the place. We can call, like, Japan if we want. Do you have anyone to call?*

I thought about it. I Think My Dad Lives In Louisiana, I said. I imagined a phone ringing in a little shack, a shack balancing on stilts smack in the center of the swamp. My dad knocked out on a wooden boat, oblivious, an alligator making ripples in the water. But I Don't Know For Sure, I said. My Mom Lies A Lot.

Rose nodded. *My mom's girlfriend is in Iraq. Do you think we could call there on it?*

I shrugged. Why Not? I asked. If You Can Call Anywhere?

Find out where your Dad is, get all the long-distance numbers you can and we'll meet up tonight and make tons of phone calls! We'll call fucking everywhere!

Okay, I said. All Right. We made plans to meet and I left her there, dredging for that block of fish with a pair of long metal tongs, cursing as the oil spattered her arms.

Nice to meet you! Gina hollered. I cut quick through the court and was out of there.

Eighteen

The walk back home from the mall sucked. It sucks even on a regular day, and this day was not regular because I was wearing a skirt that crawled up my rear and a shirt that sparkled, drawing the attention of every ape on the streets to my boobs. I don't know if there are creeps everywhere or if Mogsfield is some kind of unfortunate creep central, but dudes were just blatantly staring at my chest and there were cars on the street piloted by guys who felt the need to holler at me out their windows as they sped by. At least they didn't stop. At least I couldn't actually hear whatever it was they felt compelled to tell me. The speed they zoomed at made their cries sound like *Heeeeeeyyerabababafreaarrma! Hahahaha!* At least none of the guys on the street showed me their dick or flashed me their ass. As a girl I had a lot to be grateful for, plonking home in my flops. Once I was walking in my neighborhood and this skinny white guy in a pair of nylon running shorts and no shirt, not even those useless tank tops that guys like to wear, the ones that scoop way down and are slit down the sides, he jogged past me, took the edges of his shorts beneath his cheeks and lifted them real quick, flashing me his moony white ass. I cut my walk short, went back to my room and stayed there. It had made me feel pretty depressed, to be honest. This walk home wasn't having such a powerful effect on me thank god, and I think it was thanks to Rose. I was starting to see the benefit in having friends, or just one friend, really. Too many friends seemed to get troublesome. Rivalries occur, and then comes backstabbing and shit-talking and other dramatic events. I've seen it on TV and at school. If you're going to indulge in friend-having, it seems best to keep it to a manageable single individual. But having Rose to think about took my mind clear off the lousy guys I had to shuffle past, and helped me to not spend too much time thinking about if the dude who drove by in the van had called me a douche bag or an old hag. Or maybe a fag. Seriously. There's no logic to these people.

When I got home I was greeted by Donnie, shirtless, drinking a beer on the porch. Thank god we don't have an actual front yard. He'd be out there like a mechanical lawn ornament, drinking and waving to passersby and getting pink and peely with the sun. At least this way he is set back from the street.

Hi Donnie, I said.

Hey kiddo, he smiled and scratched at the snarl of hair

on his chest. Donnie lived life nude to the waist whenever possible. He scratched at himself like something from *Animal Planet*, then rubbed his sweaty-wet beer can across the tangle, making it all damp and matted. *You walk all the way home?* He squinted at me.

Yeah, I shrugged. I Just Worked Half A Day. To Start.

So tell me all about it, he lifted the can to his wet mouth and slurped at the opening. I could smell the thin and tinny stink of the beer and I wanted one. I figured I'd simply swipe one from the fridge and then I noticed that Donnie had stashed the whole six-pack in the shade beneath his sagging lawn chair.

Oh, It Was All Right, I said vaguely. I Made Friends With This Girl, We're Going To Hang Out Tonight.

How's the work? he asked. *Easy, hard? They treat you all right?*

I nodded. Can I Have One Of Those? I pointed down at the splintery wood of the porch, wiggled my fingertip in the direction of the beer.

Kid, you work now, you gotta buy your own refreshments, he shook his head and grimaced, like he was cluing me in to some sort of difficult life lesson and it pained him to do it.

Donnie I Can't, I reminded him. I'm Fourteen, They Won't Sell To Me.

Well you can chip in a bit, howbout? Toss me a few dollars? You're probably making more money than I am. He jammed the can into the crotch of his cutoffs and held his hand out like I was going to slap some cash down on his palm.

I could not hide the sourness, it creeped across my face like a bad smell. Sure, Donnie, I said. I pulled a phony good-kid grin up over my sourpuss. Once I Get My First Paycheck I'll Kick Down, Okay?

Donnie emitted a sound like someone was letting the air out of him. *Listen, I'm taking up some space in your room. Just a little corner. Just 'til the weekend.* With a grunt he bent down and yanked a beer loose from the plastic rings. *We'll consider this a rental fee.* He tossed it to me but I wasn't ready, so it sort of hit me in the chest and rolled across the porch. Pieces of glitter from the *Baby* T-shirt stuck to the can.

Great, Donnie quipped. *Nice going. Good catch. That's gonna blow up when you open it now. Don't ask me for another one.*

A Rental Fee? I asked in a crabby voice. I hated the thought of Donnie in my room, getting his vibes on my things. I scrambled across the porch for my rollaway can of beer.

Some batteries fell off the back of a truck. He shot me an awkward wink, like a mosquito buzzed into his eyeball.

How's Ma? I asked him.

See for yourself, he invited, and gestured toward the door. Then he tipped his can way back, sucking the dregs, and with a flick of his wrist tossed the empty out into the street with a clatter. *Score!* he chortled. A wide smile ate his face. It's always a happy day when stuff falls off a truck.

Ma sat in the dim living room, her nightgown rumpled and her hair tangled and still pretty despite it all. Still plump and perfect, rolling with woman-ness, wrapped in peach. The couch was draped in a faded floral sheet 'cause in the summer the old woolliness of it makes you itch and feel gross. The living room was dim, the sun kept off the television screen and also out of Ma's eyes. The sun gave her headaches. The shades were drawn, Donnie's silhouette out there on the chair like an alcoholic puppet show, his can lifting and descending. The television was on, always on, always turned to talk shows or news, something real, no chipper family sitcoms or emergency room dramas, only the real dramas of real living, everything going wrong all the time, everywhere. And yet I see very little on TV about how creepy men are in the streets or about the basic daily obstacle course a female is forced to run through. About how you can be walking along absolutely not thinking about your *pussy* your *ass* your *tits,* but then, wham, thanks to the drooly curbside dude, now you are. Now your mind is consumed with the idea, the reality of your *pussy, ass, tits;* the possibility of *blow jobs,* of *getting fucked.* I wish more attention would be paid to this phenomenon. That there would be long-term psychological studies on the mental effects of this, the changes in brain waves it produces in girl-brains. I can go days without leaving my room and never think of my boobs once. Then I leave the house and it's all anyone wants to talk about.

From what I gather, all Ma watches on TV are reports of the new big scares, terrorism and ebola and gun-toting six-year-olds and how the Bible or Nostradamus or the ancient Aztecs predicted the world is going to end next year. The glow of the television flickered over Ma, who was sipping tea from a cup and watching a talk show. It was like a burning log in a stately fireplace, casting its warm light around the room. On the screen a lady in a tight lady-suit bustled all over the studio audience, clutching a microphone. She dipped into the rows of civilians, the opinionated people. Ma said, *Opinions are like assholes, everybody's got one.* A heavily made-up woman with a short, bleached hairdo asked a question, her voice shaky with the weight of the cameras upon them. The camera swung around to the stage, where a heavyset lady daubed the damp corners of her eyes with a wad of toilet paper. Then it happened. I looked for too long at the television and it stole my soul. It turned me to stone, like some terrible myth. That was why I avoided this room. It wasn't only because Ma is depressing and Donnie annoying, it's the frigging television. I glanced at it and suddenly I was interested in something you couldn't give two shits about, say, the health of that crying woman on the talk show, and before I knew it hours have gone by and I've become an expert on, like, carpal tunnel syndrome. Who cares. It's probably why Ma hasn't been able to really get off the couch in so long. She's frozen there, held in the malevolent shine of the TV. She craned her neck around to see me there, all decked out in Kristy's skanky clothes. It's strange how the same clothes that make Kristy look like a normal, well-adjusted teenaged female make me look like a hooker.

I have autism, Ma informed me. She turned back to the screen and rested against the sheet draped like a toga over the back of the couch. *It's very interesting. I'm learning all about it. Want to watch some with me?* She patted the cool, worn-away sheet bunched next to her.

I Got To Get Out Of Kristy's Clothes. I said this to Ma but my face was hitched to the television. Television is like a great gooey snare, the light shining off it clingy spiderweb vibrations. I didn't even care about this emotional woman on the TV but then I couldn't take my eyes off her. I guess she had autism too, just like my mom. The beer I had begged off Donnie was growing warm in my sweaty hand, in the dead, dense air of the house. I wondered if it was still too shook-up to open it, thought it could be refreshing perhaps to feel the tickly bubble-spray over my body, soaking the stupid *Baby* shirt in sticky beer.

Trisha, Ma continued. She had a little offended catch in her voice. *I would think you'd be happy to hear this. I thought it was maybe ADD but now, I really think I should be tested for this new kind of autism.*

I Don't Know, Ma, I said skeptically. Usually I just nod and say something vacant, but every now and then her claims are so out-there, like when she got on a Tourette's kick. She had seen some *20/20* episode about Tourette's syndrome and decided that was her problem all this time. I was like, But Ma, You Don't Walk Around Screaming Swear Words, and her answer to that was, *But I always want to.* Huh. Then I guess I had Tourette's too, right? Who doesn't feel on the verge of screaming *fuck* or *shit* or *fucking shit* half the time? That's not a disease, that's like the opposite of having a disease. Ma dropped the Tourette's story line after a week of halfhearted mumbling, of swearing a bit more than usual. It was so forced. Now autism. I thought autism was little kids rocking back and forth in their playroom or hitting their toddler heads against the wall.

Ma, You're Not Autistic, I told her firmly. It was too hot out for this shit. You're Too Functional To Be Autistic. Believe It Or Not.

It's very interesting, she repeated, ignoring me. *There's many different sorts of autism, actually. Some people are highly functional, highly intelligent really. They just had this woman on,* she nodded her chin at the screen. *She was brilliant. Some sort of scientist.*

Uh-huh, I grumbled. The woman on the television was giving a brave, tight smile, the camera pulled close to her face. I wondered what that was like, working a camera for a talk show. Crouched behind the tall black equipment, zooming here and there, spinning around, listening to crazy people all day. I bet I'd like it. I took a stab at my beer can. I cracked it gently and foam fizzed out of the split.

And — you're not gonna like this, Trish — they think lots of Alzheimer's cases are really mad cow disease. How you like that?

Not So Much, I said. I licked the froth from the top of the can.

Don't do that, Ma scolded. She doesn't miss a trick. *Those cans sit in warehouses. Mice shit on them. I tell Donnie, you should wash those first.*

Okay, I said. I started to leave the room. My First Day At Work Was Fabulous, I told her. In Case You Cared. I Was Promoted. I Got A Raise. I Got Employee Of The Day.

I knew you could do it! Ma shouted at my back.

In my room I found a small sculpture of car batteries. Hard bulks of machinery shrink-wrapped in heavy, puckered plastic. There were about fifteen of them. Donnie had done an okay job of backing them into the corner, they weren't much in the way. Still, they were ugly and stolen. When I was younger I thought that trucks were the most shabby and unreliable vehicles of all, things always tumbling from their backsides. I imagined the rear doors of semis crushing open beneath a tide of food processors, hair dryers, computer printers. I fantasized about the epic traffic jam, the excited carloads of people scooping booty into their trunks. Then Kristy told me the goods were actually stolen. She was really upset about it. This was when she was about twelve and going through a Jesus phase. She was going to a church around the block and making friends with nuns and other old ladies. She told me the stuff Donnie stashed in our bedrooms was ripped-off and illegal, and at the very least he was going to hell for it. She wasn't sure about the rest of us, but she was worried. She said it didn't look good. Ma and Donnie started getting nervous that she was going to confess to a priest or something, so she got grounded and wasn't allowed to go to church anymore. She had to stay in the living room with Ma watching talk shows where women recount all the horrible things that happened to them in foster homes. *You want that?* Ma would wave the remote at the screen. *You want the state to take you away? Just because of some boxes in your room? Put them under your bed if you don't like looking at them.* Donnie brought her a truck-fallen curling iron, then a boom box. She chilled out. I never minded the piles of loot occasionally materializing in my bedroom. They had an outlaw sheen, and Donnie tended to be a bit more ass-kissy when he needed to use our rooms for stashing.

I stripped off Kristy's stupid clothes. I threw them — balled up and reeking of my brief time backstage at Clown in the Box, stained with the gritty sugar drool of my Baby-Muffin — onto her bedroom floor. The force of my hurl created a wind that fluttered the rows of supermodels hung by drying tape from the walls. At least that was over. No more dressing in Kristy's clothes. Back in my room I grabbed a pair of sweats and then a pair of scissors and I went to work chopping them into new summertime shorts. It wasn't so easy, the scissors being wicked dull and the sweatpants material being pretty good quality, actually. I'd got them for Christmas. Every winter I get a brand-new pair of sweats and every summer I chop them into shorts. So autumn, for me, is a sweatsless season. I had to cut and cut the sweats with little chops, so the end result was pretty Frankenstein. Then I did the next leg and it was equally jagged but in a totally different manner. I pulled them on and then that Weight-Watchers T-shirt. I wondered what it meant that I went to work in a T-shirt that said *BABY* and after work put on a T-shirt that said *I'M A LOSER*. In the mirror above my dresser I looked at myself. I saw my darkish hair done up in that hairdo, and I dismantled it. It was scrunchy and stiff with product. I mussed it all up hard with my finger tips, and then I came at it with the dull blades of the scissors, chopping off an inch and then another inch and then another. I didn't have much of a plan, it was an intuitive haircutting. I chopped at it until it was too short for Kristy to strangle it into a french braid or lasso it into some Audrey Hepburnish little cupcake of hair on the top of my skull, all anchored in place with a squad of clippies. My new hair swung thickly into my face at about chin level, jagged like my sweats. I thought that perhaps at a certain angle I might resemble a young prince from a children's book. Or, like a girl forced by the circumstances of her time to take on the appearance of a young prince in order to carry out certain adventures. My face under my hair was the same. I didn't much love it but there's nothing to be done about a face. Kristy of course would argue with that but we're of different persuasions when it comes to cosmetology. My eyes are sort of squinty and my cheeks a bit chubby. I guess my nose is okay. It harbors blackheads but the shape is fine. Same with my chin. It's not an ugly face, just kind of boring.

With my new haircut and my new sweats, I felt pretty excellent. The can of beer had finally settled and I peeled the shiny tab away and took a hearty gulp. Maybe Ma was autistic. What did I know? Maybe there's a type of autistic hypochondria she is in the midst of. I lay on my back in my bed, crunching upward to slurp at my beer, thinking about Ma's health and feeling an excited trembling in my stomach, an anticipation of my coming hours with Rose plus the result of eating candy and shit that had had any nutritional value boiled away into a vat of oil. I thought about Rose at her home, wherever that was, somehow funneling power into Kim Porciatti's cellular phone, sparking it alive, juicing it up. I tried to think about people in other places who I could call, but came up empty. Supposedly my Dad was in Louisiana, but there was no point in asking Ma about it. Maybe she threw his number away or maybe he had never left it with her. There was even a chance that he didn't actually exist, that he was some lie she'd dreamed up and placed in the muggy South. And then there was the possibility that he was dead. People who shoot drugs die all the time. It seems like they either die or they stop, and if he'd stopped, wouldn't the first thing he'd want to do be to find his family? I sat up on my bed, in my dreamy state I knocked a slug of beer out the window. It rained down in a pissy stream, sizzling on the hot concrete below, evaporating into the day. That's For You, Dad, I said out loud. Then I sucked the rest of the can empty and flung the tin out the window too. Thinking of Dad could get me a little sad, but the beer made me feel light, pleasant, and full, my stomach settled. I felt ready. There was a rap at my sticky bedroom door, and then the pressure of what I figured was Kristy's physique behind it. The door opened with a sucking pop. I burped a gust of beery breath into the air.

Hey, Kristy said. She was smiling, which meant she had no idea I'd been fired. I figured I wouldn't tell her. She got me started on the lying track, anyway. Before this whole little job scam I'd never had cause to lie and so I never had lied. I'm serious. I know it's probably hard to believe, but when you're allowed to do anything you want, why lie? Lies are for people who are trapped and cornered. But after I'd spent the day wildly crafting lies and counter-lies and clean-up lies, why stop?

Tell me everything, Kristy demanded. She settled onto my bed. She seemed not to notice my new hairdo, or the aura of beer in the air. Kristy seemed preoccupied. *Should I go first?* she asked.

Yeah, You Go First, I said. I gathered my legs beneath

me. My newly shorn sweats looked like they'd been chewed by a giant pit bull. They were my new favorite shorts.

Well, she began, *Mercedes is — she's great in a way, like she tells stories all day, she's had this crazy life but — she's really mean.*

Yeah? I asked.

Yeah, she's not just mean, she's, like, cruel. She just insults the girls that work there. She told this one girl, after she'd done a perm on this old lady, that — oh, I can't even say it.

Please, I said. I had no time for Kristy's modesty dramatics. Spare Me. What Did She Say?

She said she'd made the lady's head look like a poodle's twat.

Wow, I said. That's An Image For You.

And the girls just kiss her ass. And the girls are mean too. One went back into the trash can and pulled out a fistful of hair and threw it on the ground for me to sweep back up again.

Why?

She said I missed her area when I was sweeping. She said I was ignoring her on purpose.

She Must Be Really Insecure, I said.

That's what I think! Kristy burst brightly. Maybe Kristy was a little manic, or hadn't eaten properly today, either. Nobody in our house ate properly. *I'm just going to be wicked sweet to them, all of them, until they like me. That's my plan.* She smiled. Kristy could tolerate the weird laws of the female jungle. Be nice to girls who are jerks to you until you're all friends. I myself tend to avoid mean people, which is probably why I've spent the past fourteen years of life in my bedroom and have only just today made a friend.

Now you, you've got to tell me, how did it go? She tugged at my trusty, perfectly worn Weight Watchers tee. *Wait, you cut your hair! Oh my god.* Kristy brought a horrified hand to her raspberry mouth. *Trisha,* she said. *I would have. Oh, no.* She reached out and grabbed a lock, examined the up-and-down of the ends, the multiple angles. I yanked my head away.

I Like It Like This, I said. I Did It On Purpose. Somehow I thought that if Kristy believed it was a *style* she'd leave me alone. It Matches My Sweats. I stuck my leg out, offering her my chopped shorts for inspection.

Oh, god, Kristy groaned. *Trisha, I don't know what I'm going to do with that. What about Ohmigod!* —

Well, It Was Kind Of Fucked Up, I jumped in. I Mean, That Girl Kim's Friends All Came In And They Know Something Screwed Up Is Going On And Seriously, They Might Want To Kick My Ass —

No, Kristy interrupted, solemnly shaking her head, swinging her hair. *No way, they wouldn't do that. They're not like that.*

Right, I said. Katie Adrienzen's Not Like That. She Went To Anger Management Classes And Now She Deals With Her Rage By Kicking Homeless People While They're Passed Out In The Street. I'm Sure I'm Totally Safe. I pulled a smile onto my face but it was more like a grimace. Aside From Their Visit It Was Great. Bernice Said I Did A Good Job. I Made Friends With This Girl Who Works In Another Store —

W*hat store?* Kristy was excited.

I Don't Remember, I lied.

That kind of stuff is important! Kristy chastised.

I Know, I nodded. I'll Get Back To You On It. And, Lastly, Ma Has Autism.

Kristy cocked her head like a curious dog. *Autism? Is that, like, from eating bad food?*

No. It's Sort Of Like A Form Of Retardation. But More...Interesting. Autistic People Can Be Really Smart, Even Geniuses.

So Ma is like a retarded genius?

Maybe.

Are you fucking with me?

Go Talk To Her About It, I shrugged. And she did. But first she went into her bedroom to grab the video camera. I grabbed my backpack and left the house.

Nineteen

At the bus stop bench across the street from Spritzie's Spa I sat in the fading light and waited for Rose. The bus stop was a wooden bench with splinters so thick they poked through even the very nice, very thick material of my best sweats, harpooning me in the ass. Everytime I shifted I had to stand and pull a tiny wooden spear from my butt cheek. I wondered if I could get tetanus from bus stop splinters. Figured Ma would know and then decided to forget it. It would only result in Ma somehow having tetanus. I was a little embarrassed to be so early, so eager. I concentrated on looking aloof, like a loner, lost in my own deep thoughts. The world around me encouraged this by ignoring me completely. Man, what a difference it makes to not look like a giant girl. I know that any female is vulnerable to the occasional ass-flasher, but really, the amount of lousy shit I get when I walk around in Kristy's clothes versus the relative peace and quiet when I scoot around clad in sweats is staggering. It's like these dudes are programmed to scan for glitter or certain shades of pink, and as long as you're wearing a trusty pair of sweats and some gender-ambiguous flops you don't trip their radar. I leaned back against the bench, where a large ad for a real estate agent was plastered. Someone had carved *Bitch* across the woman's forehead. The carving went through the plasticky ad and into the wood behind it, deep and precise, and I thought it probably took the person quite a while to complete. It took some time, a good tool, and strong hands. And a hatred for real estate agents. I ran my fingers in the grooves. A couple of little kids trotted by, their clothes deliberately swimming on them, huge pants hung low and baggy, netted sports shirts. They kept walking 'til they were out of sight. I spaced out at the blur of cars zooming by on Main Street, the bits of radio tossed from their cranked-down windows and evaporating at the curb. Then there was Rose across the street, coming out of Spritzie's. She looked like some lost street kid who had wandered out of the house in her pajamas. The dress she wore was shapeless and gauzy and the palest blue. It looked like one of Ma's more ragged, throwaway nighties. I watched through the strands of bang draped across my eyeballs. It for sure was her, that same weird strut, like a mean chicken. She wandered back into Spritzie's and then wandered back out. A little electronic beep echoed in the humid street as she passed in and out of the shop. Rose! I hollered. I gave a wave from my bench, flopped my hair out of my face. She squinted and leaned forward and then trotted toward me.

Wow, man, you look totally different. She stood with her hands on her hips and stared at me. Rose looked different too. Without the hairnet plastering her hair flat and matted, it swung loose, a dark brown, thick and wavy and chopped off at the same place I'd just chopped mine. The front bits were pulled back from her face like curtains, stuck with bobby pins the color of rust. She had her eyebrows back on, delicate black arches crayoned across her forehead. Black ran in thin, wet circles around her eyes.

You cut your hair, she said, nodding. She reached out with her tiny fingers and plucked a chunk from my scalp, held it into the air for inspection. The past couple days of extreme preening with the hair had sort of messed up its texture. Hair spray and other concoctions had dried it out, it was wounded from the battery of Kristy's heartless fingers, her pins and clamps, combs with rows of sharp little piranha teeth.

It sort of looks like mine, she commented, and gave her head a wet-dog shake. When ladies on shampoo commercials do a move like that their hair settles all layered and elegant on their shoulders. When Rose did it her hair ruffled and sank.

I Wasn't Copying You, I said, quickly thinking that it looked like maybe I had. Like I was *Single White Female*-ing her or something. Trying to be her. I Couldn't Even Tell What Your Hair Looked Like Today. 'Cause It Was All Up In That Thing.

The fucking hairnet, she said. *The hairnet is evil.*

Customers were finding deep-fried hairs in their fry balls. There were complaints. So now we all have to wear them. She took her hand and scruffed the back of her neck with it, fluffing the hair around. *Now my hair can breathe.* She returned to looking at me. *Just in general, you look really different, man. Like you got a twin sister you sent over. You looked like one of those Ohmigod! hos and now you hardly even look like a girl.*

Those Were My Sister's Clothes, I told her. I Was Just Wearing Them To Work. This Is What I Wear Normally. The whole story, about the lies and Kim Porciatti and my screwy family, seemed too overwhelming to tell. The thought of such a long story, with me at the center, sort of took my breath away.

Well you look better than earlier. For real.

I Wear These Exact Sweats And This Exact T-Shirt, I said proudly. And These Flops. I clapped the rubber against my heels. That's It. I Don't Think A Person Needs A Huge Wardrobe.

Hmmm, Rose nodded. She sat down next to me on the bench, then popped right up again. There's Splinters, I told her, as she dug one from her rear and placed herself back down more gentle. Rose clutched in her hand the pink plastic purse I'd left behind at the Clown. Rose had crammed it full of stuff 'til you couldn't pull the zipper shut. I saw a pack of cigarettes, a wad of dull green cash, and a Chapstick. Rose had a coating of the waxy goo across her lips. She would scrape a bit off with the tip of her tooth and chew it like a mouse. The Chapstick was cherry flavored. I smelled it in the air, along with a good, clean smell that seemed to be coming right off Rose. And the nice, leafy smell of the tree that hung above the bench. The smell of tree leaves that have been baking in the sun all day, all green stinking and pulpy.

You got beer? Rose asked. *You smell like you have some.*

I Drank It, I said, impressed with Rose's nose-sleuthing. I Bummed One Off My — I paused. Who was Donnie to me? What was he? He's Not My Anything, I said. He's My Mom's Boyfriend. I Don't Know What To Call Him.

Probably "my mom's boyfriend," Rose nodded. *I call my mom's girlfriend "my mom's girlfriend." Her name is Irene.*

Oh Yeah? I asked.

Yeah.

She's The Person In Iraq?

Rose nodded. *She's in the war.*

Is Your Mom Worried?

Rose nodded. *They get to talk sometimes on the phone. That's why I was psyched to get this* — she tugged the phone from the purse, knocking cigarettes to the sidewalk. I took the cell from her while she scrambled around under the bench, fetching the tumbling smokes. The screen on the phone was lit up and alive, with little electronic fountains on either side shooting all the way to the top.

Rose sat back up. *But you can't call Iraq with it. The plan's not too good. It doesn't matter,* she shrugged. *There's no real phone number for Irene, anyway. She just calls when she calls. What do you think of the war?*

I pulled my face away from the telephone. I thought about the war. I'd seen some of it on TV, everything a sandy color, people ducking as things exploded, crazy footage of people running. Mostly I thought of the newscasters who talked about it, the women with helmet hair and dudes like aged Ken dolls. How the dramatic music with the horns starts playing and giant words that look like metal swoop down and then there's some image of like a flapping flag or a mean-looking eagle or something red with a tank on it. Those images that sit behind the newscaster when they yak. They say, Operation Desert Muck. Sand-Land Attack. Operation Freedumb What-What. It's like the war was a cheesy television show I knew better than to watch. Not even Ma watched it. Ma kept the tube tuned to *Dr. Phil.* It was weird to think of having someone you knew in the war. It was like they were on TV but trapped inside it, the way I thought about the television when I was a kid. How I thought that all the little people on the screen were somehow caught behind the glass. Even though they didn't seem to mind, it scared me. I wanted to smash the screen and free them. Having someone in the war seemed like they had gotten sucked into the television and far away to a place no one could see, the way that little girl in the *Poltergeist* movie did.

The War Seems Really Stupid, I said. No Offense To Irene. I Mean, My Mom's Boyfriend Is All For It, Which Makes Me Think It's Probably A Bad Idea. It Seems Like Everyone Who Likes It Is Kind Of The Wrong Sort Of Person. If You Know What I Mean.

Yeah, Rose said. She kept one cigarette out of the pack, and then climbed over the back of the bench and sat on the ground behind me, her feet stretched out onto the roots of the tree. The roots were busting through the sidewalk, pushing up chunks of cement like a tiny earthquake. *I have to hide,* she explained. *I'm not supposed to smoke.*

Okay, I said. I kneeled backward on the bench.

I need to decide if I'm for the war or against the war, because the news is coming to our house tomorrow to film us.

They Are? That sounded exciting. That's Lucky. Right? I asked. How Come?

They're doing a piece on people who have family in Iraq and they wanted to do a special bit on gay people so they picked my mom.

Wow, I said. Well, Does Your Mom Like The War?

She hates it. Rose struck match after match against the worn strip on the back of the book. The air smelled all tangy and disgusting with the sulfur smell. Finally she got it going. *My mother hates all that kind of stuff. She got arrested when she was pregnant with me, she was trying to shut down the nuclear power plant in New Hampshire.*

Whoa, I said. She Brought You To A Nuclear Place When You Were Just A Fetus? I wondered if that was why Rose was so scrawny. That plus all the smoking.

She thought the cops wouldn't arrest her if she was pregnant, she said. Her face was all screwed up and her voice sounded salty. *Can you believe that? I bet they had extra fun arresting her. I bet they couldn't wait.*

Wow, So You Went To Jail In The Womb, I said. That's Cool.

Rose laughed. Then she got serious again, took a short, serious drag off her smoke. *I just don't want to be all anti-war just because my mother is. I mean . . . it's like she doesn't really think about things. She just goes with her heart all the time. Like, probably the war isn't a good idea, right, but I don't even think she really thought about it. She just assumed it's bad 'cause it's a war and all wars are bad. Like, how is she going to explain that to the news people? She's going to sound like a frigging flower person.* A gray cloud flew out from her mouth and floated up toward the tree leaves. Rose was smoking like she was mad at the cigarette. It didn't look too relaxing.

And I feel bad for Irene. She really might die. That's really the truth. Rose looked at me like I would maybe argue with her. My mouth gaped like a little dying guppy and I felt sweaty. People didn't normally look at me head-on so much. Especially challenging people like Rose. I never talked to anyone who knew a person that might die. I didn't really get it. I felt like we were part of the war show now, sitting under a tree, getting intense.

I nodded. Yeah, I said. I didn't know what else to say. I always felt weird and confused when the news showed the families of soldiers who got killed on the TV. You know, crying moms with permed hairdos sitting in paneled living rooms, pictures of their sons in fancy white cop-hats hung on the walls. They would cry and cry and I thought it was sad of course that anyone ever dies but also, what did they think was going to happen? It was like even the parents had thought the war was just a television show.

People Die A Lot, I said carefully. I Mean, It's A War.

Rose seemed relieved that I wasn't going to try to tell her that Irene would be okay. *They don't even count it unless you get shot by one of the enemy dudes, or blown up or some-*

thing. Like, if an American shoots you by mistake, it doesn't count. They don't say it on the news. Or, like, if you get your arm blown off but you live, and then it gets all infected and you die, they don't count that. It doesn't count if people kill themselves. If they're like, I'm over this shit and then shoot themself in the head. None of it counts. Rose's cigarette was almost over. She seemed tenser than ever.

Why Don't You Just Say All That On The News, I suggested. That's A Pretty Good Speech. I Didn't Know All That.

Rose nodded. *Maybe I will. I just know Irene is scared shitless. She doesn't even want to be there. She signed up 'cause these army guys grabbed her outside the Stop & Shop and talked to her all about it and made it sound so cool. She was bartending at this gay bar and then it got sold and isn't gay anymore and the new people didn't like how gay she was and she didn't know what else to do. Pretty fucking stupid. I could have gotten her a job at the Clown. I told her that too.*

A car cruised by with hip-hop tumbling out from its speakers. The bass was so deep I could feel it run from the tires into the ground. It rumbled up the bench and into my knees, making all my bones vibrate. I laughed and then Rose laughed. The heavy music shook the heaviness right out of our heads. I didn't understand how the person in the car could even hear the song. I craned my head around and looked at him. He had a baseball hat low with hair spilling out the back, and his eyes were fixed on the street in front of him. His face looked like a rock. I bet he was wicked stoned.

This is that girl Kim's cell phone, huh? Rose asked, snatching it from my hand. *The one who tried to kill herself?*

She smoked and studied its face. The cigarette was all but a butt and Rose kept getting another drag out of it.

Do you Know How To Use It? I asked. Who Should We Call?

Rose hit some buttons and a series of names flashed across the small face of the phone. She held it in one hand, and in the other the squat cigarette sent a vine of smoke treeward. She kept her face down when she said, *How did you get this? What's up with you, with your split personality and shit?* Then she looked up and seized my eyes with hers. Her brown eyes were a different brown than mine. You wouldn't think something like brown eyes could vary or be special, but Rose's were so large, they seemed to have a pulse about them. They were these separately alive orbs on her face, swirling in the dark.

It's A Long, Fucked-Up Story, I said simply. I stretched out my hands and they bonked a low-hanging branch of the tree. I plucked a leaf and set to nervously shredding it, my fingers turning yellow and damp from its damp insides. I Got A Sister Who Is, Like, Really Normal? I paused to see if Rose would know what I meant by that. She nodded, took another drag from her smoke. The cell phone screen grew dark in her palm. She's A Hairdresser And Shit. She Got Me That Job, At Ohmigod! 'Cause She Knows Bernice. She Lied, She Told Her I Was Kim Porciatti's Best Friend And So I Had To Dress Up Like Those Girls And Pretend To Care About Kim Porciatti's Suicide Attempt.

You don't?

No, I said.

I don't either. I don't really get it. She flung the phone around in her hands like a little gymnast, flipping it in circles. *Maybe if I had actually seen her try to kill herself I'd feel bad about it. Do you know how she did it?*

I shook my head. I was sick of Kim Porciatti's dramatic attempt to scoot out of life. Today Was A Horrible Day, I said. And Now I Don't Have A Job And Kim's Friends Want To Kick My Ass And I'm Not Allowed Back In Ohmigod! Ever Again.

Rose laughed. *You could kick those girls' asses!* she hooted. *I bet you'd win in a fight. Don't you normally? You look like a boy. You could take them.* She nodded with authority, sizing me up.

I've Never Been In A Fight Before, I confessed. I Don't Know If I Could Do It. I was seriously flattered that Rose thought I was so tough.

No way, Rose insisted. *It's nothing. Those little bitches, you just take them down by their hair. All that hair, you just wrap your fists in it and yank them onto the ground.* She was getting excited, motioning with her hands. The cell phone tumbled into a crook of the roots and her smoldering cigarette danced, the smoke twirling. *Then you kick them.* She looked at my feet. *You should maybe not wear flip-flops if you think someone's after you,* she said. *They fall off and then you're barefoot and they can stomp on your toes. Or you twist in them and fall. And you can't kick.*

Is Kicking Fair?

Kicking's fair, she nodded. *Anything's fair, especially if they start. You gotta protect yourself.* She paused for a minute. *You got friends to back you up?*

The leaf was a wet pile of mulch in my fist. Totally smashed. No, I said.

You just move to Mogsfield?

No, I said again. I Just Don't Go Out A Lot. I cleared my throat. I'm A Loner, I said. It sounded cool. It was cool, a cool thing to say. I'm A Loner.

Rose nodded. *Yeah, me too,* she said. *I have people here and there.*

You Hang Out With The People You Work With?

She shook her head. *Nah. Not much. Once in a while. You know.* Her cigarette was done, she ground it into the trunk of the tree. Poor tree, I thought. The crunched butt fell into one of the holes in the sidewalk. And then, the phone rang. It wasn't a ring like a normal phone, it was a crazy, frenzied series of blips and bleeps, like the noise a video game makes when you clear all the levels. The ring sounded like a mistake, like a machine gone berserk.

Ack! I shrieked. Ack, Stop That Thing! It was so loud. Rose lifted it. The letters XXX ran across the electronic face.

What Do We Do? I whispered, like the phone itself could hear us. The phone, with its unpredictable trills and squeals, felt sinister. It was connected to Kim and all the girls who hated me by invisible cellular rays, rays that wrapped all around us, thinner than air.

Rose tossed the phone at me. It was like that game hot potato that I'd had when I was a kid. A plastic potato that you passed from person to person and then suddenly it made a big alarming honk in someone's unlucky hands, spazzing violently like a living thing having a freak-out. This was like that but the opposite, it came at you already angry and wailing and you had to shut it up. *Answer it!* Rose cried. I looked at the buttons. One had the image of a little green phone on it. Only it looked like an old-fashioned telephone, not like a cell phone. Weird. *C'mon, man!* Rose urged. What did I care? I pressed the button, held the phone to my ear. It was so tiny. The tip of it didn't even go to my mouth, it lay flat and warm against my cheek.

Kimmy, baby, the voice spoke through the tiny gadget. Rose's raccoon eyes were wide and excited. She hopped up and swished over to me, tried to cram her ear into the phone with mine but it was just so small. Like you could accidentally inhale it and choke to death.

Hellloooooo, the voice said again. It was like the voice of the devil. I know that sounds dramatic, but the voice on the other end of Kim Porciatti's cell phone would have sounded totally great and appropriate coming out of some monstrous animal-man-thing from hell. It was deep and adult, a guy voice. It sounded crusty, like its throat was a long cave packed with stalagmites and mucusy drippings, and the words had to fight through all that muck to get free. The voice sounded drunk, slow and slurry, sort of crunchy. Its edges rasped. Rose poked me in my side.

Hello, I choke-whispered. What did Kim Porciatti sound like? I couldn't remember ever talking to her, only seeing her swishing by under the terrible lights of the mall.

You got someone there? The monster asked. *You got something going on? I haven't seen you. You never pick up your phone.* There was a pause. My heart was beating like crazy. Rose stretched her hand around my waist and pulled me closer to her, close as could be, so she could hear. Our heads were knocked together like the conjoined twins Ma was watching on Oprah last week. Stuck together forever by the top of their skulls. Our hair rubbed and mingled, tangling. I imagined being Siamese twins with Rose.

Your motha there? You got family there? You at your home?

Yeah. I pushed the word from my mouth like a little burp.

You want to come by later? Do some stuff?

Rose pulled away from me abruptly, jolting her head up and down. *Yes, yes!* she whispered furiously.

Yeah, Sure, I mumbled. I looked at Rose for guidance. She was miming something furiously. What? I whispered. The voice on the other end chuckled.

I didn't say nothin', sweetheart.

No, I stuttered. Not You.

Where does he live? Rose whispered.

You got one of your girlfriends over there? asked Monster Man.

Ah — No, I said. I kept my voice hushed. Like maybe all mumbly girl voices sound the same. Where, Where Should I Meet You? I asked.

Same as always, he said smoothly. A smooth gargle. *You forget about me already? Where you been?*

Tell Me Where To Go, I whispered. And he gave me an address. Mogsfield? I asked. He laughed. *Revere,* he said. *On the beach, darlin. Like all the time. You hit your head or something?*

Okay, Okay, I said. I Gotta Go. When?

Rose was nodding her head encouragingly. The voice

spoke. *I'll be here all night,* it said. *Just watchin TV and, you know.*

Right. See You Soon, Then.

Bye, Kimmy. It sounded like a taunt but I think he was flirting. Ick. I held the phone away from me like something radioactive. I tossed it to Rose. Make It Stop, I said, and she fumbled with some buttons. Fumbled with the buttons then collapsed back onto the cracked sidewalk.

Fuck Fuck What The Fuck! I yelled. I yelled it right when an old lady was sort of heaving by us with the aid of an aluminum pole. She was putting all her weight onto her homemade cane and shuffling by slowly. She did not like my swearing. She scowled at me. Sorry, I told her. It somehow made it worse. I guess she hadn't wanted me to talk to her.

You're terrible, she snapped at me. I could see the round egg of her naked scalp where her hair became thin. Her hair was a cotton-candy fluff melting away under the sky, exposing the shiny skin beneath. It was too much to look at. I turned away from her. She filled me with a bad concoction of feelings, like hatred and sadness and anger all at once. Fucking old people. They always pull this crazy emotional combo out of me. It's too much. Rose was still collapsed against the old tree, huffing and puffing and generally cracking up. She looked like a marionette who had its string cut. Just a jumbled pile of girl against a tree. She took a wheezy breath.

You Should Stop Smoking, I told her. You Can't Even Laugh Normal.

That was your only chance to say that, she pointed a

bony finger at me. *If you say it any more times we don't ever hang out again.* She gathered her bones together and hurled herself up, shaking the dirt and grime and cigarette ash off the ass of her weirdo dress. *You want to go to his place or what?*

I laughed. I still had all the jangly nerves of the phone call running around inside my body, like a cage of tiny animals set free inside me, scurrying across my arms, freaking out in my belly. We're Not Kim, I reminded her. We Can't.

Sure we can, Rose shrugged with a smile. *We can do whatever we want.* I thought, this is a girl I met because she stole something from me. Because I let her steal the stuff I was supposed to be protecting. I read in one of Kristy's *Cosmo* magazines that girl-boy love relationships have deep patterns that form in like the first five minutes. That first encounter sort of dooms or blesses the whole rest of their life. I wondered if the same was for girl-girl friendships. If Rose would forever be the sassy thieving chain-smoker and me the inept and halfhearted official person. A person there under false pretenses, there because of a giant lie, pretending to be a girl I'm not.

Rose, That Guy Was A Creep, I said. You Couldn't Really Hear His Voice But There Was Something Wrong With It. He Sounded Like A Swamp Monster. Remembering his phlegmy tones made my skin go bumpy all over again. He was what Ma would call *a bad actor.* Maybe even *a sick puppy.*

He can't be that bad, she reasoned. *He lives on Revere Beach. Right in those big condos I bet. Those are expensive.*

My head was shaking like it was its own battery-powered instrument. I wasn't even aware of shaking it. My body was refusing to go.

C'mon man, where's your sense of adventure? Don't you know how to lie? We'll just lie. It'll be cool. Maybe he has beer.

I liked the idea of beer but there had to be another way to score some. I mean, I managed to drink beer all the time and I've never had to go over to this creep's beachfront creepshack.

No, I said wearily. I Can't Lie. I Really Can't. I'm Not Good At It. It's Exhausting. That's Why I Got Fired Today, 'Cause I'm Such A Bad Liar. I Can't Keep It Together. You Don't Want Me On Your Lie Team. I'll Bring You Down.

Rose crammed the phone back into the plastic purse. Every time she pushed something into the useless bag, something else toppled out. The Chapstick rolled down the sidewalk. The roll of cash spilled out, unfurling on the ground. I gasped a little at the wad of cash, the underwear money, the pantie-bulge. It uncurled from its tight bundle like something alive, a magical money-flower blooming on the cement. That's A Bunch Of Money, I said.

And I'm going to lose it all in this stupid purse. What's up with this? She stuffed it all back in and wrenched the zipper shut. Its metal teeth split in the middle, opening like a plasticky pink mouth. I hoped Kristy didn't care too much about this particular broken purse. I thought she probably was too wise to my capacity for destruction to leave me with anything she truly cared about.

Fuck, Rose mumbled.

I'll Put It In My Bag, I said. My backpack was limp and empty. There was nothing in it but my house key pinging around inside the cavernous darkness like a little satellite in outer space. Rose handed me the purse. It was sort of shaped like a hot dog and the cigarettes and cash poked out the top like the fixings on a truly bizarre mall food item. The ultimate food court meal. Dirty money and Marlboros in a hot pink plastic bun. I put Rose's ratty cigarette pack in my pack's inside zipper pocket, then tucked the roll of bills and the cherry Chapstick in there with it. Rose's items were all nestled together. Her own house key was dangling around her neck on a piece of stringy rope, like a little kid. I threw the telephone and the busted purse inside the pack and zipped the whole thing up.

Let's hitch to the beach, Rose decided. I felt locked into something scary, like the minute after the lap bar comes down across your thighs. How it doesn't ever come down low enough, how you can feel all the wiggle room you've got, how you can imagine that when the coaster does its famous loop you'll just slide right out of the car. And you wave your hands wildly to tell the tweaker dude working the ride that maybe your lap bar isn't down all the way, that it feels a little loose, and he just thinks you're another slavering yahoo with your hands in the air. And he yanks his crank and the car begins to climb.

Twenty

Rose said about hitchhiking: *it's no big shit.* She said she does it all the time, that once she hitchhiked all the way up to Nahant, wherever that is. *In Massachusetts,* she told me. Massachusetts is where we live, but I never think about it like that. I just live in Mogsfield. Sometimes I wind up over in Medford, or Malden, and I think I've been to Everett once. Revere is always there with the beach and the crappy carnivals, and Boston is of course a famous city, but I've only made it there on a couple of school field trips. I know from history that Massachusetts contains a lot of well-known areas. Salem, where all the witches were killed. Somewhere is Plymouth Rock where the Pilgrims climbed off their boat, somewhere else is where the later Pilgrims went nuts and dumped a bunch of tea into the ocean. I've heard of a village where everyone wears bonnets and churns butter and pretends like it's the olden days all the time. They're not Amish, they do it for show. You can pay an admission to enter their village and watch them milk cows. It's sort of weird if you think about it. Imagine if Mogsfield became an old-timey village like that. Like in the future there were townies lining up in their radiation-proof spacesuits to watch people decked out in the sweats and flops of yesteryear doing crazy long-ago things like sitting on their asses on a busted couch watching the tube, or tossing frozen foods into giant vats of oil over at Ye Olde Shopping Malle. Anyway my point is, Rose was living in a larger world. I might live in Mogsfield but Rose, it seemed, lived in Massachusetts. She got around. It added greatly to her sophistication, this hitchhiked trip to Nahant.

What's In Nahant? I asked.

The ocean, she said.

Big Whoop, I said. The Ocean's Right In Revere.

No, this is the real *ocean,* she told me. *It's the ocean the way you see it in books and nature magazines. It's the natural ocean.*

Like Waves And Cliffs And Stuff?

Yes, she nodded. *Big rocky cliffs. Nobody's around. There's grass and flowers and shit growing out of the rocks. Tons of bugs.*

Lots Of Bugs And No People, I summarized.

Yeah, Rose said. She took a breath. She looked like she'd like to be there in Nahant right now, all alone with the bugs on a side of a cliff.

Weren't You Scared, Being Alone On A Cliff?

No, she laughed. *Why?*

Well, What If You Fell In? Off The Cliff? People fall off cliffs all the time in nature. I once knew a girl named Cora whose mom died when she fell off a cliff. Ma told me she died hiking. Who knows how Ma gets gossip when she doesn't leave the house, but she does. It's like it comes through the mail slot with her checks and paperwork. She told me Cora's mom died hiking but I thought that meant hitchhiking. I was pretty fascinated with hitchhiking, having seen an old CHiPs rerun featuring a really amazing blond girl in tiny shorts and roller skates who went hitchhiking and got into some sort of trouble and had to get rescued by Ponch and Jon. I think in my head Cora's dead mom became the hitchhiking blond girl, who seemed very glamorous, and I figured death by hitchhiking was a sort of cool, TV-land way to die. And so I told the other kids in the neighborhood all about it. So Cora found out that I was telling everyone that her mom was a hitchhiking rollerblader and that's how she died. Cora had long and wavy brown hair and a light blue plasticky jacket with *Hello Kitty* on the back in a pair of overalls. Her face was all splashed up with tears and she was telling me her mom hadn't died from hitchhiking. Yeah, She Did, Cora, I told her. I thought maybe nobody'd ever told her the truth about how her mom died. I thought I was breaking some real life-changing news to her, I remember infusing my voice with gentleness. And still Cora cried. *She fell off a cliff!* she shrieked. Her snot and her tears mingled, her face was a waterfall, the features blurred under the rush of fluids. I shrugged my shoulders. I knew what my Ma said. I Know What My Ma

Said, I said. Later, that night, I told Ma what happened. *She did fall off a cliff!* she snapped at me. *She died hiking, not hitchhiking! You're a real pip.* I stared blankly. I didn't know what hiking was. And I still haven't ever done either, haven't ever hiked or hitchhiked, both sports being branded with badness and general death-producing danger in my head. And here was Rose, a girl who hitchhiked in order to go hiking.

I don't fall, said Rose. *I'm a Capricorn. A mountain goat. We can do anything. What sign are you?*

Pisces, I said. Rose laughed.

Yeah, you'd fall. You'd fall right in and drown.

Thanks, I said, stung. Thanks But I Actually Wouldn't. I Can Swim Fine.

It was a joke, Rose said. I decided against elaborating on my other concerns about her trip to natural Nahant, such as serial killers and other up-to-no-goods lurking along the cliffs, just waiting for some solitary city teenager to stroll by for their sick happiness. Clearly Rose paid no heed to the possibility of serial killers and their friends. It occurred to me that really I had my whole dumb equation ass-backwards. Rose was the loner here, Rose was the glamorous mystery. She stood at the curb with her tiny thumb hustled out, her chin pointed up like she had a real attitude problem. Her nonhitching hand was stuck to her hip, the bony piece of which jutted up like a shark fin from the fabric of her nightgown-dress. I tried to imagine if I would pick Rose up. I would not. She looked like something crazy would happen once she climbed into the car. The bearer of dramas that you'd become tangled up in.

There in the setting sunlight she looked like some neglected twelve-year-old who was hitching to the local jail to visit her pops. Once you picked her up you'd be buying her hamburgers, you'd be saving her alcoholic mom, dragging her sloppy stinky body to Alcoholics Anonymous, you'd be buying Rose a real dress and leaving that gauzy number in a Dumpster somewhere. A whole cinematic idea arced around Rose. I was bummed that I had such a hard time seeing my own theatrical potential. It's probably hard to get that sort of understanding about yourself. What was easier and more immediate was to become Rose's cinematic sidekick. I stepped off the curb, my backpack limp on my shoulder.

The first car that stopped, Rose was, like, forget it. It was some crapped-out number that firstly didn't even look like it'd make it to Revere Beach, and secondly was already crammed with people, dude-people who looked wicked unsavory.

Heeeeeeey! the dude in the front passenger seat hooted out the window. *You ladies off to the Palace?*

Um, no, Rose said. There was so much in those two words.

We're going to the Palace, but we could drop you ladies off somewhere first. If you're sure you don't want to come along?

If you're sure you're a lady, the kid in the backseat said. He said it in that way, like when you pretend to be coughing but you're really saying something shitty. He choked the words into his hands, but there were too many words. That gag works best with words, like *douche bag* or *lezzie.* Wicked slick.

I Heard You, Slick, I snapped at him.

Slick! the kid next to him howled, poking him in his stupid tank top. All of them wore tank tops, low under the armpits, revealing an eyeful of boy-boobie. Also they sported gold chains and baseballs hats twirled at various quirky angles.

How'd you guess my name was Slick, beeyatch? The car was rumbling with laughter and I felt sick. I wanted them to leave. Even though it was true that I looked like a boy I just didn't like how they said it. When Rose said it earlier it was like I was tough, could ass-kick in a fight.

Get out of here, Rose swished her hands like she was shooing off a small dog. *We're not going with you, man.*

We don't have to go anywhere, the driver leaned past his friend, sprawling across the steering wheel. He was demonstrating a relaxed vibe. Staying slumped, he crawled the car a little closer. I moved back toward the bench. See, I knew the hitchhiking thing was a shitty idea. It's so hard to get rid of dudes when they attach themselves hostilely to you. At least they were in a car and we could run in the opposite direction if we needed to. But that's so humiliating. Running away sucks. I don't get beat up but I just feel fucked-up from it for hours. Like my mind got beat up. I looked at Rose. I gave my head a jerk in the away direction, but she was ignoring me. She was glaring at them.

Get out of here, she repeated. The guy in the front passenger side leaned further out the window. He smiled a big smug smile at her. His eyes were sort of slitted and teary and I figured they were all fucked-up. All fucked-up and on their way to the Palace, a totally stupid gigantic dance club complex right here in Mogsfield. The place was divided up into different awful dance clubs. Like there was a room with male strippers where people like my mom went to get tanked and throw themselves at the stage. One section was called Rascals and it was for kids sixteen and up. That place was famous for being date-rape central and it was probably the one where the hoopdie full of losers was heading.

Front Passenger licked his lips, which were large and chapped. Dry from dehydration, from too much drinking and smoking. *I'm going to stay here and look at you,* he google-eyed Rose. *I like looking at you. You're funny looking.* The geniuses in the back cracked up.

C'mon Rose, I said. I was getting twitchy. Shit like this is exactly why I don't leave the house. And then Rose went totally nuts. She tugged her dress up in a quick flash, her hand sunk down her drawers. When her hand came back it was clutching what looked like a dead mouse. A coagulated blood-lugey slid off the side of the mouse, which Rose was holding by its ropey tail. It was Rose's tampon. The blood splattered the sidewalk. The guys all roared. There was a second of delayed stoner reaction, and Front Passenger jumped back, hitting his head on the rearview.

What the fuck! all the dudes screamed. I heard the words *sick bitch* and maybe something really tired like *slut.* And then Rose twirled the tampon around like some perverted Wild West hero. She spun it by the string, flicking blood from the drenched cotton, and she let it fly into the car. It whacked Front Passenger in the face. It bounced off his acne-speckled cheek and came to rest on his tank top. He jerked and spazzed as the blob of tampon snagged on his gold chain, as it rode up onto the skin of his clavicle and then plunged down under the shirt.

Aaaaaaaah, the dude screamed. *Aaaaaah, aaaaaah.* It was like he was on fire.

Get the fuck out! the driver reached around him and popped the door open. Bloody Front Passenger spun toward his friend. He banged his head on the rearview again. It was bonked all out of place and the driver said, *Fuck,* and then shoved the kid in his back. He shoved him hard out the open door.

Clean yourself off, man! That's sick! That's sick! My fucking car! One of the kids from the backseat leaned over and pulled the door shut. Front Passenger stood on the curb and the tampon slid out from his shirt, landing on the sidewalk. Rose dove for it, her grubby fingers wrapping around the string. The thing still had plenty of blood left in it. It was like the Uzi of bloody tampons. She could take him out again and again. I was breathless. What a genius weapon. The car peeled out, leaving their friend in a blue fog of burnt tire and exhaust. They headed in the general direction of the Palace. Front Passenger was lifting his shirt, looking at the long smears of Rose's menstruation on his chest. He held the fabric away from the wet mess.

What the fuck? he demanded. He looked seriously pained. He looked like Rose just kicked him in the 'nads. Like she'd done something dirty, betrayed some sort of pact we'd all agreed to. The tampon swung from her fingers. She made it sway like a pendulum. Her big eyes got creepy-big.

You are getting slee-py, she droned, moving toward the

boy. He took a quick step backward, still holding his shirt up, and tripped off the back of the curb. He went down hard, on his ass. Rose laughed. She leaned over him with the tampon. He was shouting all sorts of shit at her, mean shit and curses. I started getting scared again. I don't think I'd stopped being scared, but it had morphed from a bad-scared to a sort of exciting-scared and was now starting to go sour again. That kid was going to get up and punch Rose in the head. He let his shirt drape back over his torso and used his hands to help him scramble up. He was big and wobbly. He had a tattoo on his leg, Chinese writing. It probably said "Peace" or something. He was a fucked-up white kid who liked to start shit, walking around with a Chinese peace tattoo on his leg. I hated him so much. It was cramping my hands and making me feel wild and shaky.

I Fucking Hate You, Man, I said. I went and stood closer to Rose and her tampon. At least there was two of us. I didn't know how to fight, but I bet I could scream really loud, I bet I could make help come for us. If that didn't happen I could knock his baseball hat off and rip out hunks of his Abercrombie-colored hair, like Rose said to. I could bite him in the jugular and knee him hard in the balls. I could fight a dirty panic fight if I had to.

You bitches are crazy, he said. He backed up, then halted. He looked around for traffic but there wasn't any. He dashed into the street. Rose leaned in and hurled the tampon a second time. It whacked his back, leaving another crimson smudge, and tumbled to the street.

He kept screaming back at us as he ran past Spritzie's

and down the street. Just your regulation Mogsfield trash-mouth curse words, the ones specifically for females, like we haven't heard them a million times before, like they're practically not our nicknames by now. Like calling us douche bags could hurt our feelings, make Rose feel bad about chucking a dirty tampon in his face. We stood on the curb and watched him get smaller and smaller. Rose held her hand up to shade her eyes against the last atomic-orange flare of the setting sun. The boy turned down a side street and was gone. Rose made a wet and scraping noise at the back of her throat and spit a glob onto the sidewalk. She wiped her skinny mouth with the back of her hand. An SUV cruised by and flattened the tampon. It looked like roadkill against the pavement, like a bit of pigeon or the bloodied tail of a rat.

Another car stopped, with just a solitary man inside. Rose waved him along. *He had perv vibes,* she said. I tried to get her to tell me what the perv vibrations felt like but she couldn't explain it. *It was an intuitive thing,* she said. I was happy to hear she had the ability to pick up on these invisible perverted rays since the driver had actually looked pretty okay to me. I wondered if it was reasonable to expect any sort of normal person to pick up a couple of hitchhikers. Isn't it the sort of thing a normal person avoids? A blue pickup hurtled over toward us. There was a woman inside, which Rose noted and said, *Score!* poking a tiny fist into the air. The lady leaned over as far as her seat belt would allow.

Can you take us to Revere Beach? Rose asked. She was using the voice of a different girl. It must have been her hitchhiking voice. It was softer and higher, like she'd filed down the gravelly points of her regular, more jagged, lifetime-smoker's voice.

I'll take you anywhere except over state lines, the lady smiled. Her smile and her chipper voice seemed odd and I realized it was 'cause she was crying. She was a white lady with long orangey hair and a blotchy face. Little red splotches bloomed over her cheeks and her eyes were pink and puffy. *You girls shouldn't be hitchhiking, you know that?* she scolded us, but her snot-clogged voice was teasing. I climbed up into the cab beside Rose. The lady had enormous boobs and a tight T-shirt covered with Chihuahuas. Every time she blinked, some residual tears squirted out her eyes and she wiped them away. *I'm sorry,* she laughed. Or pretended to laugh. I mean, she was freaking out. At least it looked that way to me. I snuggled up against the door as she swerved away from the curb and onto the street, the treaded tires rolling over Rose's tampon mash. I hoped she could see where she was going with all that water in her eyes. *Don't be scared,* she said. *I know it's scary to see adults cry, right?* She laughed again. *I'm a real waterhead.*

Rose seemed totally unaffected. *It's cool,* she said. *My mom cries all the time. She's very emotional.*

The lady looked at Rose and then launched into this whole story about her boyfriend and how he caught her cheating on him, only she wasn't cheating on him, it only looked like she was but she couldn't explain it because he'd taken her cell phone and he'd smashed it with a cinder block. *That's how he caught me,* she hiccuped. *The phone. How he* thinks *he caught me. He* thinks *he knows the whole story! He doesn't know shit!* This lady was giving off some serious electrical vibes. The tight cab of her pickup felt stuffed with the angry wind of her mood, dense and crackling. The floor was a carpet of trash that rolled and snapped beneath my flops. Some rap-rock was yelling from the radio. Rose offered the freaking-out lady the use of our stolen cell phone. *Oh, you are angels!* She got newly emotional and a fresh rain of tears plopped onto her splotched face. She seemed seriously unstable. It took about fifteen minutes to get into Revere, then another few to reach the water and become snared in a clot of Revere Beach traffic. Bunches of oiled-up yahoos in tight clothes cruised around trying to pick each other up. The place was a real scene and we were only at its tip. Far down the way I could see a faint sparkle of light, maybe fast-food places, maybe the carnival. The lady was punching the tiny buttons on the cell phone, she was pushing the tiny machine into her slick face.

Look for the address, Rose hushed to me. I cranked down the window and let the beachy air whip my face. My hair swirled up in little salty hurricanes, it blew around and grew thick with the ocean grit carried on the air. I licked my upper lip and tasted tangy sweat and beach. I watched the house numbers climb as the traffic crawled and the lady freaked out into the phone. First she was sorry, her voice all curled up and soft and weepy, and then she'd really lose it and start shrieking all sorts of angry words, mostly *Fuck you* and *It's not what you think.* You know whenever anyone says, *It's not what you think,* they're totally lying. Rose reached over and pinched my leg with her fingernails. She'd pushed up the raggy end of my sweats to do it, and my body jolted with the eensy pain of her fingernails, chewed short, the polish gnawed, hurting my skin, and also with the simple and superunexpected reality of her touch. I had a friend, this girl Rose, famously a *crazy bitch,* hitchhiker extraordinaire, we were so comfy and tight we touched each other, she touched me, like it was no big whoop. She shot me a look that went with the pinch, like she was going insane trying not to crack up at the lady, munching the shit out of the inside of her mouth with all the strain of keeping her laughs inside. The truck crawled past the houses and into the realm of cruddy hotels, just one or two, ramshackle bars in between them and then nothing but the bars for a while, old-fashioned looking like the hotels, places that maybe were sort of fancy a long time ago but now were dingy and sad. I imagined the people on the insides were the same way, people who used to be okay and had hopeful sparks in their hearts but then something happened and they got dingy and sad, they began to droop on the inside and after a while you could see it in their faces, the way the skin cragged and discolored, and in their bodies too, all skeletal or else weirdly chubbed, bulging with problems. There were racks of motorcycles lined up outside some of the bars, some of them had fake palm tree insignia, hula-skirt material fringing the doorway even though there weren't any palm trees or hula dancers in New England. The beer signs were constant neon twists in the windows. We crawled and crawled. People in the cars all around us were hollering out their windows, locating friends or harassing the various females shuffling around still in bathing suits. Bathing suits with heels, bathing suits with tiny cutoffs yanked over the ass, the white fringe of denim unraveling dreamily down their thighs. Everyone talking loud over the bassy rap that boomed out the car windows, the bassy rap occasionally dueling with something older and twangy or younger and screamy. I felt unreal in the midst of it all, somehow invisible in the salt air. The insane chaos of music and honking, of the hordes of squawking seagulls, their sticky feathers the same color as the poop they left all over the beach, all the mania somehow creating a calm for me. I turned to Rose. The woman was still yakking her teary yak into the phone and Rose was scavenging the landfill of fast-food styrofoam cups and burger rappers and empty cigarette packs on the truck floor. She pushed with her hands, creating trash tides that turned up pens and suspicious balls of crusty toilet paper, a cracked CD cover and a single rubbery flip-flop crusted with sand. *What, baby?* The lady asked her. *What you looking for? Shut up! Just shut the fuck up! What is it darling?* She kept the little phone clamped to her cheek the whole time, bouncing back between Rose and the man on the other end.

Tam-pon, Rose sort of mouthed. She made an awkward gesture that involved spreading her legs and moving her hands around her groin area in a plunging motion.

Tampons! Yeah! I'm sorry, okay! I'm sorry, what the fuck — baby, check the glove compartment. Over there. The only tampons you're going to find down there are dirty ones. Oh, yeah! Yeah, now I'm having an affair with a couple of twelve-year-old girls, you fucking sicko! Right! The glove compartment. She sucked her lips into her mouth, licking away the cry-snot residue. Rose clicked open the glove compartment and came out with a squat, linty tampon. One of the ones that don't come with an applicator to inject it up yourself. It was sheathed in a bit of plastic Rose tore through with her teeth.

Watch the numbers, she said, spitting the plastic onto the floor. *I bet it's in one of those big buildings up the street.*

I stuck my head back out the window. Like a dog, I thought. How they're always so happy, with their long faces poked out from a speeding car, their ears whapping around. I seem to remember having a dog, a long, long time ago. Sticking my own face out the window above it, the fur of its ears blowing into my face. I thought maybe my dad had a dog or something, but Ma said no, not ever, she hates dogs and would never live with one, so I don't know. Maybe it was a dog dream or maybe I'm always creating these phony memories for myself, trying to re-create the vanished dad. Give him a dog. He's living in Louisiana with a dog. They sit together by a river, the dog slaps at the foamy waters with his fat paws and my dad, I don't know, toots on a harmonica or something. Right. More likely he's drugged out in some shithole bar starting fights or hooking up with crazy women like the one currently driving us down Revere Beach Boulevard. The numbers were close now, we were in the heart of it. The traffic seized and people swarmed the sidewalk. Clamoring for fried ocean grub outside Kelley's. Workers in oil-stained hats were shoving plates of sand-colored nuggets through the pickup windows. It made me think of work, of Rose at work, and me unemployed. Maybe I could get a job at Kelley's. Maybe it would be cool to work on the beach, people coming to the window stinking like coconut. I locked eyes with a topless guy standing on the curb holding a paper boat of fried squiggles. He gave me a sharp nod as we passed, then slid his tongue out and licked his teeth at me.

Rose was hunched over in her seat, her ass levitating off the pleather, stuffing the tampon up inside her. She ruffled around on the floor and came up with a Burger Empire napkin to wipe her bloody finger on. Then she balled the paper up and dropped it back into the mess. It was as if it had never, ever occurred to her to give a fuck. She had no fuck inside of her to give. She was void of fuck. She scooted her ass around in her seat, getting comfortable with her new tampon.

The lady peeled the phone away from her face with a wet suck. She hit some buttons. She was answering our telephone. *Which one of you is Kim?* Rose opened her mouth. *Here take it, fuck it, you can't talk to someone who's crazy. You just can't.* She took her hands off the wheel and shook them out like they were cramped. Rose held the phone to her ear.

Hello? The sound from the other end was shrill static to me. It was like the call of a fry-happy electronic seagull. I dipped my ear down to eavesdrop.

This is not Kim! the little voice chattered. *We are going to find out who you are! You're a girl!* It was one of the mall bitches. Rose looked at me and shrugged, stamped her finger over the hang-up button and slid the phone back into my bag. When the chiming beep explosion erupted again we just let it sing.

No kidding, the lady nodded at the sound. *No point in talking to most people.* We were at the skyscrapers now. Not true skyscrapers like the ones I saw on a field trip to Boston, but they were big for a regular city. Three of them, clustered together, looming up and over the boulevard. The numbers on the first one matched what the caller had given us.

This Is Us, I said. I clicked open the door while the truck was still in motion, hopped out onto the pavement. The wild ocean air blasted my face, cool and soothing. Natural nighttime air, a relief from the tense static weather inside the lady's truck. Thanks For The Ride, I hollered in to her. It Was Really Nice Of You. Hitchhiking was clearly no big whoop, providing you stick with crazy females and avoid carfuls of crazy dudes.

Thanks for the tampon, Rose added, slamming the door on an escaping plastic bag. It whipped in the wind as the lady drove off toward the carnival. The carnival lights were candies against the sky, glowing orbs that pulsed and swirled like psychedelic fireflies. I know the rides are rickety and manned by weird prison dudes who never sleep and have swastika tattoos they gave themselves with sewing needles, and I know the games are all rigged and no matter how good your aim is you'll never knock down the wooden bottle, that the larger-than-life hot pink stuffed snake is actually unwinnable, but still I love the traveling carnival. Its lot is a year-round empty place, crapass weeds burping from cracks by the chain-link, maybe a scattered beer bottle or crushed can, but really the space isn't even interesting enough to steal a drink in, not with the wide expanse of beach splayed out across the street. The lot is a vacant nothing. Then suddenly one day you're cruising past and there are the rides, all folded up on themselves, collapsed lengths of curving track, rings of dull lights, the fried-dough stands shut tight on their wheels. Slowly the thing unfurls. The eggs of machinery crack and stretch their metal legs into rides and games, the empty glass bursts into frenzied bulbs of brightness proclaiming, THE COMET! THE HAMMER! THE WHIP! It gets all filled up with trashy people and skanky girls and kids with guns but I love it anyway.

We Gotta Hit The Carnival, I said to Rose. I gave her swishy dress a tug. She shrugged, squinting her eyes toward the lights. You could hear a faint *rat-a-tat,* the sound of cars rattling fast over slatted metal, the pale cries of the riders. Come On, Don't You Want To Go On Some Rides?

Not really, she shrugged. *I've gone there before. It's the same every summer.* Rose was more interested in our authentic creepy mystery, the guy on the other end of the cell phone. Why seek fake thrills, I guess. Why let some mechanical chair lurch you through a shabby fun house where old Halloween masks with flashlights stuck into the eyeholes dangle on poles and beep like cell phones as you jerk by. Why pay three dollars to glimpse a fake monster painted in black-light poster paints when you can visit a real monster in his oceanfront lair? Before us his apartment building rose into the night. Being so big and near to the beach my lazy mind had imagined it would be a real nice place. On television, celebrities live in buildings like this. I've seen helicopter views of the rooftop pools, ringed with palm trees. But it wasn't like that here. The door was set back from the street, we hiked the path and pushed into the hallway. The wall was filled with doorbells. I've only ever been inside an apartment once. The business I had in that one long-ago apartment was placing a dead bird into the mailbox of the lesbians who lived there. Me and this kid from school had found the bird on the street, its scrawny legs already stiff. We didn't kill it. And we'd known the lesbians were lesbians because we'd seen them and they looked the way lesbians looked together, plus there weren't ever dudes with them. I remember the two woman lesbians but I can't remember my kid-friend as anything more than a grubby smear of motion. I remember the bird, hard as feathered stone. We lifted it with sticks, we balanced it into the apartment, a crappy place with all busted mailboxes, their narrow doors unhinged or outright gone. The bird plopped inside and we left. I think it's good that I took such a long break from having friends because all I can remember from my old little-kid friendships is rotten activities like dumping dead things in gay people's mailboxes, or finding the one person with a garden in all of Mogsfield and smashing their produce on the ground, tomatoes and cucumbers pulpy on the pavement. The air smelled fresh and clean from them, a smeared salad of dead veggies. Oh, and convincing a girl that her dead mother was a hitchhiking ho. It's better that I abstained from friendships 'til now, when I'm mature enough to handle them. Those gay ladies could have been Rose's gay moms. Maybe Rose went down for the mail and her tiny kid hand, all stunted from smokes in the womb, came down against the rigor mortis wing of that bird.

Beside the doorbells were pieces of masking tape with names jotted onto them. The dude gave me a number, not a name, apartment twenty-four. We scanned the wide wall, squinting at all the scrawled and homemade doorbell tags. The name beside twenty-four was *Grafton.* It wasn't on tape, it was carved into the wall, with a little box carved around it. The doorbell itself was smashed, the tiny plastic dome half-cracked away, displaying metal beneath. Did You Ever Live In An Apartment Building? I asked Rose. She shook her head. *I always wanted to,* she said. *All the different people running around, elevators . . .* Rose hit the bell. Soon came the violent noise of the door buzzing us in. An angry, fuzzy honk. I had some more questions for Rose. They honked in my head like the door's rude open sesame. Like, what the fuck are we doing? Why are we going into a weird dude's house? Do you often go into weird dudes' houses? The hallway was lined with a jumble of telephone books, a scatter of junk mail nobody wanted. Grocery circulars with pictures of bloody pink steaks arranged on beds of lettuce, pictures of juice cartons and cookies. The elevator opened its mouth for us, and the metal doors sealed us in. The steel box lifted us into the air, leaving our stomachs back in the messy hallway. I suddenly wished the cell phone was mine, really mine, and that someone who knew me would call it. This would have to be Ma or Kristy, maybe Donnie. Someone out there who would ring me up just to say hey and check in on me. Yeah, I'm In An Elevator With My New Friend Rose, I'd say. We're Going To See Some Guy. Oh, Not For Any Reason, Just Going To See What's Up With Him, I Guess. Here's His Address And If I Never Return

Come Dig My Body Out From Under His Bed. The doors slid open and released us into the hallway. It felt like some sort of bad hotel where people lived. There was a door with a twenty-four on it. Rose's bony fist shot out and rapped the fake wood. Rose, I said. It seemed we should have a plan. An escape plan or maybe an explanation for not being Kim Porciatti. She shot a quick grin at me, wiggled her eye-pencil eyebrows, inky and arched. When she smiled her eyes themselves closed briefly, a sleepy face. I heard a scrabble behind the door and imagined someone was getting a fish-eye view at us through the peephole. The knob rattled and then there was an old man standing there, inspecting us. An old guy. He took in the sight of us and sighed. It was not a pleased sound. It was regretful and resigned. *Well.* He still had some hair and it looked like he'd even tried to fashion it, push the wiry silver wisps into a deliberate style. His face was awfully red, like he'd been steamed. He wore big glasses, and he looked at us through the plastic squares. *Hrrmph,* he noised. He shook his head. *Well.* His was not the voice on the phone. Not that thick and confident voice of sleaze, not this trembling little man.

Rose and I just stood there like some weird-ass Girl Scouts who forgot their cookies, forgot their little uniforms, forgot their purpose in life. We looked at each other and then at the old guy. *Let her in, Harry!* called another voice, *the* voice, the phone-man voice, from somewhere inside the apartment. Harry turned his back and walked his elderly-person-walk away from us. We followed him inside the apartment.

Shut the door, girls, Harry motioned. His eyes were

blue but maybe he had cataracts. Maybe he was old like that, cataract-old. He settled himself down onto a puffy leather couch and tuned into the television, ignoring us completely. The wood-paneled room we stood in was filled with cigarette smoke; it spun around us like a terrible cotton. The old man was its source; a castle of spent butts clambered up from a wide glass ashtray. He lit a new one and blew smoke at the screen.

Harry, you are polluting the house with your cigarettes. We got a porch, why don't you smoke out on the porch. The man was in the room with us. He swung out of some back area, took a quick look and saw we were no Kim Porciatti. We weren't even Katies or Yolandas. He looked us up and down with a sober expression on his face. His face was like Harry's face, only younger. Younger but not young. Old, just not about-to-kick-the-bucket old. He was old like Donnie was old. His hair was gray but also yellow-blond, and he had the old man's eyes, that cataract-blue color. His stripy hair was thick and in a long ponytail. His hair seemed angry at being captured by the elastic, it hurled itself around in unruly waves. The most alarming thing about the man was that he seemed to be pregnant. He had a belly like a hard, round rock. It protruded from his torso, he had followed it into the smokey television room. It wasn't a fleshy ball, it didn't jiggle or hang. It was like a pumpkin under his Harley T-shirt. Even a tumor would be bumpy or wiggle, I thought. *I don't know who you are,* he said simply. The old man Harry made another snorting sound and gave the dude a look of pure disgust.

We're Friends Of Kim, I said. It sounded like a secret

club or something, like I was talking code-speak. Friends of Kim. A charitable organization perhaps. The phrase felt foreign in my mouth. It came out of my stiff and awkward body like candy from the yap of a Pez dispenser. A mental expert could have investigated my posture and pointed out all the different angles of elbow and shoulder that proved what a giant liar I was. A dog could have lapped up the panic vibrations of fear coming off my skin like sweaty laser beams. But the dude with the misshapen torso was unaffected. *Come on,* he nodded his ponytailed head back toward where he came. Rose trotted off behind him but I was in no hurry to leave the room near the exit. I was in no hurry to leave Old Harry. Old Harry flipped through the television, exhaling blue clouds at the screen. He was like some wrinkled cloud-breathing creature, a myth. He was the pregnant monster's father. The room held a lot of furniture, all crammed together. Stools and armchairs piled with newspapers. End tables sporting dust thick as velvet and random souvenirs and glass-framed pictures from a long time ago.

So, Your Name's Harry? I stalled. I could hear murmured voices from the back room. The high-pitched tones of Rose. If she screamed I would run for her. If I heard glass breaking or the sounds of things being knocked around, the noise of kidnapping or rape or strangulation. Harry glanced at me briefly, then back to the TV. *Yup,* he said. His voice was soft and dry.

I Think I Saw You Once, At The Walgreens In Mogsfield? I wanted him to be that guy so bad. That guy who took so long to pay, that guy who seized me up when I had my period and was vulnerable to the sadness of everything. If I could locate Harry in my regular life then he could become a rope back to that place if I needed it.

I don't think so, he mumbled. *I go to the Walgreens here in Revere.*

Really? I pressed. Maybe You Bought A Box Of Ice Cream?

He gave a little chuckle and waggled his head. His sparse hairs in their deliberate placements didn't move. Something real strong was holding his hairdo together. Strong and greasy. It shone in the television's electric light. Football, men in tight uniforms tumbling over each other, rolling together on an endless grassy green landscape. The screen was shot through with gray pixels, little strands of bad reception. He breathed a new ghost into the room.

You Like Living So Close To The Beach? I asked. You Go Over To The Carnival Ever? He brought the butt of his cigarette to his thin lips and took a papery drag. I looked around the room. To my right was a kitchen table with a blue plastic tarp for a tablecloth, and beyond that a little stove. Above the dark iron burners hung a string of topless-lady photos, their boobs like ice-cream sundaes melting on their chests. I peered closer. They weren't photos, they were air fresheners. Still in their packaging, with the little dangly string for hanging off rearview mirrors. It was a real collection. Some girls had bouncy brown hair but most were blond. Their plastic packaging shone under the shadowy yellow light in the kitchen. They were held to the wall with pushpins. So, You Like Air Fresheners? I asked Harry. On the TV screen a bleacherful of people flung themselves from their seats and screamed. They shot their hands into the air, they flung popcorn and waved fat foam fingers. I thought about how nice it must be to feel so passionate about something.

From the side room Rose popped her little dark head into the smoke. *What the fuck, Trisha?* She marched into the TV room and clamped her hand around my arm, tugging me away from Old Harry and the getaway front door. I'll Just Be Back Here, I called to him. The burning cherry of his smoke gave a crackle as he sucked at it. Don't You Want To Hit The Carnival? I whispered to Rose. This Place Is Wrong. Her arm slung around my waist, she pulled me into the little room. I could feel the wiry strongness in her arm, in her whole body. Rose felt more alive than other people, like there was extra machinery cranking away inside her. She was born with an additional gear, twin hearts fused under her ribs making her extra brave.

You like Harry? the monster garbled at me. *He's my father.*

He Seems Like A Real Nice Guy, I said.

He keeps me alive. I'd be living on a bench across the street, wasn't for him. The monster regarded me with his deep blue eyes. His face was craggy like the inside of a cracked rock. Sedimentary layers of lines, shades of pink and tan, orange and red, settled down his cheeks. Stubble was scattered on his chin like sand. He was sitting on a twin bed, a kid's bed, his hands twined across his melon-belly. The eagle on his T-shirt glared out from the taut mound. Beside the twin bed shoved into a shadowy corner of the room there was another bed, a bigger one, clearly busted, the lumpy mattress careening downward at a severe slope. The headboard was dark plastic with fake-wood grain. Across from it a dresser held a lamp on its surface, plus a framed eight-by-ten of a young girl in a dance costume. One of those spangled jobs, canary-yellow with sparkly bits of silver all over it, fringe like Christmas tree tinsel dangling from her ass, a poof of yellow fuzz frizzing out from her redheaded head. She was one of those redheaded kids who always look like they're drooling. She held her arms out stiffly, demonstrating a dazzle of silver at her wrists. Her expression was stiff too, like someone had grabbed a big metal tool and wrenched a smile across her face. She looked cramped with happiness.

The monster cleared his throat, but when he spoke it still sounded phlegmy. *You girls do a poor imitation of Kimmy. No offense.* From the shadows behind his bed he wrestled with something on his wall. He stretched his arm and tugged, and the lamplight from the dresser washed over his skin and made the mottled colors glow there, bruises and redness in the crook of his elbow. When his hand returned from the shadows all I saw were the tits cupped in his palm. Air Freshener? I asked. But it was a Polaroid. Of Kim Porciatti. Naked Kim Porciatti. If I had ever wanted to know what lay beneath the tight jeans and the buttery cardigans, if I had ever cared, it would have been a happy moment. *Here's my Kimmy,* he said. *Maybe you never seen her this way. Maybe not, though. You girls get naked for each other all the time, don'tcha? At, like, your sleepover parties and whatnot.*

We don't get invited to Kim Porciatti's sleepover parties, Rose said. Her voice sounded dull.

I'm just saying, I know that girls are more comfortable with their bodies together than men are. Men don't like each other naked. Here, take a look. He offered us the picture, dark in its white frame. Kim Porciatti, her little tummy, her two tits staring straight at me, the nipples giving me dirty looks. Got a staring problem, the nipples asked. Take a picture, it lasts longer, they invited. Kim's face was turned to the side, her mouth slightly open, maybe she was saying something. Maybe she was saying, *I don't know,* or *Promise you won't,* or *Just one.* Her pubic hair was a spidery smudge, her arms were clasped behind her waist, pulling her shoulders back. I could see her rib cage laddering up her edges, disappearing beneath the emergence of tits. Kim Porciatti's body. It was very tan in color, like the goopy insides of candy bars. There was her famous hair in its sleek ponytail. But mostly it was her face. At first glance it looked sort of blank, the way people look in pictures that aren't posed — caught in a thought, mouth open to a passing idea. Then I felt the rising need to giggle, a terrible laugh storm growing inside me, and the Kim in the picture seemed happy, her mouth rising slightly at the corners. So I experimented. I tried to see if I could make Kim look angry. I could. I could make her look horrified. I could make her look like someone had stolen her clothes. Like a monster dude was just out of reach, her Ohmigod! threads crunched in his grubby paw, bunched in the crook of his rotting elbow, held above his head, out of reach. Her clothes stomped under his shit kickers as he aimed the hunk of camera at her. He hit the button and the Polaroid spit out a souvenir of her skankiest moment. It promised she'd live forever above a monster's pillow. In the photo before me Kim Porciatti was now on the verge of tears. I waved it away before it started bleeding from the eyes like a cursed church statue.

Wow, how'd you get her to do that? asked Rose. Her eyes were stuck to the plasticky square of Kim.

You're lucky you even saw this, the man smiled proudly. He shook it in the air like it was still wet, like there was still more naked Kim to emerge from the slick film. *You're lucky I showed that to you. I don't show it to most people.* He turned and pinned it back inside the shadows. Rose rolled her eyes.

Yeah, I feel really lucky. The guy started at the sarcasm in her voice and I felt a quick chill roll my arms. He wasn't totally dumb, he could read tone, could tell when he was being made fun of.

She's Just Kidding, I said fast. I was embarrassed at how ass-kissy my voice sounded. I shook my hair into my face and tried to look unaffected. Totally blasé about his weird bedroom, about the painfully cheery dancer girl on his dresser, about his deformed stomach and discolored arms and the liberties he'd taken with Kim Porciatti.

Serious, Rose said. She was smiling now. *How'd you get her to let you take her picture like that?*

His bear paw gave the underside of his ponytail a vicious scratching. *Why don't you tell me where she is, or how you got her phone or something? Why don't you let me ask you some questions.*

Rose shrugged. *She stole it.* She twitched her head in my direction. So casual, as if stealing was not a secret thing. As if it were not private information.

I Didn't Steal It, I protested. I swung my face toward Rose and cranked my mouth open so she could know what a jerk she was. I gave her jerk-eyes as well. I Worked With Her And She Left It Behind So I Took It.

I've been callin' and callin'. He leaned forward on his little bed, his hands on his legs. He had jeans on. Black jeans and boots and a Harley shirt. Work boots. Shit kickers. *I would think she'd have called me. She usually calls me.*

She tried to kill herself. The dude squinted his eyes at Rose, like if he focused he could see what she was telling him. His mouth was open. Rose gave a short little laugh. It was a mean sound, and it comforted me. I didn't know where I fit in the room. I wanted nothing more than to go out into the smoke glob and watch TV with Old Harry. Have him explain football to me, where the ball was supposed to go, why one man just hopped onto another man, why anybody gave a shit about it. Let his secondhand smoke spread like black lace across my lungs, who cares. A laugh chimed out of Rose, a burst and then a tinkle, like a car window getting smashed. *I can't believe you didn't know that. Everyone knows that. I don't even know Kim and I know that.*

I can't know everything, he said simply. *I can't know things nobody tells me.* Then he was quiet, he nodded his head like he was agreeing with himself. *She shoulda called me. She was only crashing. I told her to just call me whenever and I'd meet her anywhere. I don't deliver but I'd deliver to her. You can feel real low when you're crashing. You stop making any kind of sense to yourself.*

What was she crashing from? Crystal?

He snapped his head back and filled his face with a somber expression. *What about you? I don't even know you. You don't even know Kim. What, did someone hire you? I'm not saying nothin' to you.*

Please! I laughed. You Already Showed Us A Naked Picture.

Yeah, really, Rose chimed. *It's a little late to get worried. Plus we're just a couple of regular girls anyway. Are you a drug dealer?* Rose leaned against the dresser, then with a backward swoop lifted herself onto it. She kicked her legs against the drawers like a baby in a high chair. The framed picture of the canary dancing girl was lifted onto her lap. She gazed down at it, tapping the dusty glass with her chipped black fingertips. *Who's this, your daughter?*

My cousin.

You got a daughter? You got any kids or anyone?

Nah.

Just Harry out in the room?

His name ain't Harry. It's Chester. We just like to call each other Harry.

That's cute. Harry and Harry. So, this is your cousin. That — she pointed into the darkness behind the dude's head — *is Kim Porciatti. I am Rose and this is Trisha. What's your name?*

The monster's name was Paul. Paulie. And he didn't have anyone except Old Harry Chester, who slept on the wildly crooked other bed while Paulie snuggled on his narrow child's bed, beneath a creepy naked Polaroid of Kim Porciatti. Paulie confirmed that he had had a mother, but that's as far as he went with that. I hoped the lady had high-tailed it to a better place. I hoped she was hunkered at the tip of a better beach, one with a permanent carnival lacking gun-toting teenagers. I hoped she was playing bingo somewhere excellent, with a faceful of too-bright makeup and no regrets. He'd had a wife once for three months, and it didn't work out so he'd moved back in with Old Harry Chester and that was the end of their story. OHC collected old-person checks and Paulie sold something called crystal, which was not the fancy place settings rich people eat from on TV shows. It was also not the magical-looking rocks Ma once balanced on her head while she lay on the couch. It was a phase. They were beautiful, the crystals, like thick jagged glass with pink smoke trapped inside, but Ma looked like a fool laying around with them rolling on her face. She'd seen some show about crystal healing and tried it for a while and then was done with them. Kristy has them now. I've seen them in her room, on her dresser, and I bet she lays around with them on her head too. She says she only likes how pretty they are but she can't fool me.

Monster Paulie was crouched on his knees, his head stuck under his bed. This minor physical maneuver required maximum huffage and puffage. That giant ball in his belly really got in the way of basic motion. He leaned over it to dip beneath the bed, coming out with the cardboard box his shit kickers came in.

Shut the door, he said to Rose, and she did. She popped off the dresser and clicked shut the door. *How'd you meet Kim Porciatti?* she wanted to know.

You want to know everything, he said, shuffling through his box. *How did you meet me, huh? How did you two meet each other? What's your story, you two?*

Rose looked at me and shrugged and laughed. The deep randomness of all of this was staggering. I guess that's what happens in life — you do one sort of innocent thing, like get a job or rather, lie to get a job and then, wham, a giant chain of causes and effects grows and grows until you're trapped in this thing, your life. *We just met today,* Rose said. *We don't really know each other.* This is the circumstance, I thought. The one I was supposed to avoid becoming victimized by. Rose was the circumstance.

Well, you two can't really trust each other, Paulie said. *And I can't trust either of you. And I don't like to sell crystal to people I can't trust. That's no good. How am I gonna trust you? What are you gonna give me? I need to have something over you 'cause you're gonna have something over me. Life's got to be equal. Business life.*

I got money, Rose said. *I'm not asking you for free drugs.*

Everybody's got money, sweetheart.

I Don't, I offered. Paulie ignored me.

I'm just dealing with you here, right? This is between you and me?

Rose looked annoyed. She glanced at me. *Yeah, I got the money.*

I need collateral. Kimmy gave me the photo. He hefted a dark block of camera from the box.

No Way, I said. I bolted for the door.

Trisha, Rose snapped, halting me.

Don't worry, there. I just need a picture from one of you. You gonna give me a picture? The room was quiet. I could hear the vague cheers from the television, the hearty, confident jabber of a sportscaster explaining the explainable. Why the football hero had been able to do what he had done. Why the team was so mighty. What this meant for the future. His voice was spilling with joy.

Can I just flash you? Rose was negotiating. *You can take a picture from here* — she held a hand to her throat — *and here* — and one at her belly.

It's not like I need any more clients, Paulie said. *You can get out of here. Your friend wants to leave.* He looked at me. *Right?*

Yeah, Totally, I nodded. Rose sighed.

Okay quick, come on, she said. She whipped her dress-thing over her head, creating a new wind inside the stuffy room. A clean and showery smell, powdery. It flapped like a bat above her head, whooshing to the floor. No bra. I averted my eyes from Rose's boobs, just sitting there blatant on her body. I thought of Kim Porciatti's accusing nipples. I did not want to receive the glare of Rose's. I kept my eyes turned down at Paulie's crappy carpet. The bristles of fabric were thick and frayed, clumped with stains. It didn't quite cover the room, thin strips of wood were visible alongside the walls, studded with giant staples. The feel of the room was wild and swirling.

I'm not taking my sneakers off, Rose's voice was tough, like she was really putting her foot down. Her duct-taped moldy sneakers stayed on. There was a flash and a whine and I could hear the camera cough up a picture. I glanced at Rose. She was tugging up her drawers, her nightgown veiling the dresser behind her. I looked back to the carpet, to my feet in their flops, my toes still an absurd color. They looked like someone else's feet, like when I was little and would cut up Ma's *Women's Day* and *Family Circle* magazines, slicing the models into heads, torsos, and legs, then mixing and matching them. I kept them in little envelopes, smiling paper heads in one, bodies in one, legs in another. If I was a boy doing that you know they'd have flung me at a psychiatrist or something, to make sure I didn't wind up a mass murderer, but since I was female they just thought, what the hell, and let me keep chopping up all these ladies.

Why don't your friend leave? Paulie said to Rose. He had his full-throttle monster voice back on.

I'm Right Here. My head snapped up and I shot a glare at his haggard head. Monster Paulie had been through some real monster living. It was carved into his cheeks and forehead. His nose was red putty, lumpy and crooked and glowing. It was inflated with hard times. I Can Hear You, I said to him. Do You Think I'm A Moron?

Why don't you buy us alcohol? Rose changed the subject. Her nightgown outfit had drifted back over her body, and I could look at her again. I looked at her and I breathed. It was like Rose's nakedness had sucked all the air from the room. Now that she was all covered up, oxygen had returned. Paulie's bedroom had settled back into its base level of creepiness and bad vibes. It was a range I could handle.

Why would I buy you alcohol? Paulie pouted.

C'mon, she said. Monster was flapping the Polaroid in the air. He'd peek at it, chuckle, and start blowing on it. *C'mon, where is there a liquor store? Just a six-pack. We can't do the crystal without it.*

Yeah, C'mon, I chimed in. I didn't know shit about crystal but I wanted a drink so badly. I suddenly was able to pinpoint the exact feeling I'd had inside my body since the second we walked into this grim apartment, the feeling of needing a beer. What About Beer, Do You Got Any Beer Around Right Now? I knew I sounded like a beggar.

You owe me twenty-five dollars, Paulie said, and passed a little plastic sack of something to Rose. I guess since I wasn't going to leave him alone with my friend, he was just going to ignore me. That was fine. That was a good thing about looking more like a boy than a girl, dudes like Paulie tended not to want much from me. It's always good to be invisible around monsters. Rose put the baggie in my backpack, zipped it back up, and tucked it beside her. She had her roll of swiped money in her hand, she pulled out some crumpled dollars, and passed them to Paulie. *There's extra, for drinks,* she said. *Just a six-pack. We really need it.*

Out in the TV room Old Harry Chester watched endless replays of helmeted men hurtling through the air. They were slowed down, their dives made graceful, the oblong ball willfully sailing into an outstretched palm. The television's glow caught the old man's smoke, strobed it so the room looked like some weird-ass dingy sports disco, all dry ice and flashing lights. It was disorienting.

All right, Harry, Paulie said. He clapped his swollen

hands together. *You want something while I'm out? A little Seven and Seven? I'll buy you your cigarettes if you do me a favor and smoke out on the balcony. Huh? Sit on the balcony, look at the ocean. Sound nice, Harry?*

Can't see the TV out there, Harry Chester grumped.

That's true, Paulie said. He started for the door, and Rose yelped, *Our bag,* and dashed back into the bedroom. The TV moved to a commercial. A car shaped like a giant silver turd was zooming through a mountain, high above an ocean. Then it was in the desert, weaving around those big green cactuses with all the arms. Then it was in a blizzard. *That's like us, huh Harry? Last winter, huh?* Harry Chester grunted. I got a definite feeling that Harry Chester would love it if Monster Harry Paulie just dropped dead. Rose bopped back into the TV room, my backpack slung over her shoulder. It started out innocent, my backpack, but since then it had acquired a stolen phone, a wad of stolen cash, now some mystical-sounding drug. Soon alcohol would be added. There would be little room for anything else illegal.

It Was Nice to Meet You, Chester, I said. I hoped I wasn't disrespecting him by using his first name like that, all familiar.

You too, kid, he said. He looked at Paulie. *What're you doing, Harry? What're you thinking? You don't think, do you? You're a friggin' box of rocks.* He shook a cigarette out of the hole in his pack. His match cracked and filled the room with sulfur. *You girls.* He set his cloudy blue eyes on me and Rose, bouncing between us. *You girls. You better watch it.* It sounded sort of threatening, but I think it was

Old Harry Chester's way of looking out for us. Warning us against his son.

Yak, yak yak, Harry. Paulie had his hands going like a couple of little mouths, puppet hands. *Yak, yak, yak. I'll see ya later. Stay out of my room.* Paulie held the door open and we were in the hall. He was laughing. *I tell him, "Stay out of my room," but he can't, right? 'Cause it's his room too.* I thought about that old man sleeping forever in that room with Monster. The dancing girl shining in the lamplight like a little sun. It was too much. I wanted to set him free. I was glad we were out of there. We still had Monster Paulie with us, but at least we were off his turf. We were in the humming elevator and then the downstairs hallway and then we were free.

Paulie walked us down the boulevard. He seemed to know bunches of people meandering the beach. Dudes in baggy shorts, their T-shirts hanging from their back pockets like tails. Craggy beachwomen who looked like they'd fallen asleep in the sun for about forty years. Girls our age who looked embarrassed when he said hello to them. I wondered if their naked boobs were pinned to his wall too. I would not have thought it so easy for someone like Paulie to get a girl to take all her clothes off for a photo, but what did I know. Apparently it was a cinch. We halted at a market called Mickey's. A stack of *Boston Globes* sat damp and windblown in the doorway and a clock just inside said it was just past nine. I could smell its milky corner-store smell. We stood in the blue and red glow of the beer sign behind its window. *What's it called again?* Paulie asked.

Yikes, Rose repeated. *Yikes. It comes in bottles. Big bottles.*

She held her hands apart, suggesting the size of a really big bottle. *It's not beer. It's vodka plus energy drink. Got it, man?*

Paulie was nodding. *I got it,* he said. *I got you, right? Don't I got you?* Ever since he took Rose's picture, everything that fell out of his mouth was a lousy innuendo. I think he was trying to be sexy. He was a lot less intimidating outside in the real world. Now he was just another dude. They were all around us, dangling their arms out their car windows, sleazing by us on the sidewalk.

Yeah, you got me, Rose said. *What are you going to buy for me?*

Oops, said Paulie. His eyeballs were a kaleidoscope of colors eyeballs shouldn't be. Red, yellow, maybe a bit of purple. If Paulie wasn't an actual monster, then he was dying. His planetary stomach, the raw stretch of his inner arms. I took him in. There on the street, like a regular beach guy. Paulie was totally dying. He was going to wake up dead some day in that little bed. Old Harry Chester would surely outlive him, Old Harry Chester in all his clouds of cigarette. He would find his son beneath his gallery of underage nudie girls. Maybe he'd tear them up and flush them down the toilet. But Polaroids are hard to destroy.

Oops, Paulie grinned, shooting a fat finger at Rose, shotgun-style.

Yikes, Rose corrected. *Yikes!*

Yikes, Paulie headed into the store. *I might like to try something like that. Sounds interesting.*

Get your own, Rose said. *I mean it.* We ducked around the corner while Paulie did our shopping. *This is crazy,* she laughed, shaking her head. *What a crazy night. Do you always have such crazy nights?* I just looked at her. How odd that she didn't understand that the crazy night was all her fault.

I Don't, I told her. I Never Have Crazy Nights. I Don't Hang Out With Anyone.

What do you do?

Nothing. Steal Beer From My Mom's Boyfriend. Watch Television. Sit On The Front Steps And Look At People. Rose opened the backpack and pulled out her cigarettes. She lit one up and took a deep gulp of smoke. Weren't You Scared? I asked her. What If He Puts Your Picture On The Internet?

Rose laughed. *Him? He's practically brain-damaged. His brain is mush. He can't talk full sentences. I doubt he even knows anyone with a computer.*

All Sorts Of Stupid People Use Computers, I told her. Or, He Could Send It To A Magazine —

Stop tripping, she said. *Look.* She dunked her hand into the pack and plucked the Polaroid from inside. There was Rose, smiling hugely. A smile so big it ate her face. She was naked, malnourished, her arms stiffly outstretched. Oh My God, I said.

Look, look, she was gushing breath and laughter. She pulled the corner of a heavy picture frame from the pack. It was the cousin in the canary yellow leotard. Her hands were stretched the same way Rose's were in her Polaroid. Same deranged, impossible smile. She held the two pictures together.

I Can't, I covered my eyes. It's Too Much. I Can't Believe You Did That.

Rose zipped the bag shut just as Paulie rounded the

corner, a heavy paper bag resting on his giant belly-mound. At least it had a utilitarian purpose.

Ladies, Paulie crouched with a gasp and a grunt, depositing the bag with a clank beside us. *Are you smoking?* he asked Rose. His haggard face got all bunched up. *Don't smoke, whattaya crazy? You kids today know better than that. What, you gonna sue the government when you get cancer? 'Cause you will get cancer. What are you gonna do then, huh? When it's all your own fault? Who you gonna cry to?*

Wow, Rose said. She stood up, shook the sandy beach sidewalk from the back of her dress. *Don't you think it's weird that you're, like, a drug dealer and you're getting bent out of shape over smoking? Don't you think that's hypocritical? That you use teenage girls to make pornography and lecture them about smoking? You don't think that's sort of fucked-up?* I just wanted Paulie Monster to go.

It's your lungs, Paulie said. *You ever see a cancer death? It's not pretty.*

Death generally isn't, Rose smirked. *And speaking of, we'll give your regards to Kim Porciatti.*

You just keep your regards to yourself if you don't want that picture of you hung up on telephone poles all over Massachusetts, he said. He shook his head. *Listen, you crash, you start feeling bad, don't be stupid. Give me a call. I'll hook you up, anytime. But you gotta come here. I don't deliver.* He turned on his shit kickers and shit-kicked himself around the corner and away from us. His splitting was a relief we could feel. In our bodies, in the air all around us. The world felt wide open and sweet again. I relaxed and breathed more air, could detect all the parts of the world in every huff, part fried scallops and part cigarette, part yummy beachy smell and part piña colada tanning lotion, part Rose's baby powder and part my own stinky scalp blowing in the breeze. It all smelled great blended up together in the air. Rose stuffed the bag of Yikes into the backpack and handed it to me. *Your turn,* she said, even though it was all her shit in it, all of it hers and all of it somehow against the law. I thought of my room and the stacks of stolen car batteries piled up against my wall. Down the road a tremendous twinkle rose and fell, rose and fell against the starless night sky. One of those rides that spin you every which way inside a rusty old cage. It flips you up into the air and twirls you upside down and in dizzy circles, all your change tumbling from your pockets and you hope the other people in the other tumbling cages don't barf on you. You Really Don't Want To Go? I jabbed my finger at the glow. You Really Don't Like Rides?

We have crystal, Rose said. She sounded personally offended, and I guess she did go through a lot to get it, but she never even asked me if I wanted any. I didn't even know what the fuck crystal was. *We can go on rides later. We should go do some crystal and drink. It's still early.* She tugged out the evil cell phone and glanced at the time. *We've got all night to ride rides. We got to get out of here in case Paulie comes looking for his pictures.*

And so we were back on the side of the road, trapped in that cheesy pose, thumbs out, looking for a ride to Route 1. Rose wanted to break into the miniature golf course to use the crystal. The thought of it made her so happy she spun around on the sidewalk, her soft nightgown fluttering around her. She hopped in her sneakers. *Inside, at night?* she gasped. *You will love it!* I liked that Rose was so quick with an agenda. I wasn't used to making plans, and really, if it had been up to me we probably would have aimlessly wandered back to my house and sat out on Donnie's lounge chair, bored out of our minds. We passed up the ride offers of about twenty different cars of men and accepted a ride in a beat-up little Toyota with a lady who barely looked old enough to drive but insisted she was thirty.

Nuh-uh! Rose gasped. *You look like a kid! What's your beauty secret? Do you have any?*

Clean living, the driver said. *I make pottery. I don't stress out. When you stress out it creates all these hormones and chemicals in your body and they really wear you down.* She gave us stern looks. *You should probably not hitchhike if you want to stay young. I'm sure it produces stress hormones.*

We'll consider it, Rose said. She told the woman to drop us off at the gigantic Chinese restaurant on the strip, a ways down from the golf course. The restaurant was superhuge and red and I'd never eaten at it because it was some big-ass expensive deal, not like your regular pupu platter take-out job. It sounded magical. I wanted to go inside but figured they'd take one look at my shabby shorts and Rose in her nightgown and boot us right out. Instead we crossed the zillion lanes of zooming traffic heading every which way up the freeway. In the distance was the golf course, we aimed ourselves toward it, jogging, beating oncoming traffic, sprinting down the street, so close to the cars it made my heart jumpy, scrambling up a slight landscaped hill 'til we reached the length of chain-link. Behind it was the dark and gnomey garden of T-Rex Miniature Golf. I'd seen the T-Rex for as long as I could remember, always driving by it on Route 1. When we were little me and Kristy would sit excitedly in the car as it whizzed toward the giant safety-orange dinosaur that was the spot's mascot. The dinosaur's strong orange neck craned out over the chain-link fence and its jaw was a cranked-up menace, flashing fake metal teeth, jabby and dripping in white paint. Beyond the T-Rex were clusters of smaller, less threatening dinosaurs, and little troll families and a windmill, a frog pond, all of it scattered across fake plasticky grass. I got to go to the T-Rex once when I was wicked little, so little I can't remember much, just climbing on the dinosaurs while Ma and my dad smoked cigarettes and smacked the little colored balls around with the clubs. The T-Rex had a little ice-cream hut with machines that crapped out swirls of soft serve, and a batting cage where you got locked in a swear-to-god cage with a sinister machine that spit baseballs at you. The batting cage always scared me. I have a vague memory of my dad inside it, the balls coming too fast for him, and the swings of his bat struck me as violent or something. He was cursing the balls, hollering *Fucks* and *Shits* and embarrassing Ma, who was hissing *Ssssh*s at him, which he could not hear over the machinery whir of the demonic baseball contraption. That's probably why I don't like the batting cage so much.

Me and Rose climbed the fence by the dinosaur 'cause it seemed like the easiest way to do it and we were weighed down by the six-pack of drinks Paulie bought us, that brand-new mixture of vodka and energy drink all swirled up together in big bottles. The bottles clanked around in my backpack with everything else. Naked pictures, drugs. I was kind of nervous about it and thought, oh yeah great, so now if we get busted I'm the one holding everything and I get to go to jail or whatever and Rose could just skip away, back to the oily recesses of Clown in the Box, never to be seen again. But that was just one mind. My other mind was psyched to be entrusted with the wad of bills, damp with the sweat of spending an eight-hour shift at the Clown stuffed down Rose's shiny underpants. Psyched to be entrusted with the care of the top-secret one-of-a-kind Polaroid of Rose, Rose's crumpled pack of cigarettes, a book of matches jammed into the cellophane. Just happy to help out Rose, Rose in her nightgown-dress, filmy with weird, bunched-up flowers stuck around the neckline. Rose with her duct-taped sneakers, looking and smelling so different outside her Clown uniform, after her post-Clown shower. When she hauled herself up the fence in front of me I could catch a stink-cloud of baby powder and the smell of it made me feel dreamy. Unclean thoughts like Monster Paulie and Old Harry Chester could not survive a blast of baby powder off a girl like Rose, I thought. I should dust myself down with some baby powder after a shower too. Why not? I resolved to have it be my new thing. Rose shimmied down the neck of the dinosaur — looking, for one weird and excellent moment, like the air freshener Donnie had dangling from the Maverick's rearview, not a drooling tittie-girl but a chick who looks like a witchy Viking straddling a giant lizard — and stood on the Astroturf with her skinny arms extended to catch my pack. I looked down at her suspiciously.

Are You Sure? I asked. What if it squashed her. She looked like a twiggy bug there on the ground. What if all the Yikes bottles busted open and soaked the stolen money and turned the drugs into a paste and ruined her cigarettes?

C'mon, man, she shook her arms impatiently. *I'm strong, come on.* I was at the top of the fence, my flip-flops jammed into the chain links. I leaned forward and carefully shimmied the heavy clanking pack from my back. Behind me cars honked on Route 1. I could feel them honking at me. *C'mon, before someone calls the cops,* Rose barked from the dark below. Her pale arms gleamed with a glow-in-the-dark sheen. I lowered the pack by its straps until I was bent way over the fence. Rose's grasping fingers almost reached it. I let it fall and she caught it in her arms, fell backward with it onto the fake grass.

I loved climbing onto the dinosaur. I can't tell you how many times I'd daydreamed about it, cruising by on the highway below. It seemed, for all its ferocity, aching to be climbed. As I hugged its neck and heaved my legs around its strong but wobbly body, it felt oddly living to me, helpful. I Love This Dinosaur, I hollered down at Rose. I sort of slid backward down its body, then leaped beside her. She was rifling through the pack, pulled out a bottle.

We'll share, she said. She wrapped her little fingers in the fluffy nightgown-dress and yanked the cap free. The bottlecap's tiny teeth tore at the fabric but she didn't seem to give a shit. *C'mon,* she said, and started marching deeper into the golf course, leaving the pack on the ground for me to grab.

This was a dream, being in the shut-down, nighttime golf course. The freeway beyond buzzed and flashed with endless cars, but the course was its own pocket of quiet. The planks of the windmill were still, the frog fountain dry. Spotlights lit the walkways and shone into the creepily staring faces of the gnomes clustered throughout the place. I followed Rose to a backlit hippo painted the same neon orange as the T-Rex. Its goofy mouth was wide and filled with round teeth. Have You Ever Played Here? I asked Rose. She took the pack from me and nodded, fumbled around on the inside, digging for cigarettes and crystal. She held the tiny bag above the spotlight, squinting into the brightness.

Shit, she said. *Do you have, like, an ATM card or something?*

I shook my head. I Don't Have A Bank Account, I shrugged. I Don't Have Any Money.

Do you have a driver's license, something to crush this up with? I peered around the hippo at the baglet. The stuff inside was chunky, like pebbly dust from split geodes. We went to the Museum of Science on a field trip once and I really liked the geodes, that there could be fancy-ass crumbs of jewels hidden inside just your regular no-big-whoop rock.

Does It Come From Rocks? I asked. This Stuff?

Rose shook her head. *No, it comes from, like battery acid I think. Like from car batteries? That and nasal spray.*

Nasal Spray? I didn't understand how anything could come from Nasal Spray, let alone these beautiful little chips. The battery acid thing sort of scared me. Maybe Rose was fucking with me. She wasn't a fucker, though. I was glad about that. Rose was pretty straight-up, serious. You could tell that she wasn't one of those girls who do things like slap you and say, "Fuck Off" and then when you get upset say, "Ohmygod, I'm just joking with you!" so then you have to laugh and pretend that you think it's fun to be slapped and told to fuck off. I had a feeling that if Rose ever told me to fuck off it would be because she really wanted me to fuck off, and there's something real safe and relaxing about being around a person like that.

Because Rose told me to find a golf ball I walked around the course, peeking behind the gnomes and the various statuary plonked along the paths. I couldn't find any balls. I wandered around the frog fountain and bravely poked my hand into the hole at the base. My hand bonked something and I drew it out, quick. It's fucking scary to shove your hand into a dark hole. When nothing ran out from the little cave I slid my hand back in and wrapped it around the pocked golf ball. I brought it back to Rose like I'd just, I don't know, done something really great and won a prize. I had a huge smile on my face. *Yeah!* Rose hooted. She put the drugs on the hippo's back and rolled the golf ball over it again and again. With the floodlight beaming up at her, shadowing her face and lighting the curve of her head, her bird-skull with its cap of flat, black hair, Rose looked supernatural. She looked like she was casting a spell, her face bent over her repetitive movements, the skidding sound of the ball rocking.

Suddenly I wanted a cigarette. I don't know how to

explain it. Watching Rose do her weird little drug thing like I wasn't even there, focused and breathing through her thin mouth, it filled me up with a sensation I could only call compulsive. It was like I wanted something enormous, wanted a meteor to crash down at the T-Rex miniature golf course, crushing us to death and setting the world on fire. I felt an antsy, liquid energy running through my body. Can I Have A Cigarette? I asked her. She looked up from her work. *Sure,* she said. *You want to give it another try? You know where they are.*

The match flared fast in the night air. There was no wind, just this great air that pooled around us, perfect air that rose into the night sky. Slightly damp air that smelled like powdery flowers, like clean babies, like Rose. I held the match and crackled my cigarette to life, fuming away all the good smells with my toxic smoke. My mind lit on Old Harry, wasting away in his exhaled haze. I shook the image from my head. Would I have to think about Old Harry Chester every time I saw a cigarette now, for the entire rest of my life? It seemed like it would possibly be worthwhile to take up smoking simply to give my impressionable brain a series of new cigarette associations.

Rose was gently knocking the crushed crystals onto the back of the hippo. With the matchbook she shaped them into sparkling sugar snail trails. My cigarette burned like a flaming planet in the dark. This time the choke was smaller and I held it in, my eyes watering in the dark. Then I felt my head empty out and balloon up, up and away. I leaned dizzy into the hippo. I Never Knew Cigarettes Got

You High, I told Rose. I Would Have Probably Tried Them Earlier.

They only get you high the first time, she said, pulling the cash from my pack and tugging a bill from the roll. *So enjoy it.* She grinned at me. *This is going to really get you high, though. Are you ready?*

For The Battery Acid? I asked. I looked at the twin piles on the hippo's back. I dunked my finger into one, gentle, and held my finger, tipped in sparkle, in the light. Surely this couldn't be battery acid, it was too pretty. It looked like really expensive eye shadow or something. Like glitter. I reached out and dabbed it onto Rose's cheeks and her laugh was the call of some exotic animal, a rain forest cry. She swatted away my hand. *Lick your finger, don't waste it,* she told me, brushing the stuff from her face and then slurping her palms. She twisted a twenty into a tight paper straw and with one end poked into her nose she leaned over the drugs and inhaled them. She tilted her head way back, in the spotlight beaming up from the turf I could see her pale scalp, the tiny pores her thick hair sprung from. Rose was futzing with her nose, rubbing it and snorting and sniffling. *Whoa,* she said and reached for the Yikes. She plunged her finger into the neck of the bottle and flicked the stuff up her nose. Did snorting this stuff make you then want to snort everything, I wondered. I watched Rose for visible evidence of the drug's effects. Her face had new color in it, flushed like when she was at work, hustling around the fryers. Her eyes sparkled. The sparkle of the drug had dripped into her eyes and made them hard and shiny. She held out the twenty. *Do it,* she ordered. *Listen, though, don't breathe out, breathe in, hard.*

Duh, I said.

Seriously, she said, swatting at her nose some more. Her voice sounded stuffy and clogged. *The first time I did this, I don't know, I just blew out and I sprayed the stuff everywhere.*

When Was The First Time You Did It? I asked.

At work. In the bathroom. Marty, one of the cooks, had a bunch and he shared it with me. We did it in the bathroom. And then we did it in the bathroom. She laughed.

I bent my head over the shimmering tuft. Rose did it with Marty the cook. Who was Marty the cook? Would I want to do it with him too? I handed off my cigarette to Rose who took a greedy drag and then a chug off the bottle. With the twenty stuck into my nostril I inhaled like my wind would douse the fire that was burning up my chest. It shot like a bullet through my nose and then clung, stinging, to the back of my throat. Oh My God, I gasped. My nose felt seared. I touched it and felt for blood, but it was dry.

Here here here, Rose thrust the bottle at me. *Put some up your nose,* she said, but it was my throat that felt awful, like it was shriveling into itself, collapsing, the twinkling powder corroding it. Now I understood how it could be battery acid. How it could be nasal spray, medicine someone played mad scientist with until something meant to open up your sinuses instead collapsed them. I dumped the Yikes down my throat, swallowing what was left. Rose was ready with a new one. I liked this division of labor. Sure I was having to haul the illegal shit around, but Rose had fixed up the drugs on the hippo's back and was now taking care of me, ready with a vodka drink. I felt a surge of immense gratitude.

You Are So Nice, I told her. You Are Really, Really . . . Caring. I Hope That Doesn't Sound Gay. I Mean, Not Gay. I Know, Your Mom's Gay. That Must Be Kind Of Cool, Having A Gay Mom? Is It? Or Is It Hard? My Mom Isn't Gay, She's Got This Boyfriend I Totally Hate. If She Was Gay At Least, You Know, He Wouldn't Be Around, You Know? So That At Least Must Be A Good Part Of Having A Gay Mom.

I could feel my heart shaking and convulsing in my chest. Was I going to die? I felt great, but these great feelings were being interfered with by the thought that I might die. From a drug overdose, at T-Rex Miniature Golf. Maybe I'd always been attracted to it because I knew, psychically, that it was the place I would die. That I would die a druggie's death, by the orange hippo with a black-haired girl named Rose. Am I Going To Die? I asked her. She thought that was funny. She shot her hand out and placed it atop my Weight Watchers T-shirt, over the place where my heart bucked and rocked inside my rib cage.

It's your heart, she said, feeling it kicking like a baby in a pregnant woman's stomach. No shit, I wanted to say, but all my words were piled up somewhere behind the car crash that was my primary organ. I couldn't speak. I felt just deranged with what were the best and the worst feelings I ever felt, duking it out inside my body. And now Rose was leaned in to me, one hand holding my cigarette elegantly. Like a flapper, I thought. And I said, I managed to creak out, You're Like A Flapper, and she smiled at that and closed her eyes in the dark and became sealed inside her own experience of the drug, one hand holding smoke, the other flat above my heart, which was maybe starting to slow or maybe I was acclimating to its new style of beating, and Rose leaned in to me then and she kissed me.

And the real purpose of the drug became clear, the kiss banished the bad feeling of racing panic, was some sort of friendly violence I'd never experienced before. Rose's mouth chewed into mine and she tossed the cigarette to the Astroturf and I did not even care that it would maybe burst into flame. I thought that would be fine, really, and that this was the meteor I'd been craving and it had landed here on my body, was pushing me back onto the scraggy fake ground and scrambling all over me like a spider, or a sci-fi crab-girl from another planet. Rose's teeth bit into me and I swear, a new talent bloomed inside me, kissing. This was the best ever and I was good at it, I took right to it, amazing, all this time in my room and I could have been kissing someone, kissing Rose. My hands clutched a slippery bundle of her hair and held her face to mine. We bit each others' tongues and it was sloppy and spectacular and her hand slid below my heart to where my boobs were and she touched them and it was fine that she did this, totally okay with me, and I realized my body was on fire, my body was finally happening, it had arrived and Rose could have it. I thought I should touch her boobs too since she had touched mine so I did, I slid my hand under the gaping neck of her nightgown-dress and felt them hot and cold, I touched them and it made her mouth open wider and her warm breath blew into me like weather and I felt like mush, like a ruined planet, and with her bony fingers she was pinching me and it hurt and I wanted it to hurt more. It was like I felt everything and yet was numb, my body suddenly superhuman, feeling sensation so intensely that only the most intense sensations registered, the plunge of Rose's tongue and the pinch of my lip between her teeth, her claw at the skin beneath my shirt. She lifted off of me and took a frantic drink from the glass bottle and dove back into me, her hands around my neck, she pulled me into a roll and I was on top of her and she squirmed beneath me, her nightgown-dress hiked in a tangle, I saw her underwear, I saw the holes around the elastic and their dingy color glowed at the edge of the hippo's floodlight. I saw her underwear and I touched them and she gasped, she affixed her mouth to my ear and filled it with tickles. I touched her again and then again and again and realized I could touch her as much as I wanted to and I felt like the king then of some Super-Lotto-jackpot island, thought that this was our land here, a land of plastic grass and staring gnomes and helpful dinosaurs, this was our special land and I was its king, feeling the place change as I touched it, feeling it shift behind the cloth, and I admit that though I felt like its king, I was scared to move the fabric and touch beneath it, I was scared to even though I knew she did it with some guy named Marty, or maybe I was scared because of some guy named Marty, but either way I was scared to do more than just touch and touch and touch it more, so that's what I did and that seemed fine with Rose.

Twenty-one

Afterward we lay around on the plastic grass. We looked up at the wide bowl of night, squinting for stars, but you can't see any above Route 1. We'd traded stars for the tall neon sculptures that advertise the restaurants. I say who cares. It's not like we can make the stars extinct. The stars are the last bit of nature we can't fuck up; we only fuck it up for ourselves, stacking lights on top of lights 'til we blot out the sky. I think it's an okay trade-off. I like the neon, and I like knowing the stars are up there too. Shining down on some more-country part of the world. Instead of stars we lay beneath the general glow of Route 1, the combination of all the neon on the strip rising into an orangey glow of sky, like a forever sort of sunset or gust of pollution. The round, white lights shooting up from the Astroturf. Cars on the highway added extra beams into the mix, like zooming disco balls they sped by, strobing. The light seemed alive with a pulse like the one inside my body, my new pulse, or perhaps it had always been there and the crystal had highlighted it.

It's Good We Both Wore Our Pajamas, I said to Rose. I tugged on a bit of her nightgown, rubbed the fabric between my fingers to hear it scratch. We Could Just Sleep Here At The T-Rex.

Oh, we're not going to sleep, man, Rose laughed. *Not for a while. Not on this stuff.*

It didn't feel weird that we had kissed or touched. I felt really okay. I sincerely hoped that it would happen again but I also wasn't freaking out about it. I was just floating in some plasticky garden of goodness. Rose sat up and opened the backpack. She dumped its contents onto the ground in a clanking mess. The rest of the Yikes, the shimmery drugs in their jewel-bag, the smokes. The picture of Paulie's cousin and the Polaroids, two of them. I flipped them over. One was Kim. Kim and Rose, side by side on the spiky green.

You Took It, I said.

Yeah, fuck him. Why should he have that? A picture of anyone. I wish I could have taken them all.

There Were More?

Rose nodded. *What are we going to do with all this shit?* She lifted the cell phone. It had rung a ton while we were making out. She hit buttons and saw what we'd missed. Calls from Katie, calls from XXX. Calls from Home. *Fuck this phone.* She offered it to me. *Do you want to make any last calls?*

Unh-uh.

She pressed the wide, rubbery button on the top, fiddled around and the phone went dead. *I want to bury it,* she said, *but you can't dig this shit up.* Her nails dug at the turf. She stood up and walked down the slope to the windmill. When the course was turned on, the windmill twirled, its blades blocking the golf ball hole as they spun down. The windmill was all about timing. Crouching, Rose chucked the cell phone deep inside. *Okay, we got rid of that,* she stomped back up the slope. *This?* She held up the red-headed dancer, light bouncing off the glass. *Your turn.* I walked it to the shrubbery edging the path, tough little bushes of dark green leaves. They seemed almost as phony as the Astroturf but when I dug beneath the woodchips I felt real dirt, damp roots twining deep.

It's Hard To Tell What's Real In This Place, I called to Rose.

That gnome? Not real.

I pulled the velvety stand from the back of the frame and set the picture down beside the red-capped gnome. I arranged branches of bush around it, the glossy leaves framing the frame. I pushed woodchips up around its edges. The light found the dancer — she looked like a miniature girl sashaying through an enchanted, gnome-ridden bush-forest. Rose liked it. Rose was cracking up. She lit up another cigarette and I huddled beside her, received the burning treat each time she passed it my way. I rated smoking second under kissing as best activity ever. I was glad I'd waited to try it, now I had a new thing to get into. Another new thing. I liked how the smoke totally invaded your body. It swelled your insides, then burst out in a dramatic escape. It was like eating, only better. I wanted to never eat again, never sleep, only smoke and think great thoughts and kiss Rose. I passed the cigarette back to her and took a hit off the Yikes. We talked. We talked about her mom and how sad she was about Irene and maybe just about life in general. How maybe when you're depressed for long enough it just damages your brain, makes you regular sad all the time. We talked about my mom and how sick she wasn't and was. And all the talking and thinking about her made me sad in this way I hadn't felt before. Not sad like old-people sad, but some cousin of that emotion. I thought about Ma lying day in, day out on the saggy couch. Ma had a life, just like I did. That was her life. A whole life spent on a couch. I had to stop thinking about it. It was making my chest feel like a tight plank. We talked about our dads instead. Our nowhere dads. There wasn't much to talk about. We talked about Paulie's ruined arms. They were easier to think about than moms. We talked about Paulie's stomach and the fetal alien probably living inside it. About how a guy turns into a Paulie rather than a more gently offensive loser like Donnie, or a more normal guy like you might see on TV.

No mom, Rose offered. *Right?*

Too Obvious, I said. That's Like, People Could Say We're Like This — I waved around a bottle of Yikes in my one hand and the end of the cigarette in my other — Because We Got No Dads.

Rose shrugged. *Maybe we are. Who cares.* I cared. I didn't like thinking of my general personality being the result of a mistake. Ma's mistake of marrying him or his mistake of leaving, my mistake of being born from their mistaken relationship.

It's not like that, Rose shook her head and drank from the Yikes. *It's just like — life is there to mess with you. You just have to relax and let it mess you up. You can't resist it. You turn crazier when you try to stop it.* I thought about Kristy and her positive-thinking spells and how tense they made her. And Ma's stupid routine, always coming up with a new germ infestation. Maybe if she was just honest and said, Yeah I can't deal with the world, I want to lie around and watch Dr. Phil, maybe she'd be happier.

And really, any way the world fucks with you, you probably could have seen it coming if you just thought about it. My ma is crazy about Irene being in the war, but Irene was in the army when she met her. Why did she go on a date with an army person? My mom, she explained, *protests stuff. She brought me up to New Hampshire to try to shut down a nuclear power plant when I was like four. She's got bumper stickers all over the car about peace and love, and then she goes on a date with an army person and gets depressed when she goes to war.*

Whoa, I said. Totally. It seemed like an extra amount of air was getting into my lungs. My nostrils felt huge, the back of my throat wide and dry, no matter how much Yikes I drank. A bitter ooze crept down from my nose like an underground creek, dripping a crumby sludge of leftover drugs over my tonsils. It was like all you had to do was snort a little bit of crystal and it created a magical spring that kept leeching the drug into your system. I snorted and swallowed. Don't You Want To Stay Here Forever? I asked. Rose passed me the last of the cigarette. The whole cigarette thing was fine if I didn't think about it too much. The smoking process was excellent, but if I smelled my fingers or thought about my breath I become obsessively grossed out with myself. I held the smoldering butt between my thumb and pointer finger, making an Okay sign like I'd seen Rose do earlier. I flicked it. It shot from my hand like a tiny firework, arcing orange into the bushes.

Nah, let's go walk around. Rose hopped up. *Let's go into all the restaurants.* She was off and headed toward the chain-link fence, the backpack slumped on the ground for me to carry. I stuffed the items we were keeping back into the pouch of it, the Polaroids and the drugs and the money. We had three more bottles of Yikes left, and I don't know how many cigarettes. I strapped the backpack to my shoulders and hiked down the Astroturf to where Rose was already scaling the fence. I was sort of sad to be leaving our special golf garden. I wondered if the making-out was something that could only ever happen there, in the plastic hush, among the cartoon statues. A strange otherworld, like Never-Neverland where kids don't grow up. A world where a couple of girls could make out with each other and nothing tragic or stupid would happen, not even a minor conversation to take it back or trash it, nothing at all except that magical ignition of internal sparks. We'd stepped into a fairy ring where upside-down was rightside-up. I didn't want to leave it. I felt a sudden physical plummet, somewhere inside my chest. It was a drop that took me off balance and made my body feel noodley. Paulie had talked about a crash. It had made Kim Porciatti want to kill herself. Had something crashed in me? It felt like a car hitting the brakes behind my heart.

Yoo-hoo! Rose was on the other side of the fence, her sneaks poked through the links, waving her arms at me. The backlight of the rushing highway shone through her nightgown and I could see the outline of her body beneath it, like a shadow puppet. She called to me, *Don't bother with the dinosaur,* she said. *It doesn't help. Just hop the fence.* The dinosaur, our guardian, protector of the magical land of nighttime Astroturf. I knocked its orange back with my knuckles and heard the sound roll around its hollow insides. I could hop a fence no problem. Rose clambered down to the ground and I soon dropped beside her. We looked up at the T-Rex, its mouth in a forever roar, angry at the cars below, at the giant pagoda across the street.

Bye, Guy, I said. I gave a little wave. We turned to cross the highway and I knew it had our back.

Twenty-two

If you have nothing to do and nowhere to be and you're just hanging around on drugs, Route 1 is a seriously festive place to be. All the Vegasy restaurants. The Chinese restaurant with the river, the steak house with a neon cactus as tall as Monster Paulie's apartment building and a herd of fake cows grazing out front of the building, all wooden like a ranch in Texas. The Mexican restaurant built like a shabby shack strung all around with Christmas lights and blaring Mexican guitar music you can hear as you pass by the parking lot. The Italian place with a replica of that crooked tower sticking out of its roof, all wonked. Even the crappy sausage sandwich joint where you order at the window has an enormous neon sign advertising it. It's about fifteen times the size of the sausage joint itself, which looks like a food trailer from a traveling carnival. But I guess if you're going to compete in the Route 1 restaurant world, you need to have a lot of neon. We went to the Mexican restaurant first, because it was close enough for us to hear the yodeling Mexican singer. The romantic swells of his voice bobbed in the air like bubbles. We walked alongside the road, the cars careening close. We walked one in front of the other, me leading. I didn't like not being able to see Rose. I felt that falling sensation in my body again. It left my legs trembling. I guess it was maybe time to eat, but the thought seemed lousy. I didn't have an appetite. The Mexican restaurant was shrouded in a hazy glow from all the Christmas lights; I could see the colored halo shining up from the dark like the light of a UFO crashed down in an empty lot.

What Should We Do? I asked Rose. The place was squat before us. Shaggy piñatas dangled from the awning. Inside I saw waiters wearing sombreros trimmed with little pompoms.

Let's go inside, she said. *You want to eat some chips?*

Yeah, I nodded. Now I had a focus. Chips would save me.

You want real food? We can get tacos or something. I have a bunch of money still.

I thought of tacos, stuffed with blobs of white cream and globules of crumbly meat. My stomach lurched, then sealed itself off. Even chips seemed brittle and greasy if I thought about it too much. I wouldn't think, I'd just eat. We pushed into the place and were overwhelmed by the music. The place was a real party on the inside. They had it all dressed up like Friday night in Mexico. Striped blankets swagged from the splintery roof beams, spinning ceiling fans tossing their fringed ends around above our heads. Mexican words were painted on the walls, beside murals of Mexican women dancing around in fluffy dresses. The walls themselves had been painted to look old and kind of dirty. They were yellow with faint brown streaks and creases. At the bar a bunch of jocks watched sports on a TV and drank jellybean-colored drinks in margarita glasses the size of punch bowls.

Two? A waitress asked us. We nodded dumbly, were led to a wooden table in the middle of everything. Plastic donkeys smiled with big teeth on a shelf above our heads. The salt and pepper shakers were Mexican beer bottles. A man quickly placed two giant plastic cups of water onto our table, followed by a basket of chips and a dish of chunky salsa.

Yes! Rose cheered. She grabbed a chip and started poking it into the salsa. I waited for her to eat it, but she didn't. She was just piling stuff onto it, a juicy tower of tomato, onion, cucumber. When it toppled onto the table, she started over. *This place is great but I'm going to get bored of it real fast. In fact, I'm already bored. I hate that about speed. Sometimes, I just have an idea and then I'm bored with it before I even do it.*

Aren't You Going To Eat? I asked. I gulped some water. It felt like medicine, going down. My whole body went *aaaaahhh.*

No, Rose said, *but you should. You look lousy.*

My hand went up to my face, as if *lousy* was a bumpy, tangible object sitting on my cheek. I Do? Rose didn't look so hot herself. Her skin looked a little glow-in-the-dark, and there were red blotches on her face that looked scaly. The blotches ran down her arms, too. Her arms looked webbed with some awful red flush. Beneath the bright lights of the restaurant, Rose was looking *X-Files.* There's Something Wrong With Your Arms, I said.

Rose folded them into herself like a pair of grasshopper legs. She rubbed them roughly. *It's my circulation,* she explained. *The speed does something to your circulation. It's no big deal.*

I looked at my own arms, poking out of my T-shirt. They looked fine to me. My Arms Are Okay, I said.

I'm anemic, so it's worse for me, Rose said. *But really, your face looks too white or something. You should maybe eat. Did you eat today, since what I gave you at the Clown?* I shook my head. *Come on, eat then! I know it's nasty, but if you don't eat we're not going to have as much fun. C'mon, dude.* She shook the basket of chips at me. They were warm, tucked into a cloth napkin. They were so oily they shone. I looked at them like some sort of athletic dare. I would eat the chips. I began lubing them up in the chunky salsa and stuffing them into my mouth. I crunched and crunched. The stiff chips snapped beneath my teeth, tortilla splinters jabbed my gums and tore up my mouth. My mouth felt weird. That drug drip kept recurring like an underground stream. My gums felt tight, like they were shrinking away. It made my teeth feel wobbly in my head. Giant head and shrunken gums, waggly teeth, I was a jack-o'-lantern. I was sick of the violent tortilla chips. I wiped my fingers on the cloth napkin and pushed the basket back toward Rose, guzzled the rest of my water.

I Feel Weird, I said. I Want To Get Out Of Here. I Hate These Lights and I Hate These People. The people all around us were hooting with merriment. Their goblets of margarita had made them so happy and now they could cut loose and bray and be obnoxious. I was glad alcohol didn't have that effect on me. Alcohol made me woozy and spinny and perfect. I wanted to get somewhere where we could crack open another Yikes, maybe do more of the drugs. Do We Need To Do More? I asked Rose. She shook her head.

We shouldn't. It's just weird in here. Location is really important if you're on drugs and I don't think this is the ultimate location. It's boring. I swore the waitress heard Rose say the d-word. She came over to us, pompoms swaying on her decorative sombrero. Her waitress pad was tucked into what looked like a miniature Mexican blanket wound around her waist.

You girls know what you want? She barked, no-nonsense.

Ah, we're just going to leave, Rose said. The waitress looked down at the tortilla debris littering my placemat, the splatters of tomato staining the tablecloth by Rose. Our empty cups of water.

Get out then, she spat. *Jesus Christ. What are you on?* She gave us the up-and-down. *You look like shit, girls.*

I told you, Rose said, and we cracked up. The waitress looked pissed. Rose grabbed my ass as we tore through the restaurant, dodging parties of four and five, their faces grossly greenish-pink under the fluorescents, gesturing with their drinks, kids yammering and stuffing tacos into their tiny yaps, spilling beans and cheese out the other end.

The total grossness of humanity. They all looked like shit too. At least we had an excuse. Rose grabbed my ass just for show, I know, just as a way of saying fuck you to the waitress but I didn't feel used. I was glad that Rose had remembered about my ass. That it was there. I was happy to be part of her stunt.

Out in the parking lot we tore a Yikes from the backpack and wrenched it open. Rose slurped the fizz and punched her fist-wrapped bottle into the air, sang along with the Mexican music pumped out of the speakers. You Know This Song? I asked.

No. I'm just making shit up. Here — she thrust the bottle at me. I took a long gulp. I still felt shaky, but not like I had earlier, like a balloon with the air farting out from it, my life force leaking away. Now I felt shaky but excited, like I wanted to run around. I was getting the hang of the crystal, the ups and downs of it inside my body, the roller-coaster track it had laid along my veins, the loop-de-loop where my heart used to pump. We ran over to the steak house and climbed around on the big fake cows until the parking lot attendant kicked us out. It had taken a few tries to successfully get up on one. They were wide-backed and slick-surfaced, heavy metal cows painted cow-colored and spotty. There was nothing to grip. We kept sliding off like it was a bucking bronco or something, landing on our asses in the woodchips strewn about the place. That steak house is a real popular location. The skyscraper cactus shot a groovy green light down onto us, and on the other side of the fence a long line of people wrapped around the front porch, waiting to be seated. They watched us clambering around like a couple of clowns and some of them even booed the parking lot dude when he came and hauled us out. *Thank you!* Rose hollered at the crowd. She waved one scrawny arm in the air. *Thank you!* Her other arm was held tight by the parking lot dude. He had one of mine too, and was manhandling us away from the cows.

All right, guy! Rose twisted. *Shit.* She broke away.

Where are your parents? He demanded.

Where Are Your Parents? I shot back weakly.

Yeah, where are your *parents?* Rose mocked. He let us go so we could pull ourselves over the fence. The fence was a bunch of cut-down trees all crisscrossed together. Real authentic looking. That was the look here on Route 1, authentic phoniness. We hauled ourselves over the lumber and took off for the side of the road. *Fuck yooooooouuu-uuu!* Rose yodeled. Next we hit the majestic Chinese restaurant. The outside was a pagoda and that was great enough right there, a pagoda in the middle of Mogsfield. I didn't even care about the indoor river, but then there it was. It was bubbling and splashing right at the entrance, and it ran off in the direction of some dining rooms. Everything was bright red, and everything that wasn't bright red was a gold that shot the light around like we were up inside a giant neon sign. There was some green too, a jade color in the eyes of the enormous dragons that lurched in a tasseled arc above our heads. The dragon's jade eyes swirled with PCP craziness and red-golden fake flames curled out from its wide dragon nostrils. More green in the leafy plants sprouted wildly along the banks of the impossible indoor river. There was even a planked bridge spanning one little area, where the water calmed and pooled. Some little kids were standing on it, plopping shiny coins overboard, making little-kid wishes.

I had some serious wishes to make. They were all piled up behind my throat, buzzing in my brain. I wished to kiss Rose again and touch her boobs, I wished to never again see Monster Paulie, to always feel good inside and never crash like Kim Porciatti and try to kill myself. I wished that Rose would grab my ass again and that when we were done with Yikes someone would buy us more. I wished for a magical pack of unending cigarettes. I wished that I would become a new and better person, new and improved, supersized with crazycool confidence and daring. I could feel it already happening and I wished for it to never stop. I even wished that Kristy got on to *The Real World*, I wished that Mom would get better in her mind and in her body, I wished for my dad to be alive, for him to find me and call me on the telephone. Donnie, I didn't know what to wish for him. I personally wished he would leave but that would make Ma sad, and if I was wishing for Ma to be happy how could I wish for Donnie to vanish? Rose, I Want To Make A Wish, I said to her. She was stroking this giant golden statue that looked like a pug dog on steroids. Her fingers followed the curving grooves of its spiraling tongue.

This is like being in a museum or something, she breathed. She loved the pumped-up pug. *I bet these are replicas of real statues. I bet these are real works of art somewhere.* The kids on the bridge scattered away, laughing. People came and went and nobody was paying any attention to us. Rose turned from the dog. *I gotta pee,* she told me, and I brought her over the bridge, toward the carpeted hallway where the restrooms were. Inside it was pink and green, everything still polished and creamy. Rose went straight for the handicapped stall at the end of the bank of toilets. *C'mon,* she pulled me inside. She hopped onto the can and tinkled. She tugged her underwear out and took a peek. A wide spot of blood was spreading across the cotton. *Shit, I need to find a new tampon, okay? Don't let me forget.* She blotted her drawers with a square of toilet paper, then tossed it between her legs into the bowl. *Want to do more?* she mouthed at me. Her voice was lower than a whisper.

More Of What? I asked. I felt bold. I felt like all the wishes I intended to make had been granted just by me thinking about them, like I had some direct hotline to the cosmos all of a sudden. I went into the backpack and tugged open a Yikes. One more to go. I barely felt drunk, just flying and delirious with excellence. More Of Making Out? I flicked the jagged Yikes cap against the wall like I had with the cigarette earlier. It bounced against the wall and spun like a top upon the floor. Rose swiped a ball of toilet paper over her parts and tugged her stained drawers back up. *Swoosh,* the nightgown cascaded over her. I looked at the floor, my cheeks stinging. The words had flown out of my mouth, hung in the still air of the handicapped stall, gathered themselves together and bitch-slapped me.

Okay, she said, like I'd asked her for a cigarette. *But wait.* Digging in the bag she brought out the tiny diamond-sack of crystal, plus my house keys. She dunked the tip of the key into the snowy glitter and removed it. A dusting of sprinkles clung to the metal. *That's more than enough I think. If we even need to do any more.* She stuck the key into a tiny train tunnel of nose and snorted. *It barely stings,* she said. I thought perhaps the huff we did back in the golf course had seared away all our nerve endings. She offered me a freshly dunked keytip. My mother would freak if she knew I was out shoving dirty housekeys up my nose. *Your nose,* she would say, *is your first line of defense against the common cold.* The webbing of mucus stretched grotesquely over little hairs up there acts like a giant trap that snags all incoming germ-missles. Ma would kill me if she knew I was just introducing a germy ol' key right into my germ trap. She probably wouldn't even care about the battery acid-derived drugs that were hanging all over the key, no. It was the unseen microbes that would give her a shitfit.

I took a huff and the crystals tinkled into me. My body felt wrung of everything but the drugs and the Yikes. The crystal dramatically plunged downward to my general crotch area, a penny cast into my wishing pool. I grabbed Rose's scaly arms. It was like the drug had forged new paths for blood to flow in her body. It was either oddly pretty or disturbing and scary, and I didn't want to deal with disturbing and scary when I was feeling so great. I let my head knock back against the pink stall wall. I Feel Fucking Fantastic, I said, my feet bouncing in my flops. I Love This Stuff. It forced you to move, to fling out your arms, to shuffle around or really just do anything. I looked at Rose. I pulled Rose toward me by her mutant arms. I pulled her into my face and I kissed her. It was sort of bumpy at first, I knocked her with my teeth, tooth against tooth, and her nose seemed like it grew since we kissed in the golf course, but then it was fine. Then it was great again, maybe even better because I wasn't afraid I was dying. We slurped and bit and Rose banged her body up against mine again and again, like a wind was knocking her into me, like we were wind chimes dangling in a breeze. It was so great that we were both girls and could go into the women's room together. My hands were on the back of Rose's skull, so small in my hands it felt like I could crush it, and my fingers tightened around it to reassure myself of its solidity, that it was a real skull and not a collapsable doll head. I did not know where Rose's hands were until they were at the elastic waistband, burrowing beneath it, fingers running along the red grooves it had left in my belly, and then down and down again, so nervy, right there at my underwear and then underneath and then still not stopping, not gently stroking like I had on the Astroturf but prying, nimbly burrowing, and I did not know what she was doing but was curious and so I moved to accommodate her, I slid my legs apart, back against the wall, face mashed into her hotly breathing face, and my heel slid off my flop and I kicked it to the tiled floor, I kicked them both off, and Rose's fingers were crawling up inside of me and I didn't think I could take it and then I could. She was messy and graceless and it didn't matter, my body was an electric force field, it radiated everything it contacted, was melting Rose's hand, was merging into it, her hand would surely have to become part of my body after this, my body was being forever changed right here in the handicapped stall of the Chinese restaurant, Rose was breaking and entering and stealing something and replacing it with something else, something better, herself. An inside smell wafted up around us and I knew it was me and that was okay because it didn't smell the way you always hear that it smells, like tuna, like a bag of lettuce gone bad in the fridge. It just smelled sort of warm, it smelled like wet motion, a river whipping around a rock. Rose kept at it. It was drawing noises from me, they went from my mouth into her. It was a strange, subterranean way of talking. My body bloomed around her fingers like a man-eating flower. I always had believed it would hurt and smell and be terrible and lonely, and if I had gone to a psychic and heard *you will lose your virginity in the bathroom of a Chinese restaurant* I would have known it was true, the worst, and I would have never left my house and never met Rose or crystal. And now I'd done it and now Rose left me, she rested her wet paw on my hip beneath my sweats and the kissing, so crazed, began to slow and slow and stop and then we were still, heart and blood and drugs racing on the inside but still on the outside, in a bubble it seemed, a floating bubble of pink and jade tile. And it's true I felt smashed on the inside, my body a smear across my underwear, some new part of me alive and humming and yes, absolutely, this was the greatest day of my life.

Twenty-three

I teetered like a suicide on the outside edge of the bridge. *Do it!* Rose goaded me from behind. We'd decided not to cast coin wishes into the water because really, that would just be giving money away to some giant restaurant that was so superrich they could afford to plant a swear-to-god river smack through the joint, so rich that they could wash everything in gold and have chandeliers the size of spaceships swaying over our heads. Is that who we wanted to give our spare change to? Absolutely not. We'd stared at the sparkling disks of pennies and quarters wavering under the water and figured there had to be at least a hundred dollars down there. I would jump in and get it. I would do it because I had stupidly left my flops in the bathroom and was conveniently barefoot. Rose's crumpled sneakers were held together with a scab of fibrous duct tape and if she took them off she feared they would disintegrate once and for all, so why didn't I do it. Scavenge the money for us. We didn't even need it, with Rose's Clown cash we were loaded, but it just seemed like a real waste to let so much money sit there underwater. I looked down into the pool. Fat striped fish wiggled beneath the surface, orange and red and white. Their fins were as thin and gauzy as Rose's nightgown, they blew around in some mysterious underwater breeze.

There's Fish, I said. I was a little concerned.

Even better, Rose said. Her voice had moved closer, was right in my ear. *Even more fantastic. I wish we could take them too.*

I dropped off the bridge with a substantial splash. The fish darted like startled cats, but there wasn't anywhere for them to go. The pool was dammed up with rocks, phony or real. The fish were stuck with me, they bumped softly against my calves as I stooped to scoop the spare change. We were stealing the wishes of bunches of people. Quickly I had two palmfuls of nothing but quarters. Why toss a quarter when a penny would do? These were rich-people wishes. I felt fine about taking them. Maybe they'd generously wished that poor people got more money and now I was helping their dreams come true. I brought the coins, dripping, over to the bridge, where Rose stood with the wide mouth of the backpack unzipped and ready. I dumped the money inside and went back for more. I reached down into the water and petted one of the fish as it glided past, its long fishy whiskers trailing from its face. I don't think the fish minded me in their space. The people who worked there, though, were pissed.

What are you doing? a lady hollered at me. I figured she worked there because she was wearing a Chinese-style blouse, brilliant red with little loopy buttons angling up the side. It was really pretty. There were birds and tree branches printed across it. I smiled at her. *What are you doing?* she repeated. It was so obvious what I was doing. My hands were cupping a pile of silver, water streaming from between my fingers. This would be the last scavenge. The coins slid from my hands into the bag, which Rose had zipped before the angry lady strode up the bridge. *You can't do that!* she hollered. Her whole face was collapsing toward the center in a massive earthquake of a frown. I was trapped in the pool. I'd been relying on Rose to help pull me back onto the bridge but now Rose was clutching the backpack to her chest and trying to angle past the lady. The lady was blocking her way and demanding she hand over the backpack. The lady was speaking into a little walkie-talkie thingie that had been clamped to the waist of her slacks. She honked into it and it sputtered back and soon there was another lady in an identical pretty red shirt emerging from the restroom hallway, the Yikes bottle we'd drained in the bathroom in one hand and my flops in the other. Shit. I hadn't meant to be such a littering slob, I just didn't have my head too together after what Rose had done to me. My downstairs parts still felt pretty crazy from it, actually. Central, cracked open, transmitting and receiving. It was now the satellite dish of my body.

Rose tried to slip past the angry lady and the angry

lady put her hand on Rose's shoulder, stopping her. When Rose slapped the woman's hand away I knew I had to figure a way out of the river, fast. Rose's face slunk right up close to the woman's face, Rose got all up in her face and started hollering all sorts of terrible words at the woman, the kind of words that boy was hollering at us earlier. Rose's face was as close to this woman as it had been to mine in the bathroom. I knew that the woman was smelling the Yikes fumes on Rose's breath, and the cigarettes like burnt peanuts under that. I could hide under the bridge and hope nobody noticed. I could hurl myself up and over the bridge but I was pretty sure I'd break something in the process, and if the women descended on me I'd have no chance. The second woman, holding our stuff, seemed scared to go to her coworker's aid. That's 'cause Rose was so scary. Her voice was loud; it rang through the extravagant restaurant. The diners were further down the river and couldn't see the commotion. The river, where I stood, was fenced in with large faux rocks and shrubbery, but down where the people sat eating there was nothing hemming it in, and so I splashed in that direction, over the rocky miniature breakwater and into the stream, my feet trampling so much change it was hard not to bend down and sift a bit as I scrambled. I headed toward a table with a flaming centerpiece. It looked like a fake volcano, and there were piles of greasy fingerfoods heaped around its base. The man and the woman at the table stared at me, horrified. I lumbered toward them like the Swamp Thing. I was all splashed up, my raggy shorts soaked through and my T-shirt damp and clinging obscenely. My hair dripped into my eyes. The couple had stopped snacking, the woman held a chicken wing at boob-level, her lipsticked mouth catching flies. She looked at the man desperately. The man looked confused. His tan looked like the result of some accidental poisoning, a too-bright orangey shade. The lady too. They both looked like the chicken wing trembling in the lady's claw. I'm Real Sorry About This, I said as I approached. Other diners had noticed my arrival and were swiveling around in their seats. In order to get out I needed to steady myself on something and all there was was that table with its volcano of food. I put my wet hands beside it and felt it wobble as I leaned on it, up and out of the river. Thanks A Lot, I said.

Really! the chicken woman huffed. She craned her neck around for someone who could *do something.* There was a waiter holding a tray he'd just unloaded, looking at me with the same bland bewilderment everyone else was. If I were Rose I'd have had some stylish, slightly shocking exit to make but I just hopped away from the water and ran back toward the entrance. Rose was still tangoing with the angry lady, but their fight had moved from the bridge and was now located directly under the dragons. I swooped in like something out of a movie, and knocked the mad woman back so hard she banged into its tail. I grabbed Rose. She still had the backpack, clutched to her chest so tight her fingers looked skinless, pure knobby bone.

Yeah! I hooted, steering Rose toward the door. She was off balance but I kept her moving and she got her footing and dashed ahead of me, swinging open the giant glass doors. We're Sorry! I yelled back at the women. They were yelling at each other now and that one still had my flip flops.

Twenty-four

It took us forever to make our way through the giant Chinese restaurant's even more giant parking lot. The paved car platter seemed as big as the whole town of Mogsfield, stuffed with bulbous and turd-shaped SUVs, teensy compact thingies huddling close to the ground like spacebugs, an occasional beater with rusty corner and patchwork paint jobs, all gleaming under the lights hung from tall poles. I knew we weren't safe from the angry women in the quilted ruby tops until we were seriously off their property, so we ran like crazy, not speaking, not even looking at each other. Rose was in front of me, moving fast in her shabby sneakers, our stolen treasure of quarters banging around inside the backpack. I could hear their jangle as loud as the smack of her worn rubber soles on the lot's pebbly surface.

It wasn't until we were out on the side of Route 1, catching our breath in the repetitive glare of the constant cars, that I realized I'd sliced up my foot. It felt wet, but I thought it was just from the river, from the streaming drips of my soggy outfit, but then it felt sore and when I looked down I could tell it was blood, darkly pooling out from my poor naked foot. Oh, Crap, I said. I leaned against the pole of a highway sign and pulled my foot up into my hands. It was too bloody to see what was going on in there, and the longer I stopped and breathed and observed the wound the more it hurt. It had its own living pulse, like my downstairs parts, only rotten. My foot was all smeary blood plus a good coating of grime from the parking lot.

We need a first aid kit, Rose said. *We need water, a bathroom. Fuck. Sit down.* I did as she said. I came down hard on the pavement, my body suddenly shaky again. Rose was fiddling with her nightgown. She found the little tear one of the Yikes caps had put in the gauzy outer layer. She took it and gave it a hard rip, widening the hole, and kept tearing it in a long circle around her body. She was unraveling herself. With her teeth she tore the last stubborn bit free, and the ring of fabric drifted to the ground. Wispy hairs of shredded gauze undulated over the nylon.

Rose crouched before me. She lifted my sad foot onto her knobby knees and blotted at the blood with an edge of torn nightgown. She took the strip and wrapped it around the gash, pulling it snug around the ball of my foot and tying it in a bow above my toes. The tightness felt good, seemed to contain the raw pulse. *We still need help,* she said. *Let's see where we can go next. Can you walk?*

Yeah, Sure, I said. That's Great, Thank You So Much. A dull breeze hit the bow and flopped it around. Rose had taken my battered foot and replaced it with this adorable gift-foot. I wished my other foot got banged up too. I wished I had another bleeding part of myself to offer to Rose, for her to hold in her clammy palms and return it to me blotted and unbroken and topped with a girly shred of her own self.

Here, wait, she said and unzipped the backpack. She futzed around inside and came back out with a sugar-coated key. I inserted it into my nose. It made me laugh.

It's Like My Ignition, I said. I turned the key up inside my drug-crusted nose. I made revved-up motorcycle noises. My inner nose felt crystalized, like it was hung with plastic icicles, maybe sprayed with a can of that fake snow they bust out around Christmastime. It was coated in a synthetic crust. Rose cracked up at my nose-ignition gag, took the key away. I had begun to enjoy the dull sting in my sinus, same as I had begun to enjoy the accordion-throb in my downstairs, a grabby feeling, part painful, part itchy, part deeply nice. My body was teeming with sensations. Rose had inserted the key of her hand into the ignition of my downstairs and brought me to life. Even the new opening in my foot. It was like my foot had bloomed open to get closer with the world, I thought. My whole body was craving entry, it wanted to swallow the world, it wanted the world to invade my everything. Maybe I should take off the bandage and let my foot eat the concrete, swallow the pebbles, and ingest the roadside dirt. Maybe it would make me immune to urban poison. My mind was flooded with thought. The drugs had gashed open my mind, had torn it like a split foot so that all the ideas of the universe could be mashed into my head.

I Love This, I said to Rose. I Love This. My downstairs felt wild and whirling and I reached out for Rose's head, pulled it down onto mine and kissed her. I split her mouth with my tongue like a shard of glass. I ate her mouth like I was starving. I had an urge to crush her to bits, to chomp her to pulp. I pulled away. I Feel Crazy, I said, and she smiled, she looked crazy, she said, *I feel crazy too,* and she fell into me on the sidewalk. We lay there all balled up like a single throbbing monster making out with itself, the roar of the cars and the parade of their headlights like disco strobes, occasionally beeping at us. We made out forever and tasted the gritty bitter granules at the back of each other's throats, we got higher, got more fucked-up just kissing each other. I breathed the air that streamed out of her nose and she breathed the air I pushed into her lungs — we were keeping each other alive or killing each other, a suffocation machine. Eventually we sat up, pulled away. Spaced out, catching our breath, and following the whiz of vehicles before us.

Your foot, Rose said. *We have to take care of it. It can't get infected.* She popped up with a wobble and held out her hand to help me stand. I didn't take it. Rose was a stunted wisp and I'd only tumble her back onto me and then I would only kiss her again and we'd spend the next forever rolling on the side of the road, my foot getting gangrene. I shimmied upward with the help of the pole. We began our trudge down Route 1, my foot spazzing now, alive with hurt. I limped behind Rose who sometimes trotted ahead, then, remembering I was wounded, galloped back and slowed her pace, only to ramble into a sprint again. She was like one of those tiny, bouncy, Frisbee-catching dogs. I was happy to see her face every time she turned back toward me.

We heard the roar of Seamus O'Maniac's before we reached it. Seamus O'Maniac's is a fake Irish bar, pretending to be like the true Irish bars that are all over Mogsfield and probably all over Massachusetts. Seamus O'Maniac's is all olden on the outside, with weird knotted shapes etched onto the glass and a drapey awning and four-leafed everything. A little leprechaun man leaned into the big curling *S* of the *Seamus*, little bubbles floating up and bursting around his balding red head, to convey drunkeness. WHERE EVERY DAY IS ST. PATRICK'S DAY ran beneath it, in quotes. As if Seamus O'Maniac himself had said it. I had once thought Seamus O'Maniac's was just another Irish bar, but then on drives with Kristy or Donnie I spotted two or three more so I know it's a fake. People love it anyway. The place is crammed with drunk people who are proud to be Irish. They fall out the front door and stand smoking and belligerent out front. Occasionally a dude will lift both fists in the air and go *Wooo! Woooo!* for no apparent reason. I was watching one dude with curly blond hair do this exact maneuver. His cigarette was bunched in the knuckles of his fist. *Wooo! Woooo!* Another blond guy came out the green front door and clapped him on the back. *Bra!* he honked. I looked at Rose. Rose was brave, Rose was an explorer, but this was pushing it. I did not want to go inside Seamus O'Maniac's. I would hitchhike and snort strange glittering drugs and I would follow her into the cruddy skyscrapers of bloated monster drug dealers but I did not want to go inside Seamus O'Maniac's. I imagined us being grabbed by muscly white dudes, lifted onto the bar and made to dance jigs for the amusement of the date-raping clientele.

I Don't Know, Rose, I said. I caught a peeling bit of skin on my lip with my tooth and started chewing. A bit of skin came off in a long, dry strip. Lip jerky. It was oddly satisfying. Rose watched me.

We need gum, she said. *You're starting to chew on your face. That's not good.*

You Think We Should Go In There? I asked. I nodded toward Seamus O'Maniac's. Some females had exited for a smoke, and now the *Wooo*-ing guy had a target for his noises. *Woo! Woooo!* he hooted at the girls. They were wearing short everything and huddling closely as if for warmth. Their bouncy blond hairdos bounced against each other. *Wooo! Wooo!* they hooted back, then giggled.

It's Like A Mating Dance, I said. Like You See On TV, On Nature Programs. With Animals. Rose's face was stuck on the scene.

No, no, we can't go in there, she said. *We won't make it past the bouncer anyway, but even if we did we'd never make it out alive. I want to go there.* She pointed at a storefront some doors down from Seamus O'Maniac's. It was overshadowed by the hoopla from the bar, but a blue neon sign in the window burned *tattoo.* By its pale light I could make out the sign above the door, 777. Rose strut toward it and I hobbled pathetically after her. She pushed the glass door open, tinkling a bell. *Hey!* she hollered. I came in as the woman behind the counter looked up. She looked tired. She had a tense, wooden face with blue eyes that seemed extra alive compared to her skin. Maybe it was her makeup that made her skin look hard and dull. She looked dusted with fake color. Her lemony hair was shaggy and angular and poking out in different bed-heady directions. It had that fried look Kristy said came from too much bleach. She had a raspberry-colored T-shirt on, with a collar that V'd down into her cleavage. Her dark jeans had a faint sparkle and were cuffed high. She had a few tattoos on her arms but not as many as you'd expect for a person working in a tattoo shop.

Can I help you? she asked. Her mouth warbled the question in a half-yawn.

My friend, Rose pointed to the ratty bow on my bound-up foot. *She hurt her foot. Do you have first aid here?*

What, did you cut it? the lady asked. She seemed deeply bored. Maybe she had been sleeping.

Yeah, I nodded. I walked across the linoleum to the counter. The counter was piled with black-covered books. The walls around us were hung with billions of tattoo designs. Roses and dragons and geisha ladies, fairies and unicorns and clusters of objects all bunched together, like guns twined with thorny vines and then a woman's spread legs rising up behind them. There were flags and cartoon characters, panthers and mermaids and even hula girls. Hearts with empty banners.

Wow. Rose was sort of twirling around, trying to take

it all in at the same time. *Whoa.* She revolved like a fucked-up ballerina in a cranked-up jewelry box. The woman smirked.

You're going to make yourself dizzy, she said. *Come back here and I'll get the first aid kit.* She pulled open a waist-high swinging door and we herded through. The back had more of the colorful tattoo drawings tacked everywhere, plus a giant leathery chair like from a barber shop or a dentist's office. *Sit,* she said to me, and pointed to the chair. It had its bottom up, recliner-style, and I let myself collapse into it. My heart rattled inside my chest like a washing machine with a heavy load.

Rose dropped our backpack to the floor and studied the walls. The place had a sharp, clean smell. I could sniff out a faint medicine stink beneath it. I thought it was great lucky fortune that we had found a tattoo parlor of all places. A place where people went to willingly get their skin all punched up with millions of tiny holes would of course be able to help my foot. The woman came out with a small lunchbox. It had a red cross on it and looked like a toy doctor's kit. She bent down and lifted my foot. She held it in her hand and inspected it like it was a hideous gift, all wrapped up and topped with a dingy bow. *Nice job,* she tugged the fucked-up bandage. Her stumpy, square fingers began undoing the knotted gauze. With every rough tug the cut pulsed. It was like it was hollering out inside my head, the terrible scream of a wounded foot. *You do this?* She gave Rose a smile. It was a tight crack across her face, it seemed to hurt her to do it. Rose was totally engrossed with the walls. She shook her head yes. *You're a regular*

Nurse Mercy, she said. It hurt when she pulled the fabric from my cut. The tiny web of gauze had begun to weave itself into the skin. She tugged it away gently. I winced. The woman ignored me.

Who's Nurse Mercy? Rose asked. The woman stood, unraveled, bloody gauze dangling from her hand. She walked over to dump it into a safety-orange bin marked *Biohazard.* She glanced around the covered walls and finally stuck her hand out at a design.

Her. Rose of No Man's Land. Rose moved closer to get a better look and her mouth dropped open.

I'm Rose, she said. *That's me, that's my name.* She reached out and pulled the plastic-covered sheet. The tacks that held it to the wall popped off and rolled across the floor.

Hey! the lady snapped. *What are you doing! Don't be a bitch! Why be a bitch?* But she sounded more tired than mad.

No, look, Rose said. She held the sheet to her face. *I'm sorry, but look. Look. That's me, I'm Rose. Look.* She bounded over to where I lay sprawled and wounded on the leatherette chair. *Look, Trisha, it's me.*

On the sheet chaotic with skulls and anchors and even a red little donkey with the words *kiss my ass* etched around its prominent butthole, I saw what Rose was talking about. It was a girl wearing some hat that was half nurse's cap and half the veily thing nuns wore on their heads. It had a big red cross like the first aid lunchbox. But it was the face that was creepy. The girl's hair fell in waves to right where Rose's hair fell on her own face. The face was gaunt and spooky but also pretty. Her cheeks were pink and her big eyes looked like they could see the future and the future was both interesting and sad. It looked just like Rose. It had her tiny mouth. She turned to the lady.

Her name is Rose? The plasticky sheet sounded like a rainstorm when she shook it.

They call her Rose of No Man's Land, the tattoo lady said. Her hand was jammed onto her hip like she was holding the skeleton of her body together. *It's from World War One. That's what the nurses looked like, they wore those long habits and helped the men wounded on the battlefield. If they lived they would get these nurses tattooed on them. The nurses saved their life.*

I know someone in the war now, Rose said. *She's a nurse. Or she helps the nurses.*

The lady got back down to wounded-foot-level and cracked open the first aid lunchbox. I could smell the powdery makeup smell of her face. *I don't think it's the same thing anymore,* she said. *It's a different time. It's not that kind of war.*

There's no more Rose of No Man's Lands?

The woman smiled. *Just you, I think.*

It really does look like me, right? I'm not crazy?

It looks like you. But yes, you're also crazy. What are you girls on? She didn't look at us. She had torn open a little foil packet with an alcoholc wipe squared inside it. She dabbed and pressed the thing onto my cut and a new, watery sting sharpened up and into my foot.

Ow, I said.

Sorry, babe. Gotta do it. You can take it. She tipped my foot out and tried to wring alcohol from the wipe into the cut. She was clearing away blood and grime. *You've got glass in there,* she told me.

Let me see, Rose crouched down, still clutching the tattoo poster.

Right there.

Oooooh, Rose made a puckered face, like she was sucking on a sour. *Poor Trisha,* she looked at me and I felt a charge that crowded out the stinging foot pain. My heart continued to slam. The lady clattered her hand around inside the lunchbox.

You're Rose and you're Trisha, she stated. We nodded. *I'm Amber.*

Amber, we said in unison. She was holding a pair of tweezers, they glinted in the overhead light.

Rose of No Man's Land? She held the tweezers out to Rose. *Do you want to do the honors?*

Yeah, she said, clutching at the silver. *I'm wicked good at shit like this.* She looked up at me. *Okay? It's okay?* I nodded. It seemed seriously right that Rose remove the glass from my foot. It felt like becoming blood sisters or something, something momentous and bonding. I flashed on the Chinese bathroom. It was another part of my body for Rose to visit. *Here,* she said, and thrust the poster at me. *Hold this.* I gazed at the drawing, tried to distract myself from the terrible feeling of the tweezers nudging into the cut. There were flowers with curling leaves. A giant man-eating rose with a pair of dice stuck in the center blossom. The words *sworn to fun, loyal to none* twined around a giant martini glass. Another design showed a banner curled around a sword. It read *fortune honors bravery.* That was deep. That was Rose.

Rose, You Should Get This One, I told her, pointing at the weapon. Only Tweezers Instead Of A Sword. Think About It. The tattoo lady smiled.

No, I should get Rose, she said. Her breath rolled off my toes. My heel stuck to her bare knee.

No Way, I said. I Should Get Rose. I rolled up the sleeve of my T-shirt and looked at my bare arm reflected in the mirror on the wall. Right There. A sharp, splitting feeling ran hot through my whole foot. I sunk my chewed-up nails so deep into the plump of my arm that I dented little curves into the skin. Rose brandished the tweezers, waving them in the air like a wand. A sliver of glass shone beneath smears of blood.

Buried treasure, she said. I was overwhelmed with gratitude. I couldn't believe I had walked around on that.

You're My Nurse, I said. I Get Rose.

Really? Rose asked. She looked so happy. *You would get me?* I nodded.

Like hell, said Amber. *I don't tattoo cracked-out shoeless teenage girls.*

We don't smoke crack! Rose said, offended. *It's crystal. It's really good quality. I bet you'd like some.*

Hmph, Amber grunted. She retrieved a tube of something gloopy and glopped it onto the hole in my foot. It felt cool and soothing. *I bet I would too,* she said. *But also I don't take drugs from cracked-out shoeless teenage girls.*

Because You Like Them To Have All Their Drugs For Themselves? I asked. Rose laughed. She dropped the bit of glass into the biohazard bin with a plink you could hear. That fucker was big.

I am helping you kids, Amber said. *Don't fuck with me.* She took the tweezers back.

How are we fucking with you? Rose demanded. She unzipped the backpack and pulled out the roll of money. The quarters had made it wet. Rose shook it off, started peeling individual bills from the murky green bundle. *Look, we got money. We're paying customers.*

Where'd you steal that from? Amber said, glancing at the dough. She was gently placing squares of real gauze on top of my gloopy wound, sticking them into place with strips of white tape.

God, maybe I earned it. I'm a working person. I work at the mall. She waggled the damp money. *It's like two hundred dollars almost. How much for Trisha to get the Rose of Nowhereland tattoo?*

No Man's Land.

That's Even Better, I said. No Man's Land Is Better Than Nowhereland.

It would be a full two hundred dollars, Amber said. She snapped the lunchbox shut. *At least. If I tattooed teenagers, which I don't.* She looked down at my padded foot. *Where the fuck are your shoes?*

A Waitress At The Chinese Restaurant Took Them, I said.

At Weyloon's? she asked. I nodded. *I bet she had no reason,* she said. *I bet she stole them right off your feet.*

I shrugged. I Left Them In The Bathroom.

Amber shook her head. *You girls are trouble.* She

looked down at Rose counting out piles of wet quarters onto the floor. The front door tinkled open.

Wooo yeah! a guy crowed into the shop. His long legs took him up to the counter in two giant steps. He slapped his meaty hands down onto a stack of black books. *Hey sweetheart.* He was talking to Amber. *The tattoo artist in? I want to get a four-leaf clover. A shamrock?*

His friend was in the door behind him, chiming in. *Sweet! Sham-rock!* The smell of yeasty beer gushed out on hot breath and made me remember we had one Yikes left. I thought about going into the tattoo parlor bathroom with Rose and pounding it. That thought made me want a cigarette. Maybe there was a window we could smoke out of. Then we could do more crystal. We could leave Amber to tattoo shamrocks on the losers from Seamus O'Maniac's and she could come fetch us from the bathroom when she was done. Was it even legal for us to be in the tattoo shop? Were they like bars where you had to be an adult? Some of the art on the walls was wicked pornographic. Bunches of big, rosy boobs and cranked-open legs. Some weird ones with ladies getting their head chopped off, and even a flag with a Nazi sign on it. The place felt a little creepy. The two dudes from the bar didn't cheer it up.

No, the artist is gone for the day, Amber said. *We were just closing up.*

Aw, you're shittin' me, the guy said. His voice was thick with slurred disappointment. *What you got the light on for? That's false advertising.*

Sorry guys. Amber swung out the tiny saloon door and

moved across the room to the entrance. She swept the glass door open with a chime. The men sludged toward her. They were wasted.

Just a shamrock, sweetheart. How much a shamrock cost? When's the dude in?

Try tomorrow, Amber said. She leaned against the open door and sighed. *Come on, guys.*

Come on, guys, the tattoo-dude's friend said in a fake girl voice. He sort of swished himself out the door. Drunk dudes always love to pretend they're girls. Amber swung the door shut and switched the lock. She unraveled a long shade, blocking the view of the parking lot and the still-teetering, guys. They were *woo*-ing again. We could hear them outside, like we were in some sort of naturey cabin and there were packs of crazy animals prowling outside, howling. Amber hit a light switch, and the blue neon glow in the front window went cold.

I just don't have it in me to give another shamrock tattoo, Amber said, almost sadly. She sunk her blunt fingers into the dry mop of her hair and scratched her scalp wildly, shaking white-yellow clumps of hair to attention all over her head.

You Give A Lot Of Shamrock Tattoos? I asked her. She nodded. Her crazy hair bobbed on her head like bird feathers.

All those guys, they get wasted and want shamrocks. Just little, teeny shamrocks, on their arms or on their ankles. They're pussies, she said. *They're too drunk and they bleed all over the place and they smell awful.*

Fuck them! Rose chimed in, standing up from the floor. *You like us though, right? You wouldn't have fixed Trisha's foot if you didn't like us.*

It's got nothing to do with that, Amber said sternly. *I'm not going to let some kid with a huge gash in her foot hobble around Route 1 all bloody. It has nothing to do with liking you.*

But you like us, Rose insisted. She smiled. Her hands were filled with money. One grubby little fist clutched the wad of cash, her other paw dripped coins. They spilled from her grip, spinning shiny on the linoleum.

I don't know if "like" is the right word, Amber said. *What, did you rob a bank?*

The River At Weyloon's, I told her. We Robbed The River.

Trouble, Amber repeated. *That's what you girls are.*

That would be a good tattoo, huh? Rose asked. She tugged down the front of her nightgown, showing off her bony sternum. Every time she moved her hands money fell out of them. Silver shine slid down her body, beneath her shredded nightgown and onto the floor, like she was peeing quarters. *Trouble,* she said, moving her hands across her bare skin. I could imagine it, in thick looping script, or those unreadable gang boy letters.

No way, Amber said. *Final answer. I'm not dealing with your crazy cracked-out moms coming here to kill me in the morning 'cause I tattooed their babies. Or your crazy drunk dads with shotguns or whatever.*

Whoa, I said. I got up from my luxurious recliner. It had felt nice, but my body was way too zingy to keep still.

You Think We're, Like, From A Talk Show Or Something? Like *Jerry Springer*? Like From Florida?

Amber laughed and shook her head. She went for the red cross lunchbox and packed up the first aid supplies. *I just never seen more fucked-up looking girls in my life*, she laughed. *I am not tattooing you.*

Our Moms Don't Care, I told her. My Mom Won't Ever Come Here. She Just Stays On The Couch, She's Sick.

What's wrong with her?

A Bunch Of Things. Mostly Hypochondria. And Rose's Mom Is A Lesbian, So She's Not Going To Care About A Tattoo.

Amber turned to Rose. It looked like a Doberman had eaten the bottom half of her dress. *You're mom is a lesbian?* Amber asked her. Rose nodded. *Hmmmm.* Amber went thoughtful. I wondered if she was racist against lesbian people. *So, are you a lesbian too? Are you guys lesbians together?* Her hand shot out and waggled in the air between me and Rose. I was bursting with glee, a maniacal glee. I wanted to tell Amber, this stranger, all about kissing Rose at the golf course, about what she had done to me in the Weyloon's bathroom, about what she was doing to me still, my body vibrating with crazy memory. I didn't even care if it made me a lesbian. It's not like I was going to lose any popularity with the world. The world pretty much didn't give a shit about me before I lezzed out with Rose, and I gave no shit about it, either, so fuck it all is what I figured. I was on the verge of a too-much-info confession session with cranky Amber. And then Rose fucking ruined it.

I'm not a lesbian, she said. She said it in that weird way. She could have been any rotten girl from any lousy high school. We could have been in the girl's bathroom, regulation pink from the walls rosing up our faces. Rose sounded like she was looking at a toilet stall door that had ROSE WHATEVER THE FUCK HER LAST NAME IS IS A GODDAMN LESBIAN JUST LIKE HER LESBIAN MOM scratched into the flaking layers of paint. She sounded grossed out. I stared at her. I could still feel her in my downstairs parts. What if she'd messed me up down there for good.

You're Not? I asked her. I guess I sounded challenging. Amber's eyebrows went up. So did the corners of her mouth, just a little. I could tell Amber thought she knew everything that was up with us and was kind of amused by it. I hated her for thinking she knew anything and I hated her for getting it right.

No, Rose snapped at me. *I'm not a lesbian. Do you even know any lesbians?* She was weirdly accusational.

No, I said.

If you knew any lesbians then you would know I'm not a lesbian.

You have a boyfriend? Amber asked. She had this fake innocent voice on.

I mess around with a guy at work, Rose said. She didn't sound too proud of it. Her eyes were cast down at the coins that had fallen from her grip. She crouched down to fetch them.

Marty? I asked. It sounded like I was spitting or something. Hucking a loogie, a loogie named Marty. Fuck Marty, I said. A bold statement. It seemed like the hour for bold statements. It seemed like a showdown here at the 777 tattoo parlor.

Yeah, right, Rose laughed. Rose was trying to make a joke.

Are you in love with Marty? Amber asked, tauntingly. Who the fuck was Amber anyway. We were now her evening's entertainment. She owed us both free tattoos, I thought. We weren't a fucking reality show.

No, Rose scoffed. *He's just a guy.*

I felt a surge of something hopeful puff up inside me. Does Marty Have Tattoos? I asked her. She thought about it.

No, she said. *No and I don't want to talk about fucking Marty, why are we talking all about me, why don't you ask Trisha if she's a lesbian or if she has a boyfriend. Leave me alone. Everyone always wants to know about me because of my fucking mom.*

Amber looked at me. *Are you a lesbo?* she asked. I looked at Rose. I'd be one if she was, but now if she wasn't I didn't know what was up with me. Maybe I was just on a lot of drugs. Maybe crystal makes you lez. I shrugged.

I Don't Know, I said. I'd Never Considered It Before Tonight, I said. Before Rose fucked me in a Chinese restaurant, I wanted to say but amazingly managed to keep my mouth shut.

Amber was looking me up and down with that face of hers. I don't think I liked her much. Why was everyone so hateful? *You're a lesbian,* she told me. *For sure.* I didn't know what to say to that. It wasn't like some joker on the street calling me a lezzie. It was a rather calm adult informing me I was a lesbian.

Oh, Really? I said. What Do You Know?

Come on, Rose said. *Cut this shit out. Who cares. Are you going to give Trisha the tattoo or what?* She moved forward with her heaps of dough and plonked it all on the table. *We'll even give you the quarters. For laundry and parking meters and whatnot.*

Amber quietly considered the cash. *It would be nice,* she said, *not to do another fucking shamrock.*

No way! Rose said, excited. *Trisha wouldn't ever get a pussy tattoo like that. You'd give her this* — she dashed for the poster that held the original Rose. She brandished it. *Where?* she turned to me. *Where did you say?* She was next to me, tugging the sleeve of my T-shirt up, showing my naked arm to Amber. When her fingers hit me my whole body was jolted with Rose-energy. My body hopped up on its hind legs and started slobbering. Jesus. I looked at her. What about fucking Marty, I wanted to ask her. Who the fuck is Marty, what is up, who am I, what is fucking up with me, what is going on? Marty. I imagined some greasy little fry-man, with frizzy hair poofing out under a hairnet. Red-faced and zitty with one giant eyebrow, a pimply teenage clown, no, not teenage, worse than that, one of those guys who graduated a few years ago but is stunted at the same dating age, always hanging out with high schoolers, buying them beer. Marty. But maybe not. Maybe he was some lean and muscly kid with a scrawny mustache and one earring glinting in an earlobe, the not-gay earlobe. Maybe he worked the fryers with his shirt off, tucked into the back pockets of his baggy baggy pants, the waistband of his man-panties sticking out, the word TROUBLE tattooed across his chest in gang letters. Maybe even a gold chain or two. Fuck Marty. Would Marty get a picture of Rose tattooed onto him? I didn't think so. Did Marty understand Rose, did he know that she was the Rose of No Man's Land, the spooky ghost-nurse of nighttime Route 1. Marty didn't know shit. Fuck Marty.

Right There, I said. I flexed my left arm, like there was some sort of muscle under there. C'mon, I said to Amber. You'll Get To Keep Hanging Out With Us. We'll Give You Crystal Too.

Oh, fuck, Amber sighed. *Fuck you guys.* She prodded the pile of money with a finger. *All right. I'll set it up in here and you set it up in there.* She pointed to the bathroom. *You know I could get arrested. You know that, right? You get it? I'm making a big exception for you girls.*

Yeeeeah! Rose leaped into the air. She snatched up the backpack and loped off in the direction of the bathroom. I followed her.

Stay out of each others' pants in there, you little lesbos! Amber laughed. She loved that we were little lesbos. I think I hated Amber. But in a homey way, like hating Kristy or even Donnie.

In the bathroom I was quiet and looked around at all the posters on the walls, more tattoo shit, ads for tattoo conventions and big posters of skulls with snakes crawling through the empty eyeholes. A little plastic shelf piled with a jumble of crusty dusty makeup and hairbrushes furry with hairballs. A box of tampons and a gleaming pink metal can of hair spray. *Grab me a few tampons,* Rose said, looking at the mess. I plonked a handful into the backpack. I threw the hair spray in as well, just for fun. Later I would impress Rose with giant fireballs. It would be our own raw laser light show. Rose was efficiently laying out the drugs on the smooth white back of the toilet. She was scraping the powder into lines using the edge of one of the naked Polaroids. *Amber's got all the money now,* she said. *We've got nothing to snort it with. That was stupid, huh? Do you think that was stupid? I should have kept some for us.* She looked at me. *Are you scared? About the tattoo?* I thought about it. I felt scared, but not about the tattoo. I just felt scared. I tried to figure out what was scaring me.

Listen, I said. Do You Think Amber's . . . I tried to think of the word.

A bitch? Rose asked.

Unethical. That was the word.

Oh, yeah! Rose said. *But only an unethical tattoo artist would give us tattoos. So just be happy she doesn't have any morals or whatever.* The lines were perfect, sparkly stripes on the back of the can. Rose looked at me. My whole body pulsed in her direction.

I Feel Crazy, I told her.

You just need more speed, she told me. *You'll be fine.* She paused. We looked at each other. Maybe I was staring. She started to talk and then began chewing on the inside of her mouth instead. She was thinking. *I think you're tripping out,* she said. *Are you tripping out?*

Maybe, I confessed.

Cut it out, she said simply. *Don't think so much. You'll fuck everything up.*

You Think I'm Thinking Too Much? I asked her.

I don't fucking know. I'm not in your brain. But I think you might be. You kind of seem like maybe you're thinking too much.

Okay, I said. All Right. It was good to have someone sort of observing me, letting me know how or how not to be. I didn't know. Everything felt looped, like it went out of control a long, long time ago. I'll Stop Thinking, I said to Rose. Was it even possible to stop thinking? That question was a thought in itself. I had to stop thinking about thinking. Stop thinking about thinking and about Rose and about Marty. Stop thinking about Amber's morals. Just snort some more drugs and get a tattoo.

I bet the tattoo will knock the thinking right out of you, Rose said. *It's gonna hurt.* She grinned, like this was a great thing, my future pain. She looked like a little ghoul, her bony head grinning, her shredded dress. Don't think about Rose looking creepy, I told myself. Just snort the line. I loved Rose. There it was. The pileup of every thought and kiss and grab had built a love for her inside me. Even if she looked creepy. I looked down at the floor, at my naked red toes, so as not to think about her. Looked at the bandage taped neatly to my foot. Soon it would be gray and shredded with the filth of the streets but for now it was crisp and hospital-ish. The painful pulse of the wound was softer, like the cushion of bandage was muffling it. Rose's hand reached out for my shoulder. *Hey,* she said. Her voice was nicer. *You're really freaking out, huh?*

I'm Trying Not To Think, I snapped. So Don't Ask Me If I'm Freaking Out Because Then I Have To Think. Great.

Now I'm Thinking About Freaking Out. Maybe I'm Just Freaking Out Because You Suggested It And Now I'm Thinking About It.

If Amber knows you're freaking out she won't tattoo you, Rose whispered. *Get it together.*

I'm Not Freaking Out, I spat defensively. I'm Just Thinking About Freaking Out.

Stop thinking, Rose repeated.

Maybe Just Stop Talking To Me, I said. Rose looked hurt. Less creepy. Good, I thought. See how you like it. The door cranked open and Amber came inside the bathroom. She had her hands over her eyes but her fingers were cracked open, like she was peeking.

Put your clothes back on, lezzies, she said. *I don't want to see any lesbian kiddie porn happening in my bathroom!*

This is your bathroom? Rose asked. *You own this place?*

Amber shook her head. *Nah, I just work here. This guy Tony owns it.*

Do You Even Do Tattoos? I asked her. I was honestly trying not to think, but suspicious thoughts about Amber kept cropping up inside my brain.

Of course I do! she said. *Getting second thoughts? Getting a little scared?*

No, I told her. Not if I didn't think about it.

I'm an apprentice, she said. *This is a great shop. They don't let just anyone apprentice. Especially if you're a girl. You've got to be really, really good or else none of the guys take you seriously.*

That's Not Fair, I said. Was that a thought?

No shit, said Amber. *Okay, where's the go-fast?*

Go-fast? Amber sounded like some weird grown-up trying to talk like younger people. Thought! I scolded myself. Thought! But that was a thought too. It seemed fucking impossible to not think. It was like in order to not think you had to think about not thinking and that's a thought so what the fuck. It was making me crazy. I wanted to talk to Rose about it but then she would know I was thinking. Rose I guess was somehow managing to not think. Rose seemed mostly okay, though her eyeballs seemed to be growing as the night wore on, taking up too much space on her face. She was bumming a bill off Amber so we could all do the lines patiently sparkling for us on the back of the toilet.

You gave me all your money? Amber asked. *You don't even have, like, a dollar for yourselves?* Rose shook her head. Her big, big eyes seemed to slide across and swallow her bony head. *Shit. Well, I'll give you back a twenty. What if you need gas or something?*

We don't drive, Rose told her.

How did you get out here?

We hitchhiked, Rose told her.

Oh my god, Amber shook her head, scandalized. She bent over the back of the toilet so her sparkled ass was in my face, and huffed some crystal. She stood up and bent her head back, huffing and huffing up her nose. *Whoa,* she said. She looked at us straight on. Her face had gone pink and teary from the drugs. *Hitchhiking. Jesus. Well, I don't need to tell you nothing, right, ladies? 'Cause you know it all already.*

Exactly, Rose grinned. She took the bill from Amber

and dived over the drug runway. Her face swooped back up and she reached across the cramped room to flick on the faucet and wet her fingers. She stuck her wet fingers up her nose.

Classy, Amber said. The bill was on the back of the toilet, slowly unrolling. I grabbed it and tightened it up, hit the line and then wet my own fingers. I snorted the water off them and then rustled in my pack for the last Yikes.

The Last Yikes, I said solemnly. The crystal worked so quickly. I felt brighter. My perspective, I realized, had really darkened for a moment there. Wow, I said. I looked at Rose. Who cared if she was a lesbian or not? It was all a bunch of words, a bunch of boxes. Who cared. Who cared about Marty? Was Rose running around doing drugs and getting tattooed with Marty? No way. Clearly I was the winner here.

Feel better? Rose asked. I nodded.

I Was Really In A Bad Mood For A Minute There, I confessed.

Yeah, what was your problem? Rose asked. We both cracked up.

Can I have a sip of that? Amber motioned to the Yikes. *I am so ready to tattoo you.*

We're going to need more of this, Rose said. Rose was so wise. *We're out of everything,* she said. *Cigarettes, Yikes. We're out of money.* She gave Amber a look.

It's getting claustrophobic in here, Amber said, and flung the bathroom door open.

Twenty-five

The shop was filled with smoke like the skanky public bathrooms at the back of the mall, but at least I knew where all the smoke had come from. It was being cycled through the lungs of me, Amber, and Rose. Bottle caps wrenched from the necks of bottle after bottle of Amber-purchased Yikes were working as tiny ashtrays, the charred gray dust spilling out of them, butts smoked to the filter and crushed into bent accordion smokestacks. The Yikes bottles were piling up. Burps were bubbling out of our throats. Amber's proximity to me was terrible. Mostly she had a cigarette dangling out the corner of her mouth the whole time, squinting through the smoke like some lady Clint Eastwood, peering with watering eyes down at the tattoo she was fixing into my arm. The smoke drifted straight into my face and I would cough and my body would jiggle and my arm with its partial tattoo would bounce a bit and Amber would grunt, *Shit* and *Keep still.* The butt of the cigarette was clamped between her front teeth. She kept her lipsticked lips pulled back off it, showing her teeth in a crazy smile. When she wanted a drag her lips would sink around it and pull. Smoke streamed out from her nostrils. She was a smoke factory. I figured it was best to smoke my own cigarette. Then Amber's smoke was just more smoke, and smoke was something I was already involved with. Rose smoked too, looming over Amber's shoulder, watching her aim the tiny gun, the insanely vibrating contraption, a weird machine with a bare, stripped-down look, like it was missing a crucial piece. It seemed to be doing its job, though. A mass of color was now located on my formerly bare arm. It hurt terribly. It felt like a raw scrape, an awful gutting of my skin there. Not a needle on the end of the machine but a cigarette sinking third-degree burns into my poor fleshy arm. My weakling, muscle-less arm. Rose watched intently, occasionally tilting her head away for a drag of her cigarette. I watched her face. It was absorbed, then confused. I didn't like when it looked confused. When Amber wasn't smoking with her cigarette crushed between her teeth she was taking slug after slug from her bottle of Yikes, then burping. The burp-wind blew right into my face. I looked forward to the whole thing being over. Amber bitched a lot about the state of my blood; the drugs and Yikes had made it thin, and it drained out of me worse than all the thin-blooded shamrock hooligans from the bar next door.

Trisha's no pussy, though, Rose defended my honor. *Right? Look how tough she's being.* It's true that I was not crying, was not even moaning or saying ouch or anything. I just tried to breathe, listened to the nonstop rock of my heart inside my body, worked on not thinking.

You're a tough one, Amber smiled. *You're doing a great job. You're a great customer. And your skin loves ink. It takes right to it.*

Skin could love ink? I liked the thought of my skin having the ability to love, selecting its loves without any input from me. Skin plus Ink equals True Love Forever. Finally Amber put down the machine and it wasn't to light another cigarette. She was done. She took a big spray bottle of something and misted my arm with it again and again. It felt lovely. It felt cool and refreshing. My arm burned like a thousand sunburns. *You're gonna take care of this, right?* she asked, like she was giving me a puppy. I nodded and shrugged. She mopped up my arm gently with a bulk of paper towels, then spritzed me again. I felt like a window she was washing down. *Voila,* she said, crumpling the towels in her fist. Rose hopped up and down. She clapped her hands together. She was wicked excited. *Get up and take a look, what're you waiting for?* It was hard to pull myself off the recliner. My body had molded itself into the shape of the slumping chair and cramped there. I felt like an eighty-year-old man must feel. I thought about Harry Chester, hunched on his couch in Revere. He seemed like a long, long time ago.

The new searing pain in my arm had obliterated the wound in my foot, was outshining even the good hurt of

Rose breaking into my privates. All of my body's sensation had pooled into this new sheet of color on my arm. It glistened wet and beaded with blood. It was as if Amber had peeled off layers of skin and found this treasure beneath, like it had always been there, a miniature Rose looking cool and spooky in an old-timey nurse's hat, her messy hair neater, her eyes even bigger and her mouth super-red and pouty, the way it looked after we'd made out, like I'd gnawed her a fat lip. I brought my hand up to touch it. It looked like paint, like I could bring my hand across it and smear all the colors into a slick blur down my arm. Amber stopped my hand. *Don't touch!* she shrieked. *I don't know where your hands have been! That's an open wound. Do you understand that? My gun* — she motioned toward the machine; was it really held together with rubber bands? — *put like a thousand holes in your skin and filled them with color. Think of it that way. You're wounded.*

It Looks Just Like Her, I said. I pushed closer to the full-length mirror on the wall. The girl in the tattoo wore an old-fashioned white shirt, like a sailor. Yellowy light spilled out behind her like she was in heaven. The closer I got to the mirror, the more I noticed stuff. Like how her eyes were sort of lopsided. The way the red of the cross on her weird nurse-veil went outside the lines. Perhaps her lips were *too* big. Who cared, though. It was good enough, it was a tattoo, I had a tattoo, and it was Rose and now she would be in my skin forever. I angled myself toward her.

Wow, she said. She looked up at Amber. *I can't believe you can do that. I want to do that.*

You should, Amber said simply. *It's a good career. You*

make good money, you can travel around and work anywhere.

Wow, Rose repeated. Her eyes were running back and forth between the tattoo and Amber. I was starting to feel like a wall the painting was hung on. I flexed my arm and posed in the mirror,

It looks good, kid, Amber grinned. *I wish I could take a picture of it for my book, but I can't. I can't risk it. If you ever come back in here, I've never seen you. Got it? I will lie to your cute little lesbian faces.* She turned back to Rose. *You start the cleanup while I bandage her up.*

Amber globbed a bunch of gooey gel onto my arm, smearing it around with a Popsicle stick. She pressed a bandage over my whole shoulder, roping it into place with stretches of tape. I was starting to feel like a mummy. Like the survivor of a car wreck. Like I'd gotten my ass kicked. Blood and bandages. Amber was talking to me but I was zoning out. *You're not even listening to me,* she accused and I shrugged. My mind was shutting off.

What Time Is It? I asked her. The bar next door was closing, sending the drinkers out into the night, howling in the parking lot, climbing drunk into their cars to zoom down Route 1.

If you don't listen to me and take care of this tattoo you could get an infection, you know that? Not to mention destroy my beautiful work. She thrust a piece of paper at me. It was instructions.

Oh, Good, I said. She handed me a few plastic packets. They looked like ketchup packets from McDonald's but they were filled with tattoo goop. I folded them into the instructions and tossed the package into my backpack. I looked at myself again in the mirror. I looked tough with the tattoo. Tougher. There was no argument about that. I shook my hair into my face. I hunched my shoulders. I could be a guy. I could be Marty. My body was stiff and shaky and my bladder full of Yikes. I stepped into the bathroom to pee. I studied myself in the mirror. My face was suddenly full of pores. I mean, I knew they had always been there but suddenly they were making themselves known. My skin was blotchy and riddled with pores. I was perhaps looking at it too closely. Maybe the mirror was a magnifying one, or else the speed had given me supernatural eyesight. I sat on the can and tinkled. There was a slight sprinkle of blood in the crotch of my underwear.

When I came out of the bathroom Rose and Amber were finishing the last of the crystal, inhaling squat lines laid out right on the counter. The smoke hung low in the room. The bottle cap ashtrays and sticky Yikes bottles were everywhere. The place was trashed. What About Me? I asked, and Amber laughed.

You do not need any more of this stuff, she said, like she was somebody's fucking mother.

And You Guys Do? I asked. That Was Mine Too!

Not technically, Rose said. *Technically I bought it with my money. Technically I had to get naked for it. Remember?*

I nodded. I knew that. I just had become attached to the speed. I felt like it was *our* speed. Didn't my carrying it all around in the backpack count for anything?

Amber was rubbing her nose so roughly I thought she

was going to snap the cartilage. She wasn't sleepy anymore, that's for sure. She was wide awake and ruining my life. *Naked?* she asked. Her eyes were big but that might have just been the drug. *What, are you drug whores? Why were you naked?*

It's a long story, Rose smiled. But she went into the bag, the backpack, and came out with her picture. The Polaroid of her mocking the dancing girl that had lived on Monster's dresser. I wondered briefly if Monster Paulie had already forgotten about us. It seemed like a dream I'd had a long time ago. Only patches of the memory came to me — the quick wind of Rose pulling off her nightgown; Harry Chester exhaling blue into the television screen. Rose showed the Polaroid to Amber.

Dude! Amber shook her head, laughing, holding the picture away from her like it was diseased or evil. *Dude, that is sick! I don't even want to know about you two. You two are the baddest news I've heard all day.* Rose beamed brightly. Fucking fuck Amber. So she could tattoo. So what. We had already given her all the money plus the quarters that really were *mine,* of all the stuff handed over to Amber like a pirate's booty those fucking quarters were *mine,* those waitresses had almost kicked my ass over them, I lost my flops, my favorite flops, and sliced my foot open because of them, I could have been arrested, and I gave it all to Amber. Plus we shared the speed with her. She had enough, why did she get the rest? Something shifted while I was in the bathroom pondering the bloodstains Rose had put into my underwear. Something had flipped. The filthy tattoo shop was some sort of bad bizarro world. Rose liked

Amber. She liked her in that way. She liked her in that lesbian way. She can say Marty this and Marty that and as far as I'm concerned who cares about fucking Marty, who knows if Marty even exists, all I know is Rose is a fucking lesbo and now she's making lesbo-faces at Amber, Amber who is totally gross and whatever, Amber who is cheesy, who is embarrassing the way a parent might be embarrassing, and now something has happened and all the air in the room, all the energy in the room, it's for her, it's flowing psychically in her direction. I felt a trembling terribleness. The tattoo on my arm throbbed like a punch, like a car had crashed into the skin there. It was Rose on my arm, each throb was her inhaling, exhaling, inhaling, exhaling, the pulse of her heart inside her chest inside my skin.

It's Not Even That Good, I said out loud. Maybe that was an inside thought. It leaked out, though. The Eyes Are Fucked-Up And You Went Outside The Lines. It's Not Even That Good. It Doesn't Even Look Like Her.

Rose's face was shut down, cold. *Trisha, what are you talking about? It's excellent. It looks just like me, it's excellent.*

It Does Not Even Look Like You, I said. You're Fucking Blind.

Whoa, Amber said, holding up her hand. The naked Polaroid of Rose was still in her fingers, flashing at me. Flash, flash, the light hit it, it looked like a tiny porno screen in her hand, tiny porno-action Rose. *What's your problem? I did you a favor.*

You Got Paid, I said. We Paid You Just Like Anyone.

I paid, Rose said. *Why are you being such a bitch?*

Something in my eyes felt sharp. Maybe there was glass

stuck in there too, glass from the parking lot, from the sidewalk when we were rolling around, kissing. Amber put her hand on the hip of her jeans, crumpling the Polaroid.

Well you got it for life, kid. So you better start liking it. She looked back and forth at Rose and me. *Fucking shit,* she said. *I fucking knew it. I knew it. You bitches are crazy and I'm crazy. I did you a favor. You should just get out of here.*

Fine, I said. I hoped I never saw her again ever ever ever. I felt stupid feelings about her the second I saw her. I grabbed my backpack from the floor. I zipped it and flung it over my shoulders. Rose was staring at me. Her mouth was open. Come On, I said. She looked at Amber. She looked around the shop.

I was going to help clean up. I want to stay.

You Have To Go, I told her. She Just Said So, She's Kicking Us Out, Come On.

I don't care what she does, Amber nodded at Rose. *But I think you should get some sleep. Maybe try to eat a little food or something.*

Come On, I said to Rose. I was staring at her. Amber's voice was like a drill boring in the back of my skull. Come On, Rose. Rose just looked at me. What The Fuck? I touched my face. It was wet. My Eye Is Bleeding, I said to her. Is My Eye Bleeding? I looked at my fingers.

You're crying, Trisha. Rose spoke through her hands. Her hands were covering her mouth.

I'm Not Fucking Crying, I told her. I went for the door but it was locked. I rattled. Let Me Out, Then! I was yelling. I knew I shouldn't have been yelling but I was. And crying. Crying and bleeding, bleeding somewhere, a few places, who cares if I was wrong about the eye. Amber was behind me, she reached out and unlatched the door. There was a bell above my head, it jingled as I pushed my way out. I turned back to Rose. You Are Such A Fucking Lesbian, I told her. You Are Such A Liar. I walked out into the parking lot. Beyond the lot was Route 1, all shut down for the night, the neon extinguished. Above me I could see the stars, but in front of me was total darkness, torn by the lights of the cars on the road. There were less of them. I had never been out so late before. I wondered if anyone cared.

Twenty-six

I walked all the way back home. It wasn't so bad. I got lost a few times and then had to duck from cops a few times, crouching behind parked cars. I didn't have anything on me anymore, just a naked Polaroid of Kim Porciatti, which maybe I could've been totally arrested for, who knows. I just knew I couldn't talk to cops, all fucked-up. Could you be arrested just for having drugs in your system, even if there was none in your bag and you weren't bothering anybody? I wasn't bothering anybody. I was just trying to find my way home without getting another piece of glass in my foot. Just wondering how someone like Rose could live with herself, being such a liar and a hypocrite, being so slutty. She was probably busting into Amber's downstairs parts right then, right as I navigated my way down a dim Mogsfield street strewn with turned-over trash cans. I felt bad for thinking Rose was slutty. I knew it was something bigger than that. Something about the way Rose just did whatever she wanted to. Slutty was a useless idea, it had nothing to do with her. I didn't want to be another stupid person who thought that, like a boy on the street.

When I got home Kristy was on the front steps crying. I couldn't believe it. I thought: Oh my god, Kristy missed me. Kristy was worried. Kristy thought I'd been kidnapped. Kristy was wondering what she would do without me for the rest of her sunny life. Kristy looked up at me. Her hair, soaked through with tears, swirled in wet clumps down her neck.

You fucking idiot! She screamed. *Where have you been? Donnie got arrested.*

Donnie Got Arrested? I repeated dumbly.

Donnie got arrested and Ma went down to the police station.

Ma Went To The Police Station? I know it is annoying to be repeated but I was at a massive loss. Ma Is Gone? I asked. I bounded past Kristy, up the creaking wooden stairs and into our house. The coffee table was pushed halfway across the room, at a weird angle. Some stuff had tumbled from it to the floor. It didn't look like a raid from *Cops*, but it looked like something had happened. Mostly the shock was Ma. She wasn't on the couch. It was amazing. The couch was empty. The television was off, the dark glass warping the room's reflection. Like a television show broadcast from another dimension it showed Kristy entering the room behind me, half ghost, half fun-house person in the curved glass. Wow, I said. Wow, It's So Weird She's Not Here.

She wanted me to take her, Kristy hiccuped. *The cops came and dragged Donnie out and then they dragged out all the shit he had stashed in your room, whatever —*

Batteries, I said, nodding.

— And they said Ma could come to the station and she was freaking out and said "Kristy, pull the car around." She didn't even ask. She just said, "Kristy, pull the car around" like I'm her fucking slave. She pulled her wet hair back carefully, peeling it from her skin. *I was filming when they came. I was getting it all on film and one of the cops took the camera right out of my hands. He just took it.*

It's Gone? I asked. Kristy nodded. Oh No, I said. Oh No, Kristy. That Sucks.

I just told Ma, he's your fucking problem. You get him.

And She Did?

She did. She won't get off the couch for us, not ever, in like our whole life, but she'll go down to the police station to bail out her loser boyfriend.

I Can't Believe She's Gone, I said. The room was vibrating with her absence. Kristy was staring at me.

What the hell is wrong with you? she asked. *Did something happen? What happened?*

I Don't Think You Can Handle It, I told her. I'm Just Being Honest. I Don't Know If You Can Take It.

Don't be dramatic.

Serious.

Tell me.

I'm On Drugs, I said. I Got A Tattoo, I lifted my

shirtsleeve up, flashed my bandage at her. The white cotton was seeped through with blood and murky ink. I Hurt My Foot, I said, shaking it at her. I Got Glass In It, But It's Okay. I Made Friends, With This Girl — You Won't Like Her, But I Do, And Now She Likes Someone Better Than Me. And I Got Fired From Ohmigod! Bernice O'Leary Is A Fucking Bitch And I Freaked Out On Her. And I Don't Like Wearing Your Clothes. I'm Never Wearing Your Clothes Ever Again. Sorry. And, Look. I unzipped the backpack. I fished around and grabbed the photo of Kim Porciatti. Fucking Kim Porciatti. Look At That. I passed it to Kristy. She looked beyond confusion.

Where did you get this? she asked.

The Guy Who Sold Us Drugs. He's A Drug Dealer In Revere.

That's sick. We should call the cops.

Right, I said. We Should Call The Cops? I motioned around at our lightly ransacked living room.

I don't know! Kristy squirted out a faceful of fresh tears.

Just Forget About It, I told her. None Of It Matters.

I can't believe you're on drugs, Kristy said. *This is the worst night ever.* She paused. *What kind?*

Speed.

And you like it?

I Do And I Don't. I Think It's Making Me Act Weird.

Isn't that the point?

I Guess. I walked back out the open door onto the porch. The night still felt nice. It was the same night as the one in the golf course, with Rose. It was the same magical night, belly-up. I sat on the front steps and waited for Kristy to join me. Donnie's cigarettes were still on the porch, cigarettes and a lighter. They didn't even let him take his smokes. I thought about Donnie getting hauled off, about some cops being mean to him. It seemed part funny and part sad. I wondered if he'd been in one of the cruisers I'd hid from, stuffed in the backseat with his wrists locked together. I lifted his lighter, red plastic, and flicked around with it. I studied the long, perfect flame, blue to orange. I remembered the hair spray in my bag. How I was going to impress Rose. I pulled the can out. It shone under the streetlights like some sort of deadly weapon.

Is that mine? Kristy asked behind me. *Did you steal that from me?*

Not From You, I said. She was leaning in the doorway, still crying. I was glad my crying had stopped.

A tattoo, she cried. *It's like — your life is over. You've ruined your life. I hope you know that.* I wanted to tell her it wasn't true, but I really didn't know. Maybe my life was junked. Maybe her life was junked too. Probably all our lives were over already, but we wouldn't know for sure until we were around thirty. 'Til we realized we hadn't left the couch in twelve years, 'til the cops came and threw us in jail for something totally dumb, 'til we discovered we're finally too old to be eligible for MTV reality shows. Then we'd know if our lives had been ruined. I flicked the lighter and aimed the hair spray at the wavering flame. One pump turned it into a meteor, a blasting, flaming fireball. It shot out against the black sky like a living thing, a giant whorling pulse of pure heat, all orange and liquid, a little planet of fire hovering in the air before my face. Then it vanished. Kristy was beside me, the bare calf of her leg knocking into my head. Her hands were outstretched.

Let me try, she said.

ACKNOWLEDGMENTS

Thanks to Stephen Elliott for his chronic helpfulness, both to me and the world at large. Thanks to Pat Walsh for his continuing care and enthusiasm. Thanks to everyone at MacAdam/Cage for a seriously magical book publishing experience — David, Dorothy, Kate, Melissa, Julie, Jason, Scott, JP, and everyone else who makes the boat sail. Thank you to the fantastic Elizabeth Wales. Thanks to Kathleen Tomasik for being the very best sister ever. Thanks to Eric Black for his good vibes and humor. Thanks to Tara Jepsen, Sara Seinberg, Peter Pizzi, Marcus Ewert, Clint Catalyst, Peter Plate, David West, Laurenn McCubbin, and Jessica Lanyadoo for eternal encouragement and support. Thanks to Diana and John and Anastasia Kayiatos for being so sweet and so cool. Thanks to Eileen Myles for being the north star. I worked this book out on many spoken word stages and want to thank some people who create literary community in my world: Frank Andrich, Alan Black, Lynn Breedlove, Tina Butcher, Sarah Dougher, Cindy Emch, Tara Hardy, Richard Hanson, PK McBee, and the lovely Anna Joy Springer. Thanks to Ma and Rick for their love. Most of all thanks to Rocco Kayiatos for his sincerity, his sustained curiosity, his positivity, his abiding belief in me, his foxiness, and his foreverness.